HADES' STAR

HOSTILE TAKEOVER

DOUG WALLACE

Copyright © 2019 by Rogue Ink Publishing

Cheyenne, Wyoming

All rights reserved.

No part of this book may be reproduced in any form or by any electronic or mechanical means, including information storage and retrieval systems, without written permission from the author, except for the use of brief quotations in a book review.

AUTHOR'S NOTE

Legal Note: Hades' Star is a registered trademark of Parallel Space Inc. All material, including images, logos, and other in-game elements are property of Parallel Space Inc. and used by the author with permission.

Author's Note: The Hades' Star book series was inspired by the multiplayer online game of the same name, developed by Parallel Space Inc. The author continues to play the game and is active in the Hades' Star gaming community on Discord.com. Hades' Star is available for IOS, Android, and Steam, and can be downloaded wherever you get your apps.

1

RENDEZVOUS

The undiscovered country from whose bourn no traveler returns, puzzles the will and makes us rather bear those ills we have than fly to others that we know not of. Thus conscience does make cowards of us all.

— WILLIAM SHAKESPEARE IN HAMLET

My friends would tell you I've always dreamed of worlds I've never seen and longed for peoples I've never met. Some of them would even say I have the soul of an explorer. Truth is, I've just never fit in. Not in my family. Not in Montana. Not even on Earth. So, nobody was surprised when I joined the Federation Navy. It gave my life some much-needed structure, and the Hades Mission gave me a higher purpose. But it wasn't the slick recruitment vids that made me sign up for what was likely a one-way mission to an unexplored galaxy. It wasn't the promise of unmatched pay, or generous land grants on virgin worlds, or even the allure of potential first contact with alien races. No, what made me sign a twenty-year contract aboard the *TFP Icarus* was the smell of cheap perfume. Dezzie's perfume, to be exact.

"You're out of uniform, Lieutenant." Despite her playful scorn, Dezzie's voice was like honey. I could listen to her read the operations schedule for the next year and never tire of it. I rolled over onto my side, letting my arm fall off the edge of her bed. She palmed the wall and brought up a display on its capacitive surface. I scanned it for the situational awareness feed, but before I found the date and time displayed in the corner of the screen, my gaze lingered on Dezzie. My eyes soaked in the curves of her back and hips. She dried her long, black hair with a towel and pulled it up into a bun, revealing the nape of her elegant neck and her strong jaw. My fingers yearned to trace the scar that ran from her ear to the small of her back. She never talked about it. The fact that she even let me touch it proved just how close we'd grown over the last year. That thought left me grinning like a teenage boy who'd just seen his first...well, you get the idea.

My smile faded, though, when she pulled on her flight suit and zipped it up. The nanofabric of her name tag keyed off her DNA and coalesced into letters spelling *Commander Desiree Pearson*.

"You're gonna be *late*, Paul. I can't keep covering for you. Three times in one month would land anyone else on sanitation duty." Her emerald green eyes flared with a mixture of mirth and frustration.

Most people would have shuddered at the mention of sanitation duty, but the thought of cleaning toilets didn't really bother me. Donning an EV suit and mag boots to scrape the carbon scoring off the hull, though? Now *that* sent a shiver down my spine.

It'd been over a year since an EV suit failure. The last poor sap had ended up a human popsicle. Command said sanitation duty was safer than working in the engine room or maintaining the power grid. I disagreed. Burns could be healed with sprays and radiation sickness could be treated with meds. Last I checked, though, there was no pill for sucking hard vacuum.

"I won't get sanitation duty. One of the perks of being the XO's boyfriend," I said. "Besides, I have ten minutes before my shift starts."

"Takes eight just to reach bulkhead seven," she retorted, "and your duty post is another fifty meters in zero-G."

I reached for the crumpled uniform laying amidst several other articles of clothing strewn about the floor. No zero-G to contend with in the XO's quarters, which is why most of our encounters ended up here. The mechanics were just… easier with gravity.

"No, you don't," said Dezzie with a stern glance and a wagging finger. "You need a *shower*." She smoothed out the fabric of her own uniform and retrieved the pistol she kept in the nightstand next to her full-sized bed. It was a luxury I still hadn't grown used to, even after so long. My quarters were, well, more *spartan*, to say the least. The XO's cabin was palatial by comparison. It even had a window. I looked out at the massive, fiery red nebula in the distance. Its resemblance to Milton's description of hell was why we'd called this new place Hades. I stared, mesmerized. It didn't move like the stars that raced across the windows of the *Icarus*'s four spinning habitat rings. Another benefit of rank, I suppose.

"You spend too much time on decks with graviton plates," I said.

Dezzie arched an eyebrow. "Jealous?"

"Hell no!" I spat. "An enemy ship may not have gravity like this. We get too used to it, grow too soft..." I stopped for a moment, distracted by her ample chest. "No. Better to stay hard."

She rolled her eyes at my choice of words, and I'm sure I blushed. I hadn't intended for her to take it *that* way. "Don't worry," she said, pinning two gold stars to her flight-suit collar, "earn a pair of *these*, and you can spend as much time in art grav as I do."

I shrugged and played with the corner of the sheet that lay loosely across my legs. It was an attempt to appear unaffected by her comment. It failed miserably. Dezzie knew her jab had scored a hit, and so did I. I'd wanted a promotion ever since meeting her. Matching ranks would mean we wouldn't have to rely on Captain Zhao's mercy regarding our relationship. "Fraternizing with a superior officer is against regulations and may result in disciplinary action up to and including dishonorable discharge," or some bullshit like that.

I gestured toward the pistol in her hand. "You still know how to use that thing?" Of course, she did. I'd seen her range score from the previous week: forty-seven out of fifty bullseyes on both stationary and moving targets. Second best recorded on the *Icarus*. My record fifty out of fifty remained out of reach, though, if only by a hair. We both knew it was only a matter of time before she matched it, but I took no small measure of satisfaction knowing she'd never *best* it. Can't improve on perfection, after all.

Dezzie checked the charge of the pistol's battery and placed it in the mag holster on her left hip. Command staff didn't normally walk around armed to the teeth, but Captain Zhao had ordered it after coming through the Rift. Nobody knew what to expect in the Hades Galaxy. Sure, the drones had sent back petabytes of data, but nothing could replace instinct, and the hairs on the back of my neck? Well, they'd been standing on end for a week. I reached into the drawer and grabbed two cartridges, tossing them at Dezzie's head. She caught them both with her left hand without even looking up.

"You may need them. I've got a bad feeling about the rendezvous," I said.

She slid them into her thigh pocket and turned for the door. "Seriously, Paul. If you're late..."

"I won't be," I assured her. Dezzie's cabin door closed loudly behind her. I dashed for the shower. My bare feet slapped the deck in a staggered gait as I scooped up my uniform on the way. The ration meter showed twenty percent. It was an obscene amount of water—enough for a very long shower. I gritted my teeth and banged my head on the wall. Any other day, I'd have been tempted to blow off the first half-hour of my shift to indulge a bit. But today was different. Today we'd arrive at the rendezvous coordinates, and we weren't ready. To make matters worse, this morning's orders had been odd. No, they were downright strange. Yes, we'd manage to squeeze ten hours of work into the five given us. But what were we going to do with three hundred gallons of paint on a battleship?

AFTER SPENDING the rest of the morning overseeing the unpacking and distribution of hundreds of brushes and paint cans throughout the ship, my wrist com flashed an angry summons to the bridge. I took the direct route through the maintenance conduits, skipping the lift. Sure, I had to climb the equivalent of fifteen flights of stairs, but the artificial gravity created by the spinning rings of the *Icarus*'s fuselage waned as I made my way closer to the center of the ship. I practically floated the last fifty or so meters to the door of the command deck.

I grabbed onto the handles mounted on the wall next to the door's right-side control panel and palmed it open. When it was clear, I vaulted in, feet first, and landed on the edge of the nearest graviton plate. Despite what I'd said to Dezzie in her quarters earlier that morning, there wasn't a soul on board who wouldn't trade centripetal force for the real thing, and these new grav plates were as close as you could get on a ship. I just wish they'd been installed everywhere.

I was so intent on getting to the bridge on time, I almost ran into someone going the opposite way.

"Ho!" he exclaimed, snapping off a sharp salute. He was short and well-muscled, with black hair in a buzz cut. He wore a taut expression on his face. I glanced at his name badge and unit symbol. He was from Z Company. Engineering. Strange.

"Ho, Sergeant Jimenez," I said. Then, I nodded with my chin in the direction of the bridge. "What's all the fuss? Got a summons a few minutes ago. Haven't been up here in months."

"Yes, sir," he said nervously. "I mean, no, sir." His Mexican accent was thick, but not so thick I couldn't understand him. I took another look at the man's face. He couldn't have been a day over nineteen, and his eyes darted from my face to my name badge to my rank insignia and back again. Either he was very nervous around a superior officer, or Jimenez was tuned into the same shared sense of dread as the rest of us. "I've never been on the bridge, sir. Until today," he continued.

I saluted him again and waved him off. Wasn't very often that I came to deck two and got saluted first. With a few notable exceptions, command staff tended to outrank me by at least a couple of grades.

As I rounded the corner to the starboard side of the bridge, I ducked through the door and tried to sneak past the weapons station. But it was too late. Lieutenant Eamonn Stohl raised his gaze and shot me that mouth-full-of-perfect-teeth smile. I tried to act normal. But anytime Stohl was in the room, that seemed impossible.

A girlfriend's ex usually falls into one of two categories: either they're a royal asshole or, as was the case with Stohl, they're impossibly nice. I preferred the former to the latter. Made it easier to hate him. The fact that he and Dezzie used to… god, I don't even want to *think* about that! And if that weren't bad enough, his blond hair and perfect physique drew lingering glances from every single woman on the ship. He was a walking recruitment video. Every time I saw him, I wondered why Dezzie was even with a guy like me.

Stohl stared at me expectantly. Augmentations weren't allowed in the Navy, but there didn't seem to be any other way to explain the vibrant blue of his eyes. Luckily, I didn't have to salute him—we were the exact same rank and grade—and it's a good thing too. Don't know what I would've done had I been forced to show deference to that *piss sack*. I forced a smile and turned to the platform at the rear of the room.

"Where's Dezzie?" Stohl whispered loudly. His half-hearted attempt at discretion caught the attention of half the command crew. It was no secret I was dating the XO, but we did our best to remain professional. No use in flaunting it. Every guy on the ship was green with envy. And why wouldn't they be? Besides being the hottest woman to warm a berth on the *Icarus*, Dezzie was the second most important person on the entire ship. The most important, of course, was the chef, but I wasn't about to say that to Dezzie. Best if she went on thinking it was Captain Zhao.

I made a face at Stohl. "Dunno. I thought she'd be here." I shrugged as I walked away. Then, suddenly, I turned on my heel and ducked my head as Captain Zhao glanced in my direction. "That reminds me," I whispered. Not a stage whisper, like Stohl had used, but a real one. I didn't want to get on the captain's bad side any more than the next guy. "Why exactly am *I* here?"

It was a fair question. Logistics officers didn't need to come to the bridge very often. Or ever, really. The LogOps station probably had cobwebs on it for as much use as it'd seen.

"Cap called in every department head on the whole damn ship," Stohl replied, more quietly than before. "It's gonna get crowded in here in a few ticks."

No sooner had the words fallen from his lips than six more officers made their way onto the bridge. Every eye was trained on Captain Zhao. Despite Zhao's rigid posture, his eyes were dimmer than I remembered them—almost like he hadn't been sleeping well. He glanced expectantly at his pocket watch, an antique metal Rolex on a gold-colored chain. It seemed like an indulgence, but he wasn't subject to the same rules the rest of us were. Each of us was allowed one personal object onboard, and it had to weigh less than half a kilo. Made sense that they'd been such sticklers concerning weight, especially on a long-haul mission like this one. Hell, they'd even made us skip two meals and piss three times before letting us on board. That hadn't stopped me from bending the rules a bit with my personal object though. My grandpa's Beretta 92 and box of ammo weighed almost three times the limit, but I was the chief logistics officer for this mission. Who do you think *enforced* the weight limit?

Captain Zhao cleared his throat, and everyone held their breath in anticipation of what he was about to say. But, before his lips even parted, a tall man burst onto the bridge, followed by four muscular guards in helmets and gray, porcelain body armor. They carried their service rifles unholstered, which made me wonder who the newcomer was. The slender man might have been in his mid-fifties, was tall—maybe two meters—and had slicked his hair back with an entire bottle of gel. He sported a pinstripe, double-v suit—you know, the kind politicians and movie stars tend to wear—and shiny leather shoes. *Real* leather from the looks of them. No chance a man would go to that much trouble with his wardrobe and skimp on the shoes. He strode right up to the command dais and placed his hand on Zhao's shoulder. "Captain?" he smiled. If it was a genuine expression of good will, I was Santa Claus. It made me feel sick just looking at it.

Captain Zhao stood and squared himself to the taller man, clicking his heels together. He snapped off a well-practiced salute. "Sir!"

Wow. I'd only been a spacer for two years, but in all my time aboard the *Icarus*, I'd never seen Captain Zhao salute a civilian.

For his part, the taller man made a thumbs up with his fist, raised his eyebrows, and gestured towards the door. "You are relieved, sir."

If surprise were a physical, palpable thing, it would have filled the room and suffocated us all. As it was, none of the crew even seemed to be breathing. Shocked into silence, we watched helplessly as the scene unfolded before us. Zhao nodded curtly, handed the worn out, leather-bound captain's log to the other man, and strode briskly out the door. Why had he had it here to begin with? The log was symbolic; no captain ever really *used* it. And that expression on his face? Or lack of one? Zhao had *expected* this encounter. He'd known it was coming, which was unsettling to say the least. But what was even stranger still was the fact that Zhao's executive officer had missed the entire exchange. Where the *hell* was Dezzie?

After Zhao was gone, the man in the fancy suit stood in the center of the command dais with his hands clasped behind his back. "My name is Gabriel Simms," he said in a London accent. "I am President and CEO of Galaxia Corp." He paused, letting that sink in, which wasn't really necessary. Everybody'd heard of Galaxia Corp. "As of five months ago, the Terran Federation of Planets was dissolved. Like any defunct corporate entity, it has been divided and its assets sold off. While Galaxia was unsuccessful at acquiring the rights to the entire Hades Mission, we did manage to purchase the Navy, the Marine Corps, and a lion's share of future mining rights and colonial land grants in the Hades Galaxy."

A younger woman with strawberry blonde hair and a thick Irish accent raised her hand as if she were a student in a classroom. Simms looked at her patiently, then indulged her by nodding his head.

"What does that mean, Mr. Simms? For us? For the *Icarus*?" she asked. It was the question going through everyone's head at that moment, so I was glad she'd asked it. Nobody else had had the balls to.

"It means," he replied with more satisfaction than any man had a right to, "that the *Icarus* and her crew's contracts belong to Galaxia now." He sat down in the captain's chair and crossed his legs. "More importantly," he continued, "it means, for now, *I* am your new captain."

I hadn't seen so many wide eyes since that time my uncle Frank binged on Cerilian whiskey at a family reunion on Luna. He'd tossed an empty flask on the floor and stumbled right out of the airlock in front of a hundred close relatives and friends.

"Now," continued Captain Simms as he tapped a command into his wrist com, "Who's in charge of logistics around here?"

I stepped forward from my post behind him

and offered Simms a textbook salute. "I am, sir. Lieutenant Paul Johnson."

Simms continued scrolling through the memos and texts on his com. "I see the supplies are in position throughout the ship. Good." He looked up from the device, his gaze flat, almost bored. "Now, your team will remove every reference to the Terran Federation of Planets on this ship."

"Sir?" I questioned.

"All of them, Lieutenant," said Simms. "Paint over them and replace them with our corporate logo." He tapped a command on his wrist com and flicked an image of a stylized picture of two spiral galaxies connected by an arcing line. A small, antique-looking rocket ship followed the arc from one galaxy to the next.

"And the flag on the *Icarus*'s hull?" I asked, though I was afraid of the answer.

"Ah, yes," Simms responded. "Would you be so kind as to take care of that yourself, Lieutenant. I want it done right. I'm sure a smart, young man such as yourself can manage?"

Despite his tone dripping with disdain, I saluted him and responded, "Yes, sir," while making for the exit. But as I passed the captain's chair, where Simms was seated, I caught a whiff of something familiar, and my heart sank. There were very few things that could have been worse than a walk in an EV suit on the hull with a paint gun. But Simms smelling of Dezzie's cheap perfume was right at the top of that list.

2

MOVING TARGETS

A gift consists not in what is done or given, but in the intention of the giver or doer.

— SENECA THE YOUNGER IN MORAL ESSAYS, VOL. III

My living quarters had never felt so cramped. Svet Djordjijevski's spindly arms and legs spilled into the narrow aisle that separated our two bunks. Originally from Mars, he'd lived most of his life on the bigger moon of Ceridia Prime. As a result, his limbs *and* his name were ridiculously long. It was unfortunate, too, because most of the non-official rosters simply listed him as Petty Officer 3rd Class Svet D. Of course, that led to everyone calling him *Sweaty*. It kinda fit though. I don't know what they eat on the moons of Ceridia, but no matter how many showers the guy took, that musty, locker room stench just wouldn't wash off. He made our quarters smell like the time my college roommates brought home some of the artificial beef they were growing in the science labs to hide in the air vent right above my bed. To make matters worse, Svet was one of the hundred and fifty-seven crewmen from the *GSS Andromeda* ordered over to the *Icarus* by Captain Simms to instill 'corporate loyalty' among us Navy spacers. In the past five weeks, though, that had only made the original crew feel crowded and testy.

I bumped into Svet's lanky leg and nearly tripped. "Sorry, Djordi," I said. Even though he was a corporate shill, I just couldn't bring myself to call him *Sweaty*. There was an order to things in the Navy: you had your bunkmate's back no matter what. For me, that included coming up with a better nickname. So, I'd taken to calling him by a shortened version of his impossibly long surname.

"Not a problem," he said in his sing-song Ceridian accent. He tried his best to make room, but it was no use. The bunks on the *Icarus* just weren't made for people over two meters tall. Nor were its grav plates tuned for someone like Djordi. I don't even know how he managed to stand, let alone move around outside zero-G zones. Granted, there weren't that many grav plates on the *Icarus*, but they produced exactly one G—nearly twice what most outworlders were used to. Luckily, our quarters were on Inner Ring Three of Habitat Four. Its slower rate of spin meant that we barely felt point seven five most days. After spending my shift going back and forth between zero G and grav plates, though, I was just glad to have stable deck beneath my feet.

"You wanna come to the range with me?" offered Djordi. "I can show you how to use the BR-105's recoil management system."

It was tempting. The '105 was made by Browning & Ryusaki. The old US-based gun maker had been acquired by a Japanese tech company back in '34. Like almost everything else, though, BR Co. had been gobbled up by Galaxia somewhere along the way. Our corporate friends were all too fond of reminding us just how many companies Galaxia's holdings included. For the life of me, though, I couldn't understand why they'd be proud of that. No matter how you spun it, a corporation was just the rich preying on the weak. I couldn't help but wonder what that made me now that I worked for one. And not just any corporation. I worked for the biggest one of all.

Regardless of who made it, the '105 was the most state-of-the-art assault pistol that civilians could use, and some even argued it was a better gun than anything the Navy had issued us. I'm not exactly sure how it worked; something about lopping off a tiny piece of superconducting metal and slamming it through the barrel at near relativistic speeds. One might expect such a tiny projectile to be worthless against armored targets, but the '105 had enough stopping power to down a charging rhino. It. Was. Awesome. But a weapon that could punch a hole in an inch and a half of hardened steel wasn't exactly the best choice for use on a spaceship if you ask me.

I palmed the wall next to my personal locker and retrieved my Beretta and a box of ammo. Unfortunately, the bullets weren't original, but they still worked. Had to *misplace* a shipment of Canadian whiskey in exchange for the guys down in maintenance printing me off some new ones. It'd been a risky thing to do. I still don't know how they overrode the printer's safety settings. Making weapons and explosives was strictly prohibited. But the whiskey was real, and this far from Earth, it was worth its weight in gold. So, I wasn't surprised at all when they managed to fill my order the very same day.

"Think I'll use my grandpa's gun," I said.

"Have it your way," Djordi said. "I've got my certification tomorrow. I need to practice using my corporate-issued piece. Maybe afterward? I'd love to squeeze off a few rounds with that antique." He stared at the Beretta's burnished metal surface longingly. I held it out for him to examine, and he took it from me, smiling. After turning it over in his hand a few times, and stroking the top of the barrel, he returned it. "Very nice, Paul."

"Thanks," I replied. "It's really all I have left of my family." I had to be careful here. Djordi had spent the last five weeks trying to pry as much out of me about what'd happened to my family as he could, but I didn't know him well enough to share. In fact, the only person I'd told... I gritted my teeth and exhaled slowly, forcing the memories of Dezzie from my mind. I slapped Djordi on the shoulder. "Let's go kill some stuff," I said and headed for the door.

Arriving at the range we found the entrance flanked by two of the captain's personal guards. They wore grey body armor and matching humorless expressions. I wondered what it was they hated so much about their jobs. Did the armor itch? Or was following Simms around all day really that distasteful?

When they saw me, they did their duty and saluted. "Lieutenant Johnson," said the taller of the two. He had a small scar over his left eye. I almost didn't see it through the tinted faceplate of his helmet.

"Sergeant," I replied, hoping I'd gotten his rank correct. The Galaxian insignias didn't follow standard military patterns. His was a swirly, stylized galaxy with five silver chevrons in the middle: E-5 I suppose. I started to push past them to the firing range, but the shorter, stockier one grabbed my arm in a vise-like grip.

"No one's allowed in until the captain and XO are finished," he said. I looked from the man's face to his hand around my wrist and back again. His expression softened a bit, and he let go. "Captain's orders," he added.

Great. For obvious reasons, I'd been avoiding Dezzie the past few weeks; successfully, I might add. It was amazing how little the XO and ship's logistics officer really needed to engage each other in the course of duty, and what little *was* needed, could easily be accomplished via short, impersonal text messages. I turned quickly and strode briskly down the upwardly-curved corridor. I wasn't about to run into Dezzie on my leisure time if I could help it. But before I could put enough distance between myself and the door, it parted with a whoosh and out strode Simms and Dezzie. Djordi had been caught flat-footed somewhere between them and me. He joined the guards in offering a salute. But I didn't. Instead, I pressed my luck, hoping they'd think I just hadn't seen them.

"Lieutenant Johnson?" inquired a voice from behind me. Thankfully, it wasn't Dezzie's.

I may have gotten away with pretending not to see them, but there'd be no convincing anyone I hadn't *heard* them, not in such a small space anyway. I stopped abruptly, put on my best face, and turned around. I feigned surprise and saluted rigidly. "Captain," I said.

Simms nodded his head to the side in a gesture to join him as he walked. I trotted down the corridor and fell in beside him and in front of Djordi and Dezzie. "Sir?"

"I was just going to send you a bridge summons, Lieutenant. You've saved me the trouble."

"Bridge summons, sir?" I asked.

"You know, Lieutenant, there are two nasty rumors going around about you." He arched an eyebrow before continuing. What an unsettling thing to have your captain say. It was already hard enough with Dezzie walking behind me. I hadn't seen her in weeks, and frankly, if I didn't see her for the rest of the mission that would be too soon. Add to that uneasiness an accusation from the captain, and I was feeling more uncomfortable than the time I had the middle seat on a redeye flight from Billings to Paris. The man on my right coughed with every breath, and the woman to my left spilled over our shared armrest to take up more of my seat than I did.

"Rumors, sir?" I inquired. Even with the prevailing military decorum, there was no such thing as a secret on a spaceship. Gossip-mongering was a favorite pastime in the Navy.

"Well, the first," he said as he wiped down and holstered a Rio 45 with what looked like a custom handle made of Brazilian teak, "is that you're the best shot on this ship." He smiled and glanced over his shoulder at Dezzie, who was staring off into the distance somewhere in front of us. "Frankly, I didn't believe that a *logistics* guy was our best marksman until I saw your range score and then verified it with the recorded video feed. You're a natural." He pointed at my Beretta. "May I?"

I unholstered it and handed it to him before replying. "Thank you, sir. May I ask what the second rumor is?"

He admired the weapon, testing its weight and balance. "That you and Commander Pearson were in a romantic...*entanglement* before Galaxia acquired the *Icarus*. One that was against the regs, I might add. It's a wonder you made it this far into Hades with Zhao running such a loose operation."

I swallowed hard. It felt as if there were a wad of crumpled paper filled with sawdust caught in my throat. "There may be some truth to both of those notions, sir."

"Yes," came the captain's pointed reply. He returned my pistol and reached for something in his thigh pocket. Simms had taken to wearing a flight suit just like the rest of the command staff. Something about being in Rome and doing as the Romans, but that didn't make any sense to me. The *TFP Italia* wasn't even in the same galaxy, let alone the same mission. So, his reference remained a mystery. He held out his hand and I caught a glimpse of two shiny objects in it.

"Please," he motioned for me to take them, and dropped them into my outstretched hand. Somehow, I knew what they were even without looking. I'd handled Dezzie's commander stars on more than one occasion. Still, my eyes went wide when I opened my hand to reveal a pair identical to hers.

Then, Simms held out his other hand. Dangling from it was a round, gold medallion on a thick ribbon embroidered with five interlocking rings. I grabbed the medal as well and examined it in confusion.

"Not many people remember this because it was so long ago," Simms said, "but I'm actually a pretty decent shot myself, Paul." He cocked his head to one side. "May I call you *Paul*?"

"Of course, sir," I replied.

"Anyway," he continued, "I took gold in the Ryad Olympics back in '46."

My eyes must have been the size of saucers. Simms smiled with fake humility. "Gold medalist or not," he said, "I never hit fifty of fifty. Until I do, I'm going to ask that you hold onto that for me."

I didn't know what to say. The gesture was so totally unexpected it had me second-guessing my opinion of the man. "Thank you, sir," was all I could muster.

"Now, pin those stars, *Commander* Johnson. You're being transferred from logistics to B Company."

If Simms giving me his Olympic gold medal for marksmanship was confusing, imagine my surprise at being promoted out of turn. I'd skipped Lieutenant Commander altogether. And now, I'd been transferred? "Sir, B Company is a *Marine* outfit."

"And you'll be leading it, Paul. I need a logical, cool head. Someone who can mind the details. Besides, it seems like such a waste for the ship's best shot to languish away behind a desk."

"Yes, sir," I said, though it was more out of reflex than anything. I certainly didn't mean it. I didn't want to be a *Marine*! I hadn't trained for it, and I certainly didn't want my friends calling me a jarhead!

I numbly pinned the stars to my collar and saluted him. He returned the gesture sharply. Clearly, he'd been practicing; it was the best salute I'd seen a shill make. Then, he grabbed my arm and pulled me aside, whispering in my ear. "She's a wonderful woman, Paul. And now that you're the same rank, you can fraternize all you want."

I caught the briefest of sideways looks from Dezzie, and that's all it took for my stomach to tumble into a spin. It angered me that she could still make me feel like that, especially given the circumstances.

"One last thing, Commander." Simms handed me a transparapad with a biometric lock. I knew what it meant.

"Orders, Captain?" I asked.

"Yes. Have a look," he replied.

I palmed the pad to open it. The screen snapped to life and I skimmed the three paragraphs making up the order. My head was spinning. I read it again, pausing on the words *dropship*, *alien*, and *artifacts* to make sure I hadn't misread them. But the one word that stuck out more than any other was perhaps the most important. Humanity had made first contact, and the aliens had a name—*Cerberus*.

3

CALM BEFORE THE STORM

A hymn is sung before the fight
  To wisp away the soldiers' fright
  But long before the end of night
  The reaper comes a reaping.

— *Atticus Brown*, Martian Verses, vol. I

Djordi fidgeted nervously with the five-point harness of his seat, his head bowed, and eyes closed. I sat across from him in the narrow confines of the dropship's personnel compartment. To my right sat Gunnery Sergeant Jeanne Lamiraux and opposite her, Sergeant Jimenez, formerly of Z Company. Lamiraux eyed my holster suspiciously before shaking her head. "You expect to wage a one-man war, Commander?"

I shot her a look of consternation. She nodded

toward my Beretta. "You're the only officer on this boat with two sidearms." Her French accent and dark skin had me guessing she hailed from the Ivory Coast. Her hair was cut in a close-cropped style popular among young people these days, and she was small of stature. Even seated, it was easy to see she wasn't much taller than maybe one-and-a-half meters.

Djordi's head shot up. "He can carry as many sidearms as he wants. Commander's prerogative," he argued in my defense. I think he was more excited about my promotion than I was. Lamiraux frowned but didn't dare argue. Even an E-7 in the Marines had to show deference to a low-ranking naval officer like Djordi. Having won the exchange, he smiled smugly while folding his gangly arms across his narrow chest.

"Old habit," I replied, unholstering the BR-105 I'd been issued for the mission. I gazed at it fondly before returning it to the mag holster on my right thigh, images of the warped and twisted steel targets from yesterday's session at the firing range dancing through my head. "Don't get me wrong, Gunny. I'm a fan of the '105. But the Beretta was my grandpa's, and well, I don't go anywhere without it."

She grunted. "You'd never catch a *real* Marine with that piece of junk. Not with lives on the line. It belongs in a museum display case, not in live action."

Major Chan, the *former* leader of B Company, laid a hand on Lamiraux's shoulder and cocked his head to one side as if trying to remember something. "As my mother used to say, Gunny, better take that down a couple notches." I'd spent the better part of a day in briefings with Chan, but I still wasn't used to hearing that Texas drawl coming from someone who looked like my childhood Tae Kwan Do teacher. That may not have been the most culturally-sensitive thought, but hey, I *did* grow up on a ranch. As he talked, it was hard not to picture Chan out of uniform, dressed to match his voice. Texans may wear boots and big belt buckles, but everyone knew that *real* cowboys come from Montana.

"But he's a *spacer*," complained Lamiraux, as if that justified her disdain for me. The major frowned at her use of the term, which was never intended to convey respect.

"I don't give two wet shits what he is, Sergeant. How many stars do you see on that collar?" He pointed to my uniform, which was barely visible in my armor's neck joint.

"Two," came Lamiraux's begrudging response.

The major tapped the insignia on his own collar next. "And here on mine?"

"One," she sighed.

"And on yours?"

"None, sir." Her voice was laced with resignation.

Major Chan sat down in the empty seat next to Djordi, buckling his restraints with the deftness of someone who'd logged dozens of orbital drops. "I trust my point has been made, Sergeant?"

"Yes, sir," Lamiraux replied.

My wrist com buzzed loudly, signaling that it

was time for our in-flight briefing. As company commander, that was my job. I'd issued orders before, but nothing like this. As a logistics officer, the most dangerous instructions I'd ever given were where to unload a palette of sanitary wipes. It wasn't lost on me that in my new capacity, a single word from my lips might send a man to his death, and my chest tightened at the thought of it.

I tapped a couple commands into my com and flicked my finger across its touch pad, sending the briefing to the overhead monitors for everyone on this and the other two dropships to see. It displayed a three-dimensional rendering of the solar system the *Icarus* had brought us to. The system contained four planets and a star, which was a dark, ruby red, not unlike Gliese 581 back in the Milky Way. But, unlike its distant cousin, this red star was unstable. Giant columns of solar ejecta erupted from its surface, like the volcanos of Hypernica IV. But, if we thought the star in this system was unstable, the condition of the planets was downright alarming. The innermost was a rocky ball of silicon and iron, while the three furthest from the star were gas giants. The outer planets looked more like massive comets with large plumes of their gaseous matter streaming away from them in giant tan and purple tails, as if an unseen force had torn them apart. Our destination was the rocky moon of the blue gasser. It seemed no less worse for wear. Its crust was cracked like the shell of an egg spilling out an amber yoke of fiery magma.

"Several months ago," I said, after clearing my

throat, "Galaxia SciCorp discovered a faint signal coming from the innermost portions of the Hades Nebula. Probes were sent and returned with promising data, proof of the existence of sentient beings in this galaxy." I paused to let that sink in. Djordi's mouth was agape and Jimenez smiled like a kid in a toy store. Lamiraux stared at the monitor with an expressionless face. Nice. I could respect someone with that kind of professionalism, despite her initial reluctance to accept me as B Company's commanding officer.

"In the intervening weeks, the imaging techs developed a method to boost the signal—a scanner of sorts. In doing so, they not only got a better fix on the signal's point of origin, but they discovered new ones—thousands of individual artificial signals. Since the sudden appearance of the Rift near Jupiter, there's been a lot of speculation about the existence of intelligent non-human life. Personally, I always thought a stable intergalactic wormhole showing up right on our doorstep was a little too good to be true. Now we have proof positive. We aren't alone." I turned to Major Chan for the second half of the briefing. He stood and clasped his hands behind his waist before pointing to a grainy image of an alien cityscape.

"Our mission is to reconnoiter the ruins on Auriven I. It's the largest moon of the gas giant Auriven II. If we encounter any Cerberus forces, we are to avoid engagement if possible."

"*Engagement*, sir?" asked Jimenez, his voice thick with apprehension. I couldn't blame him. He was an engineer, after all, and he hadn't volunteered for duty in B Company. No, that'd had been my doing. Same for Djordi, who was perhaps the most agile man I'd ever seen in zero G. Most outworlders took to microgravity like a fish to water, but Djordi possessed a special talent that might prove useful in a pinch. Besides, I needed a friend on this mission, and after Dezzie and I had broken up, he was the closest thing I had to one.

"If necessary, Lieutenant, we'll do what the TFP... what *Galaxia* Marines always do. We'll give'm *hell*." It was a statement befitting a potential skirmish in a galaxy named for the Greek god of the Underworld. I would have smiled if my stomach hadn't been all twisted up in a knot of dread.

"What are they?" asked one of the Marines near the front hatch.

"Imma bust me some little green Martian ass!" replied another.

Lamiraux, who was used to being the ranking enlisted person in the company, shushed the men with a wave of her hand. "Did you call the enemy *Cerberus*, sir?" she asked. "As in the three-headed *hound of Hades*, guarding the gates of the Underworld?"

"That's right, Gunny," said Chan. "We're gonna find out what they are, what their weakness is, and what they're guardin'...and then we're gonna take it."

My stomach lurched. The Navy would *never* have operated like this. Smash-and-grab just wasn't our style, and it surprised me that Major Chan seemed to take to the strategy so well. But, as

I had to keep reminding myself, we worked for a corporation now, and our priorities—and tactics—had been turned on their ear. It was enough to drive me to the brink of desertion but breaking a twenty-year contract only two years after it started was grounds for a court-martial. Besides, I didn't want to spend the next thirteen months in the brig of some puddle-jumper heading back through the Rift to Jupiter Station. I'd seen the rations they feed prisoners. Cricket powder and soy milk just didn't appeal to me.

Chan continued to brief the team of our mission parameters, objectives, and rules of engagement. I tried to listen, but my mind was elsewhere. Back on the *Icarus*. Back with Dezzie. I still didn't understand why Simms had promoted me like that and then dangled a rekindled relationship with Dezzie in front of me like a carrot before a mule. It just didn't make sense. So, what if I was good with a pistol? So was everyone else in B Company, and they were used to firing at *living* targets. What value did I *really* add to the mission? My gut told me there was more to it than the top marksman score on the *Icarus*, and that I'd find out what that was sooner rather than later.

NORMALLY, anyone routinely participating in orbital drops would spend a couple of days a week pulling sessions in the CGTM. It stood for *centripetal gravity training module*, but the crew called it the *tumbler*. I'd only had time for one session before boarding the dropship, but it didn't take more than a minute inside to see why it had earned that name. To make matters worse, we were so pressed for time that the cleaning crews had only done a cursory pass through the module's cockpit. The last guy's vomit was still visible in the crevices of the passenger control panel. It didn't matter, though. Mine soon mixed with his.

So, to say that I was unprepared for the Gs we pulled on descent to Auriven I would have been an understatement. Smartly, I'd purposely put off eating to avoid a repeat of the episode in the *tumbler*. Besides having all the blood in my body smashed against the back of my cranium for ten minutes, the ride wasn't so bad. True, it was a little bumpier than I'd expected, but I didn't black out. There were bets between Lamiraux and several grunts as to how long I'd last. But when the ship's landing gear hit the ground with a solid thud, I unbuckled my harness and sprang to my feet. "Hey, Gunny," I said. "What's your credit ID? I'll send you a personal transfer to cover all the money you just lost." She didn't answer. Instead, she shot me a steely glare. I was beginning to wonder if her face was permanently frozen like that. There were snickers from somewhere at the other end of the compartment though, and I knew my barb had hit its mark. It took effort to combine alpha dog with *nice guy*, and so far, I was doing a pretty good job of it.

The team began the task of inspecting their armor, weapons, and gear. We'd all checked them a dozen times, but this was a nervous ritual, and I joined in with the rest. I really didn't know what I was doing with the armor, though. So, when Djordi tugged at my arm to pull me aside from the others—which was no easy task given the tightness of the compartment—I breathed a sigh of relief.

"Have you read the story of King David and Uriah the Hittite?" His accent was soothing. I took a mental note of that and filed it away for future use. I'm sure there'd be plenty of need for someone to calm us down.

As for his question, I was drawing a blank. Was that a televid serial or a movie I hadn't seen? "Not ringing a bell, Djordi."

"It's from the Bible," he said, as if that would explain it all. When my blank stare didn't change, he continued. "Anyway, David was King of Israel, and he was in love with Bathsheba. Problem is, she was married to a soldier named Uriah. So, to get him out of the way, David sent Uriah to the front lines of the battle where he would surely be killed. Then, with no one to stand in his way, he took Bathsheba to his bed."

It was a fascinating story, but I failed to see its relevance to our mission. Why was Djordi telling me this now? "What's your point?"

"Don't you see it, sir? Why do you think Simms promoted you? Assigned you to B Company? *You are* Uriah. And Simms and Dezzie are King David and Bathsheba."

"That doesn't make any sense," I said. "Simms

already *has* Dezzie. He doesn't need me out of the way."

"Unless Dezzie's still in love with you," offered Djordi. "It would drive a man like Simms crazy. Think about it. He's used to getting what he wants, and he doesn't want just her loyalty. He wants her heart."

I exhaled deeply, then smiled. "When did you get so smart in matters of love? You can't be over twenty-two."

"We're poor on Ceridia Prime," he answered. "All we *have* is love."

My wrist com buzzed. It was time to dismount, so I tapped a command and brought my com up to my face. "*Icarus*, you getting this?"

"We have eyes on you, Commander Johnson." It wasn't the yeoman's voice like I'd expected. It was Dezzie's. I had to pretend it didn't matter. But truth be told, of all the two hundred and twenty-three voices on the *Icarus*, hers was probably the *last* one I wanted to hear.

"Commander Pearson? Good to know you're up there. Got your finger on the big red button?" I asked. It was a reference to the fire control lock for the *Icarus*'s railgun batteries. If needed, the ship could put a thousand rounds anywhere on the surface in less than a minute. It was somewhat reassuring to know that if we ran into trouble the enemy wouldn't make it home for drinks later that night. I say *somewhat* reassuring, because the half-kilometer target radius meant *neither would we*.

I leapt from the threshold of the dropship's hatch and landed on the dusty ground with a pair of staggered thuds. The gravity was light, but manageable, and the air was breathable. Still, we wore our helmets in case of contaminants or noxious spores. No amount of perfectly-mixed nitrogen and oxygen would matter if you had an anaphylactic reaction to something floating in the air.

We didn't need to consult our com maps to find our target. The dropship pilot—a female contractor by the name of Garza—had set us down less than half a click from the alien ruins we'd seen from orbit.

"What more can you tell us, Commander?" asked Lamiraux as we fanned out for our approach on foot. "About these Cerberus. What do they look like? Tech level? Tactics? With so little intel, I'd feel less naked attacking a full regiment of Martian Shock Troops in my panties."

Now *that* was an image I wasn't expecting to have on the cusp of battle. I'd only just met the Gunny, and only seen her face. Marine body armor made all wearers look somewhat androgynous. But hers was the most striking face I'd seen in a Marine uniform, and if her face looked that good, I could only imagine the rest of her. Luckily, or *unluckily*, my imagination filled in the blanks, and damned if I couldn't get the thought out of my head. Why'd she have to go and talk about panties like that?

"I'm afraid details are sparse, Sergeant." Of course, there were things that the team was just better off not knowing. Suffice it to say, our first contact with the Cerberus was an unmitigated disaster. "But we sent a team in. Like this one. From the *Prometheus*." Together with the *Icarus* and the *London*, the *Prometheus* was one of three Hades Class ships the Navy had sent through the Rift, though the *Prometheus* had gone through about a month or so before us.

"And?" pressed Lamiraux.

Chan quickened his pace and closed the distance between us. "And they didn't make it out," he said matter-of-factly.

My eyes went wide at his admission. We'd been given strict orders from Simms and the Joint Captains to keep the fate of the *Prometheus* and her crew confidential. The details were on a need-to-know basis.

"Why weren't you going to tell us, Commander?" groused Lamiraux. Her eyes were daggers.

I had to think fast. I was losing my grip on this unit, and we were only twenty minutes out the door. "I didn't want to clean up the puddles of piss on the floor of the dropship if I told you, Sergeant. Left all my sanitary napkins when I was transferred from logistics."

That elicited a chuckle from Djordi, and a hushed snicker from some of the other men. I heard one of them say, "nice one for a *POG*." It was Marine slang for *person other than grunt*. This was good news. Humor was an effective way into the hearts and minds of your men, and I needed them to fall in behind me.

Chan shook his head. "They need to know, Commander. Anyone riskin' their life deserves no less."

I begrudgingly nodded my agreement, and he continued. "We designated the system where the first alien signal originated *Hades Prime*. Its star was a red dwarf like the one in this system."

"Let me guess," interrupted Lamiraux. "It was as unstable as a Hollywood Diva's offscreen temperament?"

Chan chuckled. "You could say that. And the planets, too. The team zeroed in on the only one in the system with an atmosphere and found the source of the signal—ruins. They also found something else—some kind of *artifact*."

"Major…" I warned. Then, I sighed in resignation. There was no stopping now. I shrugged to indicate my indifference, and he finished the story.

"The team woke somethin' up. Some sort of guards. There was a firefight. The Marines acquitted themselves just fine, until…"

"Until what," prompted Jimenez.

I jumped in to finish things out. "It gets a bit fuzzy after that. They tried making it back to the dropship with whatever it was they found in tow, but before they could saddle up for launch, an unidentified ship attacked and destroyed the *Prometheus*. All we know is it was fast. Really fast."

The look of shock on everyone's face was not unexpected. I'd felt the same way yesterday when I found out. I knew several people aboard the *Prometheus*…some of them friends. "The *Wall Street* was the closest ship and the first to receive the distress signal," I said. "They set course to retrieve the stranded dropship and search the wreckage of the *Prometheus* for survivors."

"What did the Marine landing party say when they got them on board the *Wall Street*," Djordi asked.

I stopped and tapped a command into my wrist com, bringing up the topo map, then switched the HUD in my helmet to project a thermal overlay on my visor. I hoped that any living thing—biological or mechanical—would give off a heat signature. Didn't want to be surprised. Then I answered Djordi's question. "The *Wall Street* was six days out. Hades' star went nova before they could rescue the landing party or search for escape pods from the *Prometheus*."

Lamiraux hit the switch on the side of her helmet to retract her faceplate. It slid back with a whoosh and she took a deep breath of alien air. Then, she shaded her eyes with her hand and looked up toward the crimson sun perched low in the sky. Since the planet's rotation was relatively slow, we knew we still had several hours before it would set. I couldn't read her emotion, which bothered me. "You boys sure do know how to reassure a lady," she said at last. Her attempt at 'dame speak' from the 1930s didn't quite work with a heavy French accent.

Chan slapped her on the back and smiled. "Come on, Sergeant. Everybody knows you ain't a *lady*." After a brief round of nervous chuckles and sideways looks, we made our way to the edge of the alien ruins. I glanced down absentmindedly and noted that I had one hand on the grip of my Beretta, and the other on the '105. Was I nervous? Maybe, but it felt more like excitement—like how I used to feel on Christmas Eve as a kid or like I did in a game of hide-and-seek. I didn't know exactly what I expected it to be like, but I *hadn't* expected it to feel like *that*. But it did. The ultimate game of alien hide-and-seek. Hopefully we'd soon find out what the Cerberus we're all about.

Ready or not, here we come.

4
AWAKENING

It is not good a sleeping hound to wake, nor give any one a secret to divine.

— GEOFFREY CHAUCER IN TROILUS AND CRESSIDA, BOOK III

If we'd expected the alien ruins on Auriven I to be like the ones in old sci-fi movies, well, they didn't disappoint. Tall, sweeping, metallic-looking spires dominated the center of the complex, while flat-topped, step-like buildings encircled them like a phalanx of defenders. Well-worn paths in the dusty ground funneled into several entry points in the city's perimeter wall. We chose the one closest to us.

"How many feet have walked this way?" Lamiraux asked. She'd replaced her helmet at Chan's insistence, and I could hear her breathing over the com.

"How do we even know they *had* feet?" I responded, a little too flippant for her liking. She glared at me through her visor.

Djordi's voice crackled over the same channel. "You said *had*."

"Yeah," I continued, "Doesn't look like anything living's been through here in a very long time." I stooped to examine the dirt beneath our feet. "But in its heyday, this place was a regular Times Square."

I hadn't meant it to frighten, but that comment caused everyone but me to draw their weapons. Jimenez held his '105 with a straightened-but-shaky arm. If he hadn't been wearing armored gloves, I'm sure I'd have seen knuckles whiter than snow.

"Stay alert," ordered Chan. He tapped a few commands into the touchpad on his left forearm and studied the results in its display for a second or two. "I'm not detectin' any radiation or other indicators of danger." He pointed toward the tall clump of castle-like spires. "But just because it looks calm now don't mean it's an alien Disneyland."

I smiled briefly at the comparison. The similarities were surprising, at least from its pictures. I'd grown up in Montana but hadn't ever been to California. So close by galactic standards. Went straight from high school in Kalispell to college on Luna. Part of me was sad I'd never been to Disneyland. But being among the first humans to explore an ancient alien city seemed to make up for that and my other childhood disappointments. Being here was like crack cocaine for my wanderlust.

As we ventured deeper in, the ruins began to give up their secrets. Smooth, metallic walls ceded ground to pipes and power conduits. While the paths between buildings were still dirt—whether because they actually were dirt, or they were just covered with dust from a thousand years of disuse I couldn't say—the floors inside the buildings were not unlike the metal deck plates on the *Icarus*.

Everything was quiet until a panel on the ceiling of the corridor slid open and a turret dropped down. A bright blue, fan-shaped light swept across our formation from left to right before disappearing.

There was a moment of hesitation before everyone in the group scattered like cockroaches in a cheap motel on Jupiter Station. I rolled forward toward the turret figuring it would have a hard time tracking directly beneath it. I was wrong. No sooner had I finished my well-practiced summersault than the turret ignored the others scrambling for cover and filled my chest with a dozen rounds. I felt like a piece of regolith standing between a miner's jackhammer and a deposit of helium three. Miraculously, though, my armor held. Outside of a bruised sternum and having the wind knocked out of me, I was no worse for wear.

Major Chan and Gunnery Sergeant Lamiraux were the first to gather their feet and train their weapons on the turret, spraying it with superheated slugs from their service rifles. But it was no use. Their rounds bounced off a semi-transparent shield of some kind, light blue flares of energy their only effect. The spent slugs fell on top of me like a rain of near-molten drops. One of them got caught in the flexible joint between my shoulder and chest plate and nearly burned through to my undersuit before I managed to flick it to the ground.

For its part, the turret retaliated by darkening the corridor with a thousand tiny projectiles. While most of the team hit the deck and caught only a handful of bullets on their backs, one of the grunts near the rear of our formation wasn't so lucky. Whether he hadn't seen what was coming, or he'd frozen in fear, he caught the full effect of several hundred enemy rounds slamming into him with the force a magnetic freight skid. He tumbled backward like a rag doll falling from a little girl's grip. When it was over, his lifeless form lay in a crumpled heap on the ground.

I had to think fast before anyone else was hurt. My eyes sought an answer on the wall and were drawn to a conduit running along its length at about head height. I sprang to my feet and pulled the grappler's knife from its sheath on my right boot in a single, fluid motion. Two hacks had the conduit severed, and in the second miracle of the day for me, my guess had been right. With no more power, the turret stopped its assault and drooped limply toward the floor.

Jimenez stood erect, and warily lowered his weapon. "Sure the fuck ain't Disneyland," he said in a Mexican accent that seemed to thicken with excitement. His comment elicited a chorus of nervous chuckles over the com channel.

"No," I said, making my way toward the downed Marine. "It sure as hell isn't." Lamiraux and Djordi had beaten me to him though and had already popped his faceplate and peeled off his chest armor. Blood trickled from the corner of his mouth. Djordi brought up his wrist com and keyed in a scan. It didn't take long to confirm our fears. He shook his head somberly.

I searched for his name, but his chest plate was upside down on the ground beside him. "Where's his nameplate?" I growled. "Dammit, I didn't even know his name!"

"Lance Corporal Patel, Sir," responded Lamiraux as she reached down and forced the man's eyes shut before closing his tinted faceplate. "He was from New Delhi. Had three siblings in the Corp. One was on the *Prometheus*. This mission was personal for him."

"Well, now it's personal for *me*," I whispered.

Chan and the others formed a circle around us, and I stood to address them. "We'll pick up Patel on the way back. He deserves a burial at space. I'm not about to leave him here. This is no place to bury a soldier."

There were nods of agreement from everyone in the circle. Good. It didn't matter what they thought, though. I was in charge, and it was my decision to make.

"What now?" asked Djordi. He tried to hide the nervousness in his voice, but just like when we played cards, he was as easy to read as a cheap comic book.

"Our goal hasn't changed. We continue with the mission," I said. "And now that we know it won't be a walk in the park, we'll be a little more careful."

"A *little*?" asked Jimenez.

"A lot," replied Major Chan as he keyed in a scan on his wrist com. "Where there're power lines," he continued, "there's electromagnetic interference." He inspected the end of the severed conduit and nodded with satisfaction. "Just as I thought. Hardly any shielding."

"So, we can scan for magnetic fields?" I asked.

"Yes, sir," replied the major, "and I bet if we home in on the strongest one, we'll find the source of that signal."

"And some answers," I added, as I headed past the lifeless turret. I glanced over my shoulder at our fallen comrade and thought of those we lost on the *Prometheus*. "It better be worth it."

IF HINDSIGHT IS twenty-twenty then it *was* worth it. Unfortunately, I had the unenviable job of telling that to Lance Corporal Patel's family. I toyed with the idea of sending an old-fashioned text, but my balls descended, and I instead resolved to record a vidmail as soon as we returned to the *Icarus*.

Chan followed his scans, and in turn, we followed Chan. After a few fits and starts, and a handful of questionable detours involving more of the ceiling turrets, we eventually made it to the basement of a central control facility.

"The magnetic fields are off the charts down here," said Chan.

This was work for an engineer, so Jimenez stepped forward to inspect the room and its contents. He was in his element now, and with the threat of guard turrets behind us, he seemed more at ease; even confident. "Loads of power flowing out of the room," he offered. "Through several large conduits."

"Flowing from *what*," I asked.

"From these," he said, pointing to a cluster of three, large, egg-shaped objects in one corner of the room. They were about seven feet tall and twice as big around at their centers. Jimenez removed a glove and ran his hand across the closest egg's smooth surface. "It's warm," he said in surprise.

Chan pecked at the controls of his tactical pad. "Still no indications of radiation, neutrinos, or any other harmful emissions."

By now the rest of us had removed our helmets and were breathing the alien air. "Smells like rotten eggs in here," said one of the grunts. I made a point of glancing at his name tag: *Private Cooper*. I wasn't about to lose another nameless soldier. His face bore an expression of wary curiosity, and like the others, sweat trickled down his temples.

Lieutenant Jimenez's fingers tested the egg's surface until he found a spring-loaded access panel. Purplish-pink light flooded out of the compartment the second it was opened, causing all but Lamiraux to recoil with caution. Damn, that woman was nails.

"Nothing to worry about folks," reassured Jimenez. "Just some pretty lights."

I stepped closer to get a better look. In the center of a half meter by half meter compartment in the middle of the egg was a light purple crystal suspended in the air. Four glowing nodes pointed at it, but none touched it. "What's keeping it up?" I asked.

It was probably the question everyone was wondering, but nobody had expected Jimenez to reach in with his bare hand and run it between one of the nodes and the crystal. That's exactly what he did, though. When his arm didn't explode and no alien electricity jumped out to fry his brain, he repeated the motion, encircling the entire object like one of those cheap Vegas levitation tricks. "Magnetic fields," he said grinning.

The crystal looked to weigh at least ten kilos. "Must be pretty strong to hold up a crystal that big," I said.

"Technically," replied Jimenez, "it's a tetrahedron."

"What is it?" asked Chan. "Some kind of power source?"

Jimenez shook his head as he studied readings from his wrist com. "I don't think so. The power unit seems to be built around the tetrahedron, not to take power from it, but to supply *it* with power."

"You didn't answer my first question," said Chan, a little annoyed. "What *is* it?"

Jimenez sighed and then shrugged. "If I had to guess, I'd say it's a data storage array."

"Like an old hard drive?" I said. It wasn't as far-fetched as it sounded, and actually made sense. AmPrime had been using crystalline storage modules to run the Galactic Internet for years.

"Something like that," said Jimenez. "Only this could hold a hundred thousand petabytes of data. Maybe more."

"In English," said Chan.

Jimenez tried hard not to roll his eyes. Chan outranked him by three grades. "We could put the entire Galactic Internet in this thing and still have room for Turing's Chess Bot." Chesster, as he was called by many, was the most advanced AI to date. It was said he had his own dedicated quantum core and cooling system, as well as the second-largest cloud array ever assembled.

"Which means," said Djordi eagerly, "that thing is filled with a lot of alien data. Maybe new math, science, technology. Cures for diseases in this galaxy…"

"Weapons?" added Chan. There was a hunger in his eyes that made me uneasy. I'd never seen him so wolfish.

I motioned to the other two eggs, and Jimenez opened them in succession. To our surprise, the second one contained a yellow glowing orb, and the third a blue crystal. "How are we gonna get these outta here?" asked Jimenez. "These units must weigh a ton."

I placed my hand on the surface of the one containing the yellow orb, peering into the compartment's inner workings for clues. "Maybe we could detach them from the power units and leave those behind."

Jimenez shook his head. "My readings say these power units produce more than five Hades Class battleships put together. Maybe more."

Chan frowned. "So, we can't crack the code on these alien hard drives without the big ass power modules?"

"I can't say it would be impossible," responded Jimenez, "but it *would* be really, really hard. Besides," he continued, "imagine what kinds of tech we could power with these things on a ship. You saw those shields on the ceiling turrets. Scale them up. If the secrets to that kind of technology are in these artifacts, we're gonna need something better than our fusion reactors to power them."

I pointed to my wrist com and nodded skyward for Djordi to provide an update to the *Icarus* and the Joint Captains. Maybe they'd have some ideas. Then, I pulled my knife from its sheath again and eyed one of the conduits snaking along the floor to the closest giant egg. I wished I had some duct tape. Trailing the frayed ends of an electrical wire coming from something with more power than five battleships seemed like a really *bad* idea.

"Cut it," said Lamiraux as she tapped a command on her armor's forearm pad. "I have an idea."

I'd never been so glad my knife handle was made of hard rubber. I don't think the manufacturer rated it for resistance to electrical current, but it was certainly a value-added feature right now. I sliced through the thick cable and held the severed end up for Lamiraux. A small nozzle popped out of her wrist and she proceeded to spray a heavy foam into the end of the conduit. "Emergency suit sealant," she offered.

As soon as I cut through the last cable, the lights blinked out in the chamber. The eggs must have been powering the whole compound. "I suspect the lights are out everywhere. Best if we get these moving quickly," I said.

"How exactly are we gonna do that?" asked Djordi.

Just then, my wrist com vibrated, and I tapped it on. "This is Commander Johnson," I said. That rank together with my last name still rang strangely in my ears. It was going to take some getting used to.

"Cap wants you guys to haul those artifacts back to the *Icarus* ASAP," Lieutenant Stohl said with a trace of nervousness in it that I hadn't heard before.

"I think you forgot something in that request, *Lieutenant*." I drew out the last word as a reminder of his rank. By doing so, he'd remember mine was different now and show me the respect I deserved. It was probably force of habit. Stohl was just too nice for the oversight to have been anything else. Damnit, though, I *wanted* it to be disrespect. That might justify my dislike for the guy.

"Yes, sir," he said. "Sorry, sir."

"So," I continued, ignoring Stohl's apology, "does Command have any suggestions for how we get three one-ton objects the size of industrial furnaces off this rock?"

Stohl chuckled. "Cap said you might ask about that. Don't worry, Commander, we've got you covered. Already launched you a bird for extraction. We'll set her down right next to your dropships."

"Tell Command thanks. And have'm prep cargo bay three for a funeral."

"Roger, Commander. *Icarus* out."

I nodded with my head for Major Chan to gather up the men. "Send four Marines to the LZ. The *Icarus* just sent us a truck for these artifacts. Lead the extraction team back here so we can get these things moving. I have a bad feeling about this place."

No sooner had the words fallen from my lips than the ground beneath our feet rumbled. We'd known Auriven I was unstable, and frankly, I was surprised there hadn't been a quake since landing. It was unsettling to have the ground tremble beneath you, but somehow the knowledge that the moon's crust was cracked and breaking away into space like an exit wound in a skull seemed to make it feel worse than it was.

Ten minutes later the extraction team had the artifacts loaded onto mag skids and headed back to the transport. That's when all hell broke loose. That's when we met the Cerberus for the first time.

5

PONY RIDE

Courage is being scared to death but saddling up anyway.

— JOHN WAYNE

At first, I thought they were more quakes, which would have been alarming. But when we saw the greasy black plumes of smoke winding towards the sky over the landing zone, we knew it was something else.

"Where's it coming from?" yelled Lamiraux. She had her service rifle pulled from the mag holster on her back before even finishing the question. She trained it on the mangled wreckage of our dropship then pointed it skyward in search of the offending enemy craft.

Djordi and Jimenez took cover at the base of the compound's perimeter wall, while Cooper and

Major Chan rushed to provide support for the unarmed members of the extraction team. Three of them huddled behind the first artifact, and the fourth just stood there slack-jawed. The second it was safe to do so, I ran to his side and grabbed him by the arms. That's when I saw the yellow puddle at his feet. Some people just weren't meant for combat. I shook him from his stupor while searching for his nameplate: *Stanley French*. "Get to the ship, Stan," I yelled as I shoved him across the clearing to the struts underneath the transport.

The ship they'd sent was an older model Yakisaba commercial two-ton transport. I'd seen them used mostly to haul dry goods between Jupiter Station and the outer drifts. This particular ship had seen better days. Half its hull plating seemed to either be bolted on with hex screws or missing altogether, and what little paint was left on the hull spelled out the name *Border Mule* in looping cursive script. The rear freight ramp, which had been lowered to the ground, had a makeshift-yet-inviting set of arrows in yellow duct tape pointing up to the hold. I hadn't been so disappointed since that time in college when the girl I wanted to date set me up with the one I didn't. I had good reason to be miffed. The transport was a wreck. I'd seen more space-worthy ships in the Museum of Space Exploration on Io.

What had Command sent us? Under normal circumstances, I'd have radioed Stohl back and had him send a proper ship. But these weren't normal circumstances. Faced with the option of being left on a crumbling alien planet or piling into a bucket of bolts named after people who move contraband from one system to the next, there wasn't much debate. I waved for the team to bring the artifacts. Given the transport's cargo rating, though, I had my doubts about the prudence of loading two of the eggs, much less all three.

"Command says they've spotted a bogey makin' for their position like an ice miner for a brothel on payday," Major Chan said. You had to admire his colorful language.

"So, it was an orbital bombardment?" I asked.

"Yeah," he answered. "And from the looks of it," he continued, gesturing to a half dozen smoldering craters, the smallest of which was probably fifty meters across, "the enemy has some pretty big guns. The *Icarus*'d be hard pressed to punch holes that big."

I nodded grimly and stepped down from the ramp as the extraction team muscled the first of their heavy loads into the cargo bay. "At least it's headed the other direction," I said. "The *Icarus* can handle herself." It was the truth. The crew had been hand-picked for the Hades Mission, and with Zhao captaining the ship, I'd have had no doubts. But our new corporate overlords? Well, the jury was still out on that.

The team worked frantically to tie down the artifacts with cargo netting while Major Chan spoke with the transport's pilot over his com. I couldn't hear what he said, but from the dour expression on his face and multiple shakes of his head, I knew he wasn't pleased. He shrugged his shoulders and sighed before motioning me over.

"Captain Simms wants to talk with the person in charge. That," he said with a sigh, "would be *you*, Commander."

"What does Simms want right now? Shouldn't we be focusing on getting the hell off this rock?" I said, not trying to hide my irritation. And why should I? Simms was on the *Icarus*. He couldn't hear my bitching.

"You Commander Johnson?" came the voice of a woman with a British accent. Not the hackneyed kind from London, but Imperial British.

I glanced over my shoulder and up the loading ramp to see a short, petite woman in coveralls and combat boots push past the team securing Patel's body. Her platinum blonde hair was straight and short, shaved on the sides, and sported pink-tipped bangs that fluttered in the wind. Her steely blue eyes could have frozen a solar flare.

"That's me," I said as nonchalantly as I could, though the way she came flying down that ramp, I couldn't help but cringe inside.

The short woman covered the distance between us surprisingly fast. "I need to talk to you," she demanded.

I arched an eyebrow. "Get in line. The major here tells me Captain Simms wants me to call. Whatever you need can be handled by Chan."

It wasn't the last time I ever saw it, but I'll never forget the first time I witnessed her eyes go from cool orbs to icy daggers. "He's right. But there's no need to use the com. I'm right here."

I was confused until my eyes found her name tag, haphazardly sewn to her jumpsuit over her left breast: *Captain Simms*. "*You're* Simms?" I asked, incredulous.

"Yes," she replied, rolling her eyes. "*Patricia* Simms. And before you say anything, know this: I earned this ship on my own merits. I was a transport captain well before my father's company bought your precious Navy."

This was an interesting turn of events, and I wasn't sure how to take the fact that our transport pilot was the other Captain Simms's daughter. I wasn't sure I could handle more than one of them.

"Your men all have EV suits, right?" She didn't wait for my answer. "I've only got one on the *Mule*," she said. "And it's *mine*."

"Yeah," I said. "We've got suits. Why?"

"Cabin's only big enough for five: me and the extraction team. You're going to have to ride in back with the cargo. It's not pressurized back there."

I shook my head. "This day keeps getting better and better."

Patricia nodded toward the mangled heap of metal and burning plastic that used to be our dropship. The other two had met a similar fate. "You see any other rides, Commander? Besides," she said, arching an eyebrow, "I don't want to make it an order. But I will if I have to."

It hadn't occurred to me that her title of *captain* was also a corporate rank, which, even though she only commanded a bucket of bolts with a quiche name, was something I couldn't ignore. Luckily, captain of any ship smaller than a frigate was the equivalent of my rank of commander. But when two officers of the same rank collided, the one in command of the ship always had right of way. As long as I was on the *Border Mule*, Patricia technically outranked me. I glanced at Chan, then up to the amber sky. We didn't really have time to argue. "Saddle up, Major," I said. "Daddy Simms sent us a pony. Least we can do is take it for a ride."

EV SUITS HAD vacuum nozzles inside the front of the helmet for unexpected bouts of nausea. Our Marine corps battle suits didn't. But as luck would have it, Jimenez's faceplate was down and sealed against the vacuum of the unpressurized cargo hold, so we didn't have to contend with the mess. But he'd need an extra ration of shower water to get the regurgitated MREs out of his hair.

Just like the others, I'd jury-rigged a harness out of some bungee cords and fastening loops on the cargo bay's front wall. Since there were no seats or proper restraints, it was the best we could do. And it was a good thing we'd done it. No sooner had the *Mule's* landing skids retracted than Patricia slammed the throttle forward with such force that I was convinced the thing would crumple like an aluminum soda can. But it didn't. And while the Marines were a tough lot, the ride out of Auriven I's atmosphere made my session in the *tumbler* the day before seem like the kiddy ride in that traveling carnival that bounced between bio domes on Luna.

I pulled up a three-dimensional display of local

space on my wrist com. Images of a crumbling planet and three blinking dots filled the air in front of me. The two blue dots were the *Icarus* and the *Mule*. The red one had to be the bogey that'd shot up our landing zone. It danced around the *Icarus* like a bee around honeysuckle. I tapped on my com. "*Icarus*? What's your status? We've secured the artifacts but we're coming in heavy. Need to know what we're heading into."

"Cut the chatter," came Patricia's haughty command. Her Imperial British accent only made her disdain that much more biting. "I'm in command on this ship, and I'll get us home safe and sound. So, stick to jarheads and logistics, Commander."

Chan stifled a snicker—unsuccessfully I might add—and Lamiraux's eyes peered with bemusement from behind her visor. It was the closest thing to a smile I'd seen from her, and I let it slide. Humor was a good way to blow off steam in a tense situation. And from the looks of how the battle between the Cerberus ship and the *Icarus* was unfolding, things were going to get a whole lot tenser.

The red dot representing the bogey was like a one-ship swarm. It was vastly more maneuverable than the larger battleship, which was probably twenty times as big. I wasn't the only one to notice the size discrepancy. One of the jarheads on my left interjected his own humor into the mix. "Maybe it's looking for a trench to start its run on the *Icarus*'s exhaust port. Hope it don't have proton torpedoes." The laughter his comment stirred was very fragile; our mirth could easily have swung to panic instead as the *Icarus* sustained noticeable damage on her port hull plating.

For her part, Patricia kicked in some kind of afterburners—I'd never heard of any on a freighter, so these must have been after-market mods—and the hold instantly reverberated with groans as our blood pooled in the front of our craniums and chests. It was like getting caught in one of those industrial-sized wine presses on Nuova Italia. My battle suit attempted to compensate with pressure bands in my arms and legs squeezing the blood back into my torso. I flirted with darkness for several seconds, but somehow managed to stay conscious through the entire burn maneuver. Our inertia kicked in after the thrust was done, eventually equalizing with the ship around us.

"Wasn't that a kick in the ass!" said Chan through clenched teeth. "Better than the time I flew shotgun in one of those new Saab Banshees over Ceridia."

I glanced at Djordi, who hailed from the largest moon of that system, to see how Chan's offhanded comment had been received. Many there still considered the Terran Federation of Planets to be their oppressors. Seventeen years of siege war had left their planets and economies in a shambles. But, if he'd ever born any animosity toward the Marines, it had long since dissipated. He'd never let on around me, at least.

"Look," said Lamiraux, who'd spent the entire time focused on my wrist com's rendering of the battle above Auriven I. "The red dot is breaking off its attack!"

It was true. The Cerberus ship seemed to be peeling away from the *Icarus* and arcing off towards the planet behind us. Several of the Marines let loose a classic jarhead *"Oooh Rah,"* and even Lamiraux exhaled in relief. The green line arcing between our blue dot and the *Icarus* displayed two numbers: distance and time to destination. Even at speeds faster than any transport had a right to fly, we still had nine minutes before we'd reach our target; an eternity in a skirmish. I'd had a bad feeling about this whole operation from the beginning, and it appeared my gut had been right all along. The red arc showing the Cerberus ship's plotted course seemed to be changing, moving closer to our green trajectory. If it continued to change course, our paths would intersect before we could make it back to the *Icarus*. In less than six minutes, we'd be in enemy weapons range.

"Why don't she just fuckin' turn this bucket?" offered one of the grunts.

"Can't," said Jimenez. "The Alcubierre Drive uses a strong gravity source to spin up and distort space. Once we left orbit, there was no changing course until we reached another gravity well."

It was true. *Gravity hopping*, as it was called, wasn't the most efficient method of travel, but it was the only way our ship's drive could get us up to speeds that meant anything in the vastness of space.

"What about the docking thrusters?" offered

Cooper. "Can't we just use those to nudge us out of the way of the enemy ship?"

Jimenez shook his head. "Inertia and G forces at this speed would..." he seemed to be searching for the right word.

"Squish us like a grape?" Chan asked.

"Exactly," Jimenez replied.

So, the blue line of our trajectory seemed inexorably bound to cross the red line of the enemy ship's trajectory well within its firing radius. All we could do was watch, and for a pack of seasoned Marines, that was probably the worst kind of torture. It was for me anyway.

"We're not gonna make it," lamented Jimenez. "The math just doesn't work out." Leave it to an engineer to analyze the situation using logarithms and formulas in his head.

I tapped my com. "Patricia? You got any more tricks up your sleeve?"

"It's Captain Simms, *Commander*," she replied tensely. "And no, not at the moment, though I'm working on it. I can't exactly change course at these speeds. The *Border Mule* isn't equipped with the fancy inertial dampers those cushy space liners have."

I paused the com for a moment and turned to Jimenez. "What would happen to the artifacts if she changed course at this speed?"

He shook his head. "Probably nothing. But like I said, they'd have to scrape our liquified bodies out of these suits for DNA testing to bury us in the right graves," he said.

That wasn't a visual I needed in my head right

then, and I blinked a few times to clear my mind. I had to think fast. "Surely the *Mule* has some kind of inertial nullifiers?"

Jimenez tapped in a scan on his wrist com and studied its results. "Yeah, standard, low-grade mag plates between the cargo box and outer hull."

Suddenly, I had an idea. "How big are those mag plates?"

Jimenez motioned with his hands, drawing a square the size of a pizza box in the air in front of him. "About this big, maybe."

"How fast do you think you could pull three or four of them out and fasten them to the artifact closest to the door?"

"Couple minutes each. Could work them at the same time with help, though" he replied.

"Do it. As fast as you can," I ordered. At my command, Jimenez, Djordi, and two other Marines sprang to action.

I pointed to the power cables we'd cut and Lamiraux had sprayed with sealant. "Gunny? Can you get us exposed conduit on the end of each of those? Also, we're gonna need the adaptors from some of our combat suits." Each Marine carried a universal electrical adaptor in his suit to ensure it could be recharged regardless of where combat was taking place. Some early colonies still used two-hundred and twenty volts, while others had long since converted to newer specs. "Rig the converters up to the power conduits from the artifact, and then power up the mag plates."

I turned to Jimenez, who'd already pulled a panel off the cargo bay wall and finished unfastening a mag plate. "They work like magnetic skids against the outer hull. Like Simms said, they're not inertial dampeners really, but they do smooth out the bumpy ride," he said.

"Is this gonna work?" I asked, trying not to let my desperation show. I touched the commander's stars on my collar. It would be a shame to die before they'd even settled into place.

Jimenez shrugged, almost apologetically. "If you're trying what I think you are, it all depends on our adapters being able to handle the energy coming from the artifact."

"What about everything else?" I asked.

"Well, sir, that's up to you and our pilot."

Great. Now I had to explain the plan to Patricia. Everything depended on her being able to perform a series of very tough maneuvers. I had doubts, but we had to try. "Captain Simms?" I said, trying to picture her heart-shaped face instead of her father's. Two people with the same name and title was confusing. "I've got a trick of my own, but we need a very skilled pilot. Know anyone who could step up in a pinch? Cause we're in a pinch."

"What do you have in mind, Commander?" There was an eagerness in her tone right below its icy surface.

"We've got a nice package for the Cerberus ship. Need your help with the delivery though. I hear transport pilots are pretty good at deliveries," I said.

"I think I get your meaning, Commander. Just tell me when you're ready," she replied.

"Roger," I said.

By then the counter I'd keyed up on my tactical display read three minutes. All in all, we'd done pretty well. The artifact closest to the cargo bay doors was adorned with four mag plates glommed onto its smooth surface by emergency hull epoxy. That stuff was the *only* thing in the galaxies better than duct tape, if you asked me.

Jimenez gave a thumbs up as he powered up the last of the plates using siphoned current from the artifact's power plant. "I don't know how long this will hold, or what will happen when it decides to fail, so we probably should hurry." He keyed the remote codes for each of the four power converters into his wrist com.

I nodded and ordered the artifact moved to the center of the doors and secured to the deck by cargo netting. Then, we strapped back in as well. I hoped Jimenez would stay conscious, but I had his routines keyed into my wrist com as a backup since I'd been able to get through the last high-G maneuver with my wits still about me. I tapped my com. "Flip us around, Captain."

Simms swung the *Mule* a hundred and eighty degrees on its axis so that the back of the ship was now the front. Then, she opened the cargo bay doors. "On my mark," I said over our com channel. I nodded to Lamiraux, but she couldn't seem to free up her harness. I reached for mine but found I too had been overzealous in my makeshift restraints. Precious seconds ticked away like tiny diamonds through one's fingers.

Suddenly, Djordi launched himself toward the artifact and began hacking at the netting holding it in place. He deftly flipped to the other side to finish the job. Once it was free, he returned to his harnesses and strapped in. It was quite possibly the most graceful, efficient move anyone his height had ever done. But, that's why I'd brought him on the mission, and now that decision seemed to be almost prescient.

"Jimenez? Charge the plates and flip the switch when I say." He nodded and I readied myself for deceleration. This was gonna hurt. "Now, Captain!" I yelled into my com. Patricia threw on all eight of the rear thrusters for a short burst. It was the longest three seconds of my life. I swore my eyeballs were going to pop out of my skull and my lips felt like swollen water balloons on the verge of exploding.

Just as we'd planned, the artifact's inertia carried it forward at the transport's original speed. It was as if the *Mule* had just thrown a one-ton shoe. Patricia closed the cargo bay door and continued to slow us down, though she kept the G forces to reasonable levels. Besides, there was no avoiding the bogey's firing radius now. We had to hope the pilot would be forced to choose between shooting our jury-rigged projectile, or the fat, squishy target that our weak hull presented it.

"You're up, Sergeant Jimenez," I said.

The young engineer keyed a command in his com and smiled with relief. "The magnetic field is just big enough to surround the artifact, Commander." He made as if to wipe sweat from his brow, but forgot he was wearing a helmet. His gloved hand clanked against his visor. "It won't stop high-velocity rounds, but it may slow them down enough to do the job."

"Thanks, Sergeant."

We all watched intently as a fourth blue dot suddenly appeared on the tactical display, moving out and away from the *Mule* and toward the Cerberus ship. I held my breath without even knowing it, waiting for the bogey to open fire. Part of me had hoped he'd target our transport first. We might survive long enough for our artifact bomb to work. But if the Cerb destroyed it first, we'd certainly be next.

Unfortunately, the enemy pilot had correctly assessed the danger and opted to open fire on the artifact. "You guys have to see this," said Patricia excitedly. "Let me send an optical feed to your com." A second later she'd piped one of the *Mule*'s rear camera feeds to my tactical display and magnified it. Fiery hot projectiles streamed from the enemy warship like tracer rounds from an antique WWII airplane. Luckily, and much to our mutual relief and surprise, our little plan had worked to perfection. Half the rounds punched through the magnetic barrier cast by the mag plates, but they'd been slowed enough to hit the egg with the force of a man throwing a shot-put. The other half, however, struck the shield at such a shallow angle that they skipped off like a poorly-piloted dropship off a planet's atmosphere. That was the good news. The bad news was that several rounds glanced off the artifact and struck the *Mule's* shoddy hull armor. A round penetrated the bay doors and slammed into the wall half a meter from my head, peppering my helmet and shoulder with tiny debris.

I glanced at the counter. "Twenty seconds to impact," I said. I couldn't believe it. The hare-brained plan I'd devised on the spur of the moment was working perfectly. Until the bogey decided to speed up, changing the point of impact by several seconds. Now, we were screwed. It was in that moment of realization that I knew I was going to die. We all were.

"Commander!" yelled Jimenez. "I have an idea. If I can just…"

"Do it!" I yelled. "No time to debate. Just *do it*!"

Jimenez grinned as he tapped furiously at his wrist com. We all watched, still as statues in the last moments of our lives. Whatever it was Jimenez had done didn't work, though: the trajectory lines on the tactical display still didn't intersect soon enough. But just before the artifact flew harmlessly past the enemy ship, it suddenly veered towards it. The bogey tried adjusting course, but it was no use. After a few seconds of futile chase-and-be-chased, the artifact slammed into the enemy ship's hull, erupting in a ball of purple and white energy that vaporized both objects in a flash.

"Let me guess," I said, looking at Jimenez, "That was the *tetrahedron*."

"Yes. sir," he said, grinning dumbly. "I told you it was nothing but pretty lights."

6
TERRA INCOGNITA

Man cannot discover new oceans unless he has the courage to lose sight of the shore.

— ANDRE GIDE

Patricia's voice boomed over our helmets' com channel like a god thundering down from Olympus, and somehow, her British accent made her sound even more imperious than that. "I don't know how you managed to do that, Commander…"

Jimenez jumped in to explain. "It was simple, really, I just reversed the current and flipped the polarity of the…"

"…but we've got bigger problems." She didn't even acknowledge the sergeant, running roughshod over him like wild horses from the eastern Montana prairies of my childhood.

What could possibly be worse than narrowly avoiding death at the hands of a faceless alien enemy? I motioned for Jimenez to stay quiet and nodded at him reassuringly. Didn't want him to think we weren't grateful for what he'd done to save our asses. "What's the problem, Captain Simms?"

"It's Auriven," she answered.

"We aren't going back to the moon, Captain," I said in my best command voice. I know the corporation wanted more alien artifacts, but a return trip wasn't in the cards as far as I was concerned. Even with the Cerberus threat eliminated.

"No," she said, exasperation overcoming her otherwise professional tone. "The *star*. It's going nova."

"We know," I replied. It was true. Among the myriad risks of the extraction mission was the threat of the star going nova while we were still in system. But Galaxia SciCorp was keeping an eye on that for us. So was the *Icarus* for that matter. And they'd assured us we'd be able to get in and out with plenty of time to spare.

"SciCorp was wrong, Commander. The star is going to explode in minutes, not weeks." There was a finality to her voice that almost dissuaded me from challenging her assertion.

"What makes you say that?" I asked.

"Take a look for yourself," she said as she sent me a vid from the *Icarus*. I pulled it up on my wrist com and displayed it in the air in front of me big enough for the others in the cargo hold to see. Apparently, the *Icarus* had fired off a class IV probe to monitor the star more closely. The data it sent back was startling. I wasn't an expert in astrophysics or quantum theory, but the readings scrolling by spoke of some unexpected force acting on the star, accelerating its demise.

"What's causing it?" I asked, doing my best to hide the panic I felt surging in my chest.

There was a spike of static over our channel, then Dezzie's voice responded from the bridge of the *Icarus*. "We don't really know, Commander. But there's no time to investigate."

I shook my head inside my helmet.

Shit.

"How long do we have?"

"Our best guess is…about fifteen minutes," said Dezzie.

There was a part of me that felt relieved to hear I wasn't going to die before drawing another breath. There was another part, though, that knew it didn't matter: twenty breaths a minute for fifteen minutes. One breath or three hundred; it was all the same.

Jimenez shook his head. "Even if we spun up the Alcubierre Drive, there aren't any gravity sources nearby. The graviton acceleration wouldn't cascade properly."

If our only option was the *Icarus*'s fusion thrusters, we were toast. We needed to reach a significant fraction of the speed of light, maybe even .5C in the next ten minutes. Without the graviton drive, that would be impossible.

"It may not be as bad as you think, Commander," continued Dezzie. "Auriven II is about half the size of Jupiter with a powerful gravity well. We think we can make it there in time."

"We'd better dock up if you expect us to join you on that ride. We'll need to set a new waypoint after we finish our current hop. No offense to the captain of the *Border Mule*, but the *Icarus* can make better time, even with only her fusion thrusters. That said, we'll be cutting it close."

"No offense taken," said Patricia. "I'll have you on the *Icarus* before you can say 'promoted before my time.'"

Her barb drew wide-eyed looks from the members of B Company, who seemed caught between agreeing with Patricia and taking offense at her shaming their new CO. But we didn't have more than a couple seconds of awkward silence before we were all thrown against the makeshift harnesses that kept us from splatting against the back of the hold.

True to her word, we were docked with the *Icarus* in less than two minutes. The second the *Mule's* clamps were engaged, our piggy-back ride began. I made my way through the airlocks, completed standard decontamination protocols, and sprinted to the bridge. If there were a ship's record for fastest time from airlock to Deck Two, I'm sure I broke it.

"Nice work down there, Commander," said the elder Captain Simms. Having two of them was confusing as hell, and despite her posturing, I'd already decided Patricia and I were on a first-name basis, if for no other reason than to keep things straight in my head.

I saluted before responding. "Thank you, sir. It wasn't easy."

He nodded gravely. "Patel?"

"I'll take care of notification and the funeral, Sir. That happened on my watch. His death is on *me*."

"Indeed, Commander, but let's focus on the task at hand." It wasn't until that moment that I realized how similarly Captain Simms and Patricia spoke. Not only were their accents nearly identical, but so were their expressions. There was no denying she was his daughter. I'd hoped her apple had fallen a little further from the tree, though, and perhaps it had. But I decided there'd be time to see just how far later.

I saluted again, Captain Simms dismissed me, and, out of force of habit, I trotted across the bridge to the LogOps station. Of course, it was occupied by Lieutenant Rasmussen, who'd been promoted into my old position as Logistics Chief. So, I found a spot halfway behind the com station and the captain's dais and stood at attention, facing the main view screen. At any other time, it might have felt awkward, but we were all about to be vaporized by a dying star, so any unease I might have felt just didn't stick.

Auriven II was about 1.5 light seconds from Auriven I. Our helmsman acted as if the devil were on his heals: I'm sure we closed that distance in record time for a vessel as big as the *Icarus*. Though she was a fairly new ship—and until today's encounter with the Cerberus—in pristine condition, the Hades Class Battleship moaned under the strain of our ricochet to the other side of the big gas giant.

"What the...?" said Dezzie. Her hands danced across the capacitive surface of her console in a series of graceful moves that ended with a flick of her finger, which sent an optical feed up to the main viewer. As we entered eclipse on Auriven II's dark side, our screens were suddenly filled with the image of a massive, ring-shaped object.

"Reduce magnification," commanded Simms.

"Already done sir. It's just really *big*," said Stohl, who'd already started scanning the anomaly. "Bigger than the *Icarus*."

"That's not all, Captain," added Dezzie. "It's located right where the planet's gravity is strongest."

I shifted uncomfortably on my feet and ran my fingers through my hair, which was still damp from decon back in the airlock.

"What are the chances someone would choose to build something like that right at the confluence of two massive graviton fields?" asked Simms. "Unless..."

"Already on it, sir. Scans show it's not completely inert. Trace amounts of power. It has to be a *gate*," Stohl said. Everyone who'd seen any sci-fi serial knew what it was the minute they laid eyes on it. He turned toward the captain expectantly. *Everyone* looked at him expectantly.

I don't know what made me do it. Maybe it was latent heroism? Maybe it was a strong sense of self-preservation? Or maybe I just liked pissing my commanding officers off. Regardless, I stepped forward assertively and replied, "We should go through it."

Simms briefly arched an eyebrow before nodding in agreement and tapping open his ship-wide channel. "This is Captain Simms. We've discovered what appears to be an alien portal of some kind. We don't know where it leads, or if it will lead us anywhere at all, but given the alternative…" He gave the signal for general quarters. "Batten down the hatches," he continued. "We're going through."

He then nodded slightly toward the helmsman, who eased the *Icarus* closer to the anomaly.

"Make haste, Lieutenant," said Simms. "The crew in the aft sections of the ship are already applying SPF 500." Then, he amended his order. "But don't go too fast. We don't know what kind of physics are at play inside the anomaly."

I steadied myself against the tug of inertia as the ship's four fusion thrusters propelled us forward toward the gate. I stole a glance at Dezzie. If we were going to die, part of me wanted her face to be the last thing that I saw.

When we were less than a kilometer away our scanners went haywire with spikes for every energy type we were equipped to measure.

"Didn't even have to ring the doorbell," I said. I half expected a reprimand from the captain, but he was too busy staring at the screen. The space inside the massive ring had begun to shimmer, like the heated air over a campfire. Except this was more like the surface of a cobalt ocean, rippling with some unseen power.

Static hissed over the com as Auriven's star began to erupt. It pulsed once then started to expand like a balloon at a child's birthday party.

"Twenty seconds to contact with the gate," Stohl warned. The temperature on the tactical display near the front of the bridge read a perfect 23 degrees Celsius. But that didn't stop giant beads of sweat from trickling down my temples and forehead, ending in my eyes and leaving me blinking like the LED of a network cable.

"Ten," Stohl continued, "nine, eight…"

I wondered if the star had already gone nova. At nearly two standard AU's away, it would take a little over sixteen minutes for the shockwave to reach us. And there was no knowing for certain if or when the star had exploded. We'd only know it when it vaporized us. I couldn't help but imagine a split second of searing agony. How long would the pain last?

"Three, two, one…"

There was a flash of light that left everything on the bridge bathed in a soft white glow. My ears rang and my mouth was suddenly dry. There were gagging heaves to my left, near Stohl's tactical station. If I'd been able to smile, I would have. I reveled in discovering that Mister Perfect had a weaker stomach than me. But I was too busy fighting back my own sudden bout of nausea to jeer. Then, just as quickly as it had begun, it was over.

"Contact," finished Stohl about a half second too late.

The gate was behind us now. Its dark metallic

surface had returned to the original, near-inert state, and the space on the other side was as pitch black as any the void had to offer.

Two seconds of silent shock were followed by a ship-wide cheer. "Hell yesssss!" yelled the helmsman. In an instant, everyone was on their feet jumping up and down and pumping their fists in a writhing tangle of humanity not unlike the rave I went to in high school. I hadn't taken any blaze pills today, but damned if I didn't feel just as high as I did that night. And then it happened. Without even knowing it, and before I could stop myself, I was hugging Lieutenant Stohl. We looked at each other for a very awkward second, then turned to congratulate our fellow crew-mates. I imagined our brief show of mutual respect would remain securely locked in the vault of 'don't-say-a-damn-word-about-it'. At least it would for me.

Captain Simms returned from where he'd been congratulating Dezzie with what I thought looked like an all-too-lingering hug and ascended to the captain's dais. He raised his arms over his head and called for everyone to quiet. "Wonderful job, everyone," he said, tugging at the wrists of his uniform's sleeves. "We've managed not to die. But there will be plenty of other opportunities to assay the metal you're made of. For now," he continued, tapping in commands at his console, "we need to determine where that gate landed us."

Stohl had already begun initial scans of the area and was ready with their first results. "Already got some preliminaries, Sir." He flicked his finger across the console and the main viewer snapped to life. A rendering of a star and several planets filled the screen.

"It's *yellow*," said Dezzie with obvious relief. After narrowly escaping a dying red giant, who could blame her?

Simms stood and strode to the front of the bridge, his footsteps on the metal deck plating almost keeping pace with my racing heartbeats. He pointed at the second planet from the star. "Is that what I think it is?" he asked in awe.

"Sir," answered Stohl, "That's a *Terran* planet."

My heart jumped. This was what we'd hoped for, what every explorer and colonist dreamed of. Terran worlds were among the rarest in the Milky Way. Sure, there were millions of Earth-like planets, but none were truly *Terran*. Either they were too cool like Proxima Prime, or tidally locked, creating huge temperature gradients that spawned massive, deadly storms like on Pinnacle III. Or, they were simply too massive, with crushing gravity that made unaided movement nearly impossible, and long-term colonization impractical. But a *Terran* planet was none of those things. In practical terms, we'd found the statistically improbable. We'd found another Earth.

7

IN THE GARDEN

One of the advantages of being disorganized is that one is always having surprising discoveries.

— A. A. Milne

The sky on Eden II was a deep azure that darkened rapidly as the sun set. They'd said to expect it to look a lot like Earth's, but I was skeptical. I'd always thought the sky on Earth was blue because of the oceans, and Eden II's water was mostly in lakes and rivers. I was wrong. Earth's oceans were blue because of the sky, not the other way around. Something about blue light waves scattering more easily because they're shorter than the others. Regardless, the view on Eden was breathtaking. Montana's state motto was Big Sky Country. It may not have been bigger, but this one gave it a run for its money.

"It's gonna get pretty crowded down here soon," I lamented. Growing up in the wide-open spaces of the American mountain west had given me an aversion to crowds. How I'd even managed in the confined spaces of the *Icarus* for so long was a mystery to me, but I had. Soaking in the expansive views of a horizon and grassy plains and trees and the twinkling of the first stars in the evening sky only served to remind me of what I missed most about home.

Dezzie squeezed my hand. The softness of her skin on mine was electrifying—always was. I could still taste her lips, from minutes before when the alien sky had only been a second thought.

"A hundred thousand colonists isn't a lot when you think about it, Paul." She gestured toward the pre-dusk horizon, which had streaked with magenta and rose. The virgin scenery was only marred by the faint lights of distant temporary shelters. Seven colony ships loomed darkly behind them, silhouetted against the setting sun. "There's room for millions here," she added, a trace of satisfaction in her voice.

I knew how she felt. We all did. Building a new world was exhilarating. Still, I sighed. "I'm just glad I didn't have to hitch a ride on one of those," I said, nodding toward the boxy colony ships. "They're like giant cattle trailers." Of course, the suggestion was that the colonists were nothing more than cattle on the Galaxian ranch. I wondered if Captain Simms had a cowboy hat. I didn't want to know if he had any chaps.

"You know they actually are, in a way," said Dezzie. "Cattle trailers."

I looked at her questioningly. Hadn't expected that response.

"Each colony ship brought millions of frozen embryos, some of which were cows."

I shook my head. She giggled, and for a moment the difficulties of the last three months melted away. We'd reconciled shortly after coming through the gate from Auriven. But Dezzie was holding back today, and I could tell. She swore she and Simms were never a 'thing' and that he'd just been enforcing the regulation for non-fraternization between officers of differing ranks. But I'd seen the way he'd looked at her, and there was the time on the bridge when we'd first met him. The time he'd smelled of her perfume. I thrust the thought from my head, determined to enjoy the present. I was lucky to have Dezzie in my life again. Eden was a new world. Why couldn't our relationship have a new start too?

"The last ship in the fleet arrives tomorrow," she said. Over the last month or so, a dozen Galaxian ships had trickled in after being ordered to congregate at Eden. Seven colony ships, four frigates like the *Andromeda*, several planetary skiffs —which those of us in the Navy called puddle jumpers—and the remaining Hades Class battleships, the *London* and the *Italia*. My mind drifted toward the friends I'd lost on the *Prometheus*, and I resolved again to make the Cerberus pay. We may not have known much about them—who they were, what they looked like—but there was one thing of which I was certain: with that many warships patrolling the system, I pitied an enemy that crossed us now.

I moved a strand of hair that had fallen out of Dezzie's regulation bun and gently caressed her face. She smiled. I wasn't about to claim to be an expert on women. Frankly, I had no idea how I'd struck gold twice. But here we were, and I wasn't about to second guess any of it.

"You planning on putting in for a transfer?" I teased.

"Not on your life, *Commander*," she replied, flicking the metal stars on my collar.

"Good," I said, and we kissed again.

My wrist com buzzed very inconveniently. Great. Simms had summoned me back to town. He'd set up a temporary Fleet Command Center in a cargo box ejected from one of the colony ships. Dezzie's com buzzed too.

"You're gonna be late, Commander Pearson," I said. "I can't keep covering for you. If you aren't careful, you'll end up on sanitation duty."

The replay of our last morning together before the rendezvous with Galaxia wasn't lost on Dezzie. She arched an eyebrow, pursed her lips, then shot me a wicked smile. "I just have to get there before you do. It's the last man in who draws the captain's ire," she said as she whirled about and sprinted down the hill. It was true; Simms would probably be angriest with the last one in the room, but I didn't try to catch up with Dezzie. Instead, I followed several steps behind her the whole way back. The view was simply too amazing to ignore. And the scenery on Eden wasn't so bad either.

Simms stood at the front of the largest room in the makeshift Command Center. The plan had always been to build a more permanent CC would be erected somewhere in the Hades Galaxy, and since luck had seen fit to bring us to a Terran planet, Eden was the most likely spot. Captain Simms paced impatiently back and forth in front of a large tactical display that'd been slapped on the wall with wing nuts and epoxy. Cables snaked haphazardly along the wall to one side, supplying the room with power and broad-com data feeds. Somewhere just outside the building, the fusion units that powered the entangled particle array produced a high-voltage hum that served as counterpoint to the silent apprehension that hung in the air like a dense fog.

Several rows of folding chairs occupied the center of the room, and a leather sofa sat quite out of place in the front right corner. It was classic Simms to have brought it from Earth. While the Navy had limited personal items on the *Icarus* due to weight concerns, he'd loaded down the *Andromeda* with creature comforts befitting the CEO of the most powerful conglomerate in the galaxy. *Two* galaxies now. Still, his eccentricities never ceased to amaze me. As he turned on his heel to pace across the front of the room for the twentieth time, I noticed something different about his uniform. Not only was it a slightly different color—more grey than blue—but the three stars on his collar had been replaced by a constellation of five stars in the shape of a diamond.

By now the room had filled with nearly forty officers, which set my hackles on end. Every part of me screamed to choose a spot near the exit, or at least on the back row. Something about people sitting behind me in a crowd rubbed me the wrong way. But I knew better than that. I didn't want to draw the attention that sitting in the back would bring me, or the scrutiny of sitting near the front. So, I chose a seat as close to the middle of the group as I could. Dezzie and I always made a point of sitting separately in formal meetings, so she chose a spot a couple rows away.

Luckily, I wasn't the last person in the room. That honor belonged to Patricia. I smiled and started to wave, but she shot me a cold look before I could finish the movement. She'd been this way for weeks, and I didn't know why. There were untold secrets in this new galaxy, and I had no doubts we'd solve them. But I was convinced that the one mystery that would forever remain out of reach was what made a woman tick.

Captain Simms arched an eyebrow at his daughter's tardiness but didn't offer a reprimand. Instead, he launched into a polished and well-prepared speech.

"Tomorrow marks the beginning of a new day for humankind. The last vessel in our corporate fleet will arrive and merge with those Naval ships Galaxia acquired recently." He smiled broadly, clearly proud of what his corporation had accomplished. "As such," he gestured toward the twelve officers on the front row, "I have expanded the Council of Joint Captains." He clasped his hands in front of him and bowed his head as if in prayer. "And they have unanimously voted to create the position of Corporate Fleet Admiral. I am the first to hold that rank."

The room erupted in hearty applause, which he attempted to set aside. But the crowd would not be silenced. I don't know if it was all for Simms, though. The shared excitement we felt in this place was palpable. And why not? We were doing what no one had ever done before. I wondered if this is what early human colonists had felt like. But Ceridia and Proxima, though they were the jewels of human expansion in the Milky Way, were nothing compared to Eden. Nothing compared to the wonders of the Hades Galaxy.

Simms nodded his gratitude several times before finally regaining the crowd. "Friends," he said solemnly, "we have much work to do. The Hades Galaxy is vast, nearly twice as big as our own Milky Way. Its physics are similar, but there are hints that even the fundamental laws we taken for granted may not all apply here. Its chemistry is familiar, yet alien. Its resources?" By now a wide, almost ravenous smile split his face. "Its resources are plentiful and its worlds *rich*."

Again, the room erupted, but this time in a low murmur of approval. "By now you've all heard of the exploits carried out by the brave crew of the *Icarus*, of the alien artifacts retrieved from a dying star." My chest swelled with pride at his mention of our mission to Auriven. "Humanity has yearned to search the stars, to find its place in the Universe. And now, we've confirmed that we are not alone. But before we can reap the benefits of our efforts, we must first unlock the secrets of those artifacts. To that end, the Board of Directors has funded the construction of a state-of-the-art research station, to be built in orbit above Eden. Galaxia SciCorp will call it home, and some of you will be joining its ranks."

Simms tapped a command on his wrist com and the main viewer displayed the faces of half a dozen men and women. While important, none of this had truly interested me; I wasn't a scientist, and frankly, I just wanted to get back on the *Icarus*, to get back out there. I'd spent the last three months waiting for repairs on the battleship to be finished. Not having a space dock was proving more of a hindrance than ever imagined, and at last report, the *Icarus* was only just now ready for launch.

But when I saw Sergeant Jimenez's face among those being reassigned to the SciCorp Research Station, my heart sank. It made sense though. Jimenez was the first engineer to lay hands on the artifacts, the first to deduce what they were—without any specialized equipment—and, he was the first to manipulate their power units for our own purposes. He'd be a perfect fit in SciCorp. I'd miss the guy though. A lot.

"The rest of you have new orders sent to your personal com units. See your CO with any questions." Simms squared himself with the crowd and rigidly saluted, holding it for a response. Forty pairs of feet planted on the metal floor of the CC as every person in the room shot to their feet at crisp attention. We all saluted our new corporate admiral.

When he released us from attention the room bubbled into a cacophony of cheers, greeting of old friends, and congratulatory gestures. I scanned the room and found Djordi. He sported a snappy new uniform that actually fit his lanky arms and legs, and a pair of Lieutenant's bars on his collar.

"Congratulations, Lieutenant!" I said, shaking his hand firmly. He smiled as if he'd just won the lottery on Luna. "I can't believe they actually listened to my recommendation," I added.

Djordi grimaced mockingly. "I'm not going to let you take credit for this one, Paul." It was so good to hear that sing-song accent again. He'd been assigned double shifts teaching zero-G fundamentals to new recruits, and because the line to the temporary Corporate Recruiting Office snaked around the corner and down the main thoroughfare most days, Djordi had been quite busy. Too busy even for me.

"Still with the *Icarus*, I hope?" I asked. With all the unannounced reassignments, it was a valid question.

He frowned, but there was a glint of mirth in his eye. "I'd follow you into the core of a red giant, Commander."

"You almost *did*," I said with a chuckle.

"What about you? New orders?" Djordi asked.

In my excitement, I'd almost forgotten that my wrist com had buzzed with a new priority communique from Naval Command.

"Haven't even looked," I confessed, scanning my thumbprint to open the notification. To my relief, there was no huge surprise. I still had B Company, minus Jimenez, and a new grunt named Hirishu Tanaka. From his personnel photo it was hard to tell where his neck began, and his shoulders ended. I didn't want to prejudge, but he looked like the typical jarhead. But that wasn't a bad thing, really.

"Nope," I replied flatly, "I'm still stuck you piss sacks and knuckle-draggers in B Company."

Djordi smiled at that. "Good. After Auriven, nobody wanted to serve with anyone else. In fact, rumor has it that over seventy Marines requested a transfer to our unit."

"They must've all heard about your little move in the cargo hold of the *Mule*." He looked at the ground sheepishly. "If you want to be the best, you have to train with the best." I slapped him on the back. "With guys like you and Chan, it's not surprising they want into B Company."

He straightened and offered a salute. "Thank you, Commander Johnson," he said. I dismissed him and headed for the landing platform. The stars were out in full by now, and with so little manmade light to contend with, they shone brighter than ever. I wanted to sit down and gaze for a while, but I didn't. If there was one thing I knew about orders without a suspense date, it was that one should treat them as an immediate summons. So that's exactly what I did. Eden may have been appropriately named, but my paradise was in the stars. And so was my *Eve*.

8

SPOILS OF WAR

To the victor belong the spoils. In a war or other contest, the winner gets the booty.

— W*illiam* L. M*arcy*

The *Icarus* was in high orbit above Eden, so I'd have about an hour to think things through. Galaxia had spared no expense on their frigates. The *Andromeda* and the *Wall Street* were top notch vessels, if a bit on the smaller side. At least compared to a Hades Class Battleship anyway. But the corporate shuttles brought through the Rift were another story. Boarding the *GS Sprinter* was like getting into a dank, worn-out shoebox. Not only was the odor rank—the dehumidifiers had probably been broken for years from the looks of it—but I swear I saw black mold growing in the corners of the passenger compartment. Cool droplets of water formed on the slits of the air vents, dripping periodically onto the seats and grated metal floor, and onto my head until I figured out what was happening.

But annoying as they were, the water drops weren't what was bothering me the most right now. I was worried about the vacancy in the *Icarus*'s captain's chair—not that I expected to be promoted to captain myself. No, that would be a joke. But there was a real possibility that Dezzie *would* be, and that was no laughing matter to me. While it might be the best thing for her career, a promotion would mean the end of our recently-rekindled relationship.

A strange thought suddenly forced its way into my mind. What if I asked Dezzie to marry me? It was the only legal way around the regulations. If one of us ever got promoted, they'd just transfer the one who didn't. Sure, we'd see each other less, but at least we'd be *together*. I mulled it over in my mind, my heart pounding faster and faster as I did. But just as my hopes surged enough to push me over the cliff of resolve, I stepped back, disappointed. If I asked Dezzie to marry me, it would likely stymy her career. Rather than place undue stress on a marriage, the brass would just pass us over for promotion altogether. The more I thought about it, the more I realized it just wouldn't be fair of me to make Dezzie choose between me and her career. I hated to admit it, but I wasn't convinced she'd make the same choice I would, which made me nothing more than a *boyfriend of convenience.*

I pushed those thoughts from my head as best I

could. After making the mistake of sitting in the puddle directly beneath the vent, I found a drier spot. But by the time I'd buckled my five-point harness, another poor soul had made the same mistake I had. His curses were loud and forceful... and very *familiar*.

"Captain Zhao?"

He was shorter than I remembered him but that stern Asian face and almost robotic demeanor were still the same. "Johnson?" he said, eyes searching for my collar. "*Commander* Johnson?"

I tried to stand but was constrained by my harness. So, I just saluted him where I sat. He dismissed my show of respect with a nod of his head and moved from the wet seat to a drier one directly across from me. I say drier, but as I had just found out, that term seemed to be relative on the *Sprinter*.

"Yes, sir," I said, trying not to seem too eager to discuss my promotion. I didn't take his surprise as an insult, but I could have. Simms may have elevated me out of turn, but the fact was I'd acquitted myself just fine on Auriven.

"Hmmm..." he said, examining the new rank on my collar. "Suits you, I suppose." Zhao wasn't one to hand out compliments, so that was about as close as I was going to get from him. How Dezzie'd convinced the guy to let us carry on against regulations was beyond me. But one simply does not look a gift horse in the mouth, so I'd never asked.

"Sir," I said, "where have you been? With all due respect, you look like you've been through...a lot." His eyes were sunken, his face was more gaunt than usual, and his hair was longer than I'd seen him wear it before. The hint of a five-o'clock-shadow—a normal thing for most men—was what made me ask, though. Zhao had always looked like he just came from the ship's barber.

A slightly bemused smile replaced his flat expression. "Yes, I'm quite sure that I do."

He ignored my question, though, and turned to secure the shoulder straps of his harness. That's when I noticed the twin adhesive bandages on his neck right below the jawline. "Cryo sleep, sir?"

He nodded. "Given the choice between that and a six-month trip through the Rift back to Jupiter Station on a third-rate ship not much better than this tin can," he looked at the cabin around him with visible disdain, "I chose a long nap. You ever tasted the rations on a long-haul shot like that?"

I had, but turbulence jarred us right as I was about to say so. Amidst the ensuing creaks and moans of bulkheads and popping of water in coolant hoses, our pilot reassured us that everything was fine, though the expressions of all the passengers—none of whom were wearing EV suits—belied a lack of faith in his assertion.

A few seconds later the water on the seat below the air vent glommed together into several large globules that floated toward the ceiling. When they were head high, the pilot kicked on the maneuvering thrusters to point us in the direction of the *Icarus*. The inertia of the maneuver sent the globules of water slamming into my face and, since I was harnessed in, there was nothing I could do about it. Several people stifled their amusement, but a few snickers managed to get through. I shook my head and laughed out loud. "Needed a bath anyway."

We rode the rest of the way in silence. The *Sprinter*'s docking arms clamping onto the struts around the airlock was the only sound. A quad of armed Marines in full dress uniform met us just inside. It was a kind of honor guard for Captain Zhao; someone wanted him to know how pleased they were he was back. Zhao enjoyed the respect of the entire crew. He'd earned it. But things had been different with Simms as captain. Galaxia owned our work contracts, so many of us had come to feel like a piece of property to be tabulated on Simms's corporate ledger. It was good to have a real captain again, and I smiled.

As I vaulted through the airlock, I grabbed the handle on the wall right before the grav plate. Floating from zero G onto one of those was like falling off a five-foot table onto a metal floor. Not fun. Once my feet were oriented toward the deck, I pushed off and landed with a staggered thud on the floor. Ahead of me, Captain Zhao saluted the Marines and strode away briskly down the corridor. Before he was out of earshot, though, he yelled over his shoulder. "Your uniform is a mess, Commander. Don't step onto my bridge until you're fit for inspection."

"Yes, sir."

Normally, I'd have been bothered by a scolding like that, but I was walking on clouds right now.

I'd take a stern Zhao over losing Dezzie to the captain's chair any day of the week. I grinned widely, and somehow, I could smell her cheap perfume from here.

I TOOK Captain Zhao's reprimand as a summons to the bridge, so after cleaning up I made my way to deck two. Stohl wasn't in his tactical station, but sat at the helm, beaming. His perfect teeth were almost blinding. I felt like a college frat boy turning on the lights after a night of drinking. What had him so chipper? Dezzie was in her XO chair, head down, reviewing prelaunch protocols, and Zhao was staring into the distance, as if his mind were elsewhere.

There was no specific place for me on the bridge, a fact that at first left me feeling a bit awkward. But I was used to it now, having made my place a prestigious spot on the floor half a step behind the captain's chair, but in front of the com station. Before the repairs to the *Icarus*, there'd been a small scratch on the deck plating there. I'd used it to mark my spot. But now, it was as pristine as a stainless-steel surgical tray.

The missing scratch wasn't the only thing I noticed that was different. Several modifications had been made to the bridge, but I didn't have time to fully take them in before Zhao stood and motioned for the doors to be closed. I caught a glimpse of armed guards stationed just outside them right before their heavy metal hatches slammed shut. The lights dimmed and the main view screen snapped to life with a picture of the blue and yellow artifacts we'd retrieved from Auriven.

"While you folks have been taking shore leave on the surface and sipping little frilly drinks with umbrellas, SciCorp has been hard at work deciphering the data inside the remaining relics the *Icarus* recovered on her last mission."

I thought Simms had just told the officer corps something different—that the artifacts would be deciphered soon. That's why he'd ordered the Research Station built. I wondered if that part of his speech had been deliberate misinformation. But why cover up the fact that we'd already made progress with our research?

Captain Zhao continued. "Our own Sergeant...*Lieutenant* Jimenez correctly deduced that the objects are immensely powerful storage arrays. The Builders were attempting to catalog the knowledge of an entire civilization. For what purpose, we do not know."

Builders? I understood the intent but would have chosen something more original. 'Builders' was the name given to every damn mysterious ancient alien race in every sci-fi show I'd ever seen. That fact seemed to be lost on Zhao, though. He stood and tapped a command on the arm console of his chair. An image of blueprints labeled with looping alien script appeared on the screen. "It took us over a month, but we deciphered their language." He tapped another command in and the script was translated into Terran Standard. I skimmed what I could before the images cycled, but I saw words like 'heavy battery', 'alpha shields' and 'hydrogen hypercell.'

"SciCorp has managed to graft much of the Builder's tech into our own ships. The *Icarus* has benefited from several of these modifications."

He turned to Stohl and nodded. "Lieutenant, if you please."

Stohl was grinning ear to ear. His fingers danced across the surface of his console. The screen displayed a video of space flight, likely some pre-recorded departure from Eden. "How many of you felt that?" he asked.

"Felt what?" asked the woman at the com station behind me.

"Exactly," Stohl replied. "The *Icarus* has been outfitted with inertial nullifiers. We're actually traveling at .3C away from Eden, towards her closest moon, Adam." The other moon was called Eve, a naming scheme that I didn't agree with, but at least it kept with the biblical motif.

"Not only do the nullifiers make acceleration almost imperceptible, they allow us to reach speeds that would normally be…fatal to the crew," Stohl explained. He slid his finger across the pitch control touchpad and gave the thrusters a nudge. We shot towards the moon, reaching .5C in less than twenty seconds.

"Does this mean we can maneuver while at speed?" I asked.

Stohl looked as if I'd broken his favorite toy on Christmas morning. "No. The *nullifiers* don't get rid of all the inertia. They just convert it into pseudo gravitons, which get shunted into the Alcubierre Drive." He frowned. "We still can't maneuver without slowing down."

"And we need a gravity well to do that," I replied. "Asteroid hopping it is then." It wasn't so bad, I suppose. Traveling from one gravity well to another at .5C was better than the alternative. The Alcubierre Drive may not have been the most flexible means of travel, but it was the only way to reach speeds that actually mattered in the vastness of space.

Twenty seconds later, when the *Icarus* slowed to a stop in orbit around Eden's second moon, the crew grinned at each other dumbly, amazed by the upgrade. I couldn't help but think how it would have helped during our skirmish with the Cerberus ship on Auriven II.

"If you think that's cool, wait until you see this," Stohl said, a little less professionally than Zhao would have liked. Zhao raised an eyebrow but didn't say anything. Stohl magnified the screen until a large asteroid was visible. It looked to be about the size of Eros. He nodded to the fresh-faced woman manning the weapons console. Her nameplate read Ensign Kearns.

Kearns tapped about on her console and looked up at Captain Zhao for the order.

"Fire," Zhao said.

Our railgun batteries were capable of firing hundreds of man-sized slugs at relativistic speeds in rapid succession. They carried no warheads, just the kinetic energy intrinsic to the physics of something that size going that fast. But even with that kind of power, our old weapons would have taken several minutes to deal enough damage to break up something as large as an Eros-sized asteroid. When Kearns fired the new batteries, though, the target was obliterated in a matter of seconds.

I don't know if many people will ever understand the feeling shared by the bridge crew of the *Icarus* at that moment. It was like riding on a cloud, the deadliest, most awesomely-powerful storm cloud ever made by man. Somehow, the name *Icarus* didn't seem to fit anymore. We should have rechristened her *Zeus*. We were gods now.

The crew sat in stunned silence before letting out a cheer. It couldn't be helped. It was impossible to contain that much adrenaline-induced exuberance. Zhao raised his hand to silence us and nodded at Lieutenant Stohl. "Time to target?" he asked.

Stohl replied quickly, having anticipated the captain's question. He was starting to make a habit of that. I may not have liked the guy on a personal level, but I couldn't argue with his performance as an officer on a battleship. "Twenty-seven minutes."

"Very good," Zhao replied. "Engines full."

The main viewer flickered to an image of a teal green gas giant with large rings. The tactical display indicated it was equal in almost every way to our own Jupiter, and that it sat at 2.5AU from Eden. I did a double take and ran some numbers in my head. My math teacher at the Naval Academy would've smiled widely if she knew I was calculating velocity by longhand. We were going .7C. I was floored. The fastest the *Icarus* had ever gone before was .5C, and then she could only reach that after a sustained burn of two days. Not something the crew was very fond of. Sitting or lying down, strapped in with feeding tubes and a catheter, unable to get up or move due to the crushing force of acceleration wasn't on anyone's top ten list. But here we were, going faster than that, having reached speed in less than a minute with no rotating in an acceleration chair like a rotisserie chicken to keep the blood from pooling in one place of your body. The moon's modest gravity well had been enough to trigger the engine's graviton cascade. This was truly amazing.

"Commander Pearson," Zhao said. "Brief the command staff on our next mission." Then, he got up and headed for the door. "You have the com."

In unison, the crew stood and snapped off a salute as the captain exited the room. "As you were," he said over his shoulder, and disappeared behind the heavy metal hatch.

Dezzie moved to the captain's chair. Seeing her there almost gave me a panic attack. I tried to find something to occupy myself with, but I couldn't look away. With her hair up in a regulation bun, I could see that jagged scar dipping below the collar of her uniform. Someday, she'd tell me about how she'd gotten it. Maybe then I'd finally crack her code. Until then, there were parts of her that remained locked up tighter than a presidential courier's briefcase.

"Ok, everyone. We've done this before," she said, pulling up an image of a red dwarf star. "Our target is RDS-0175." I wondered why we'd abandoned calling red stars by real names, like Auriven. Perhaps the fact that they'd erupt soon made it pointless to name them.

"It's about a tenth the size of the last one, and only has two satellites." The viewer displayed an image of a pair of dying planets. The larger of the two looked like a crumbling confection on one side. Magenta cracks spiderwebbed across its surface allowing a molten layer of magma to peek through. A wispy tail of gas trailed off into space where the planet's atmosphere seemed to be leaking out like an untied balloon. I remembered the dusty surface of Auriven I. For the most part, it had held steady during our extraction of the artifacts. What would this one be like?

"Another signal?" I asked. "Like the one on Auriven I?"

Dezzie nodded. "Yes. It's a pretty strong one, too."

That meant there'd be another alien facility, more artifacts, and, more automated defenses. It also meant there'd likely be a Cerberus ship guarding the planet. I sure hoped we'd figured out where those assholes were stationed. With our new weapons and speed, all I could think of was making a not-so-friendly house call.

Dezzie went on for several minutes, relaying information about our target, our mission parameters, timeframe, and suspected artifact load. I was only half listening—this was all stuff I'd either seen before or surmised without the aid of her detailed briefing. Instead, my mind wandered to B Company's roster, and how we'd approach the extraction differently this time. No way was I letting something like Patel's death happen again. But as I was running through tactics and armament lists in my head, I noted RDS-0175's coordinates in the top left of our tactical display. It was all wrong. The first set of numbers in the system's galactic address put it in the far end of the furthest quadrant from Eden. Even at .7C, the *Icarus* would rust and crumble to dust before getting a tenth of the way there.

"Commander Pearson," I said, interrupting her briefing. "That star is on the opposite side of the galaxy. How are we going to…?"

Dezzie just tapped on her console and nodded at the main viewer. We'd arrived at the gas giant, which had been named Nineveh by the same misguided soul who'd named Eden and its moons, or so I guessed. Several large asteroids meandered in erratic orbit around the blue-green planet. A small Mako Class miner was working hard at extracting something from the closest one. It had to be valuable for Simms and Galaxia to send the ship all the way out here.

But the miner wasn't what Dezzie had meant for me to see. As we shot around Nineveh, an enormous gate filled our screen. Just as with the one we'd discovered at Auriven II, the space in the center of the ring shimmered like a bowl of gelatinous mother-of-pearl.

"There was a Builder's gate here all along? We could have…"

Dezzie interrupted me. "Not a Builder's gate," she said smiling. "They didn't build it. *We* did."

9

BUSINESS AS USUAL

Making money is art and working is art, and good business is the best art.

— *Andy Warhol*

We weren't the first people to go through a completely manmade interstellar transit gate, but that didn't tarnish the experience for me one bit. The gate may not have been as impressive as the Rift between the Milky Way and Hades, but it sure beat crawling around at .7C.

As we passed through the gate, I saw the same flash of eerie light, and felt the same dry mouth and stomach lurching as I had when we'd gone through the one from Auriven. But this time I'd known what to expect, so it didn't seem quite so bad. Even the ride down from orbit in the *Border*

Mule had proven tolerable so far, though a few minutes before we entered the atmosphere, my stomach tumbled like an Olympic gymnast. I don't think anybody's ever requested a session in the *clothes dryer*, but the gut-wrenching queasiness of orbital insertion left me wishing I'd been better prepared for landfall.

After refitting the *Mule* with a dynamic, accordion-style cargo bay extension that could resize the hold on demand, as well as pressure cycling gear and retractable jump seats on the foreword bay wall, we'd abandoned the old Navy dropships in favor of the modified transports. Hell, they'd even installed a grav plate down the center of the hold with a reversible field to help lift heavy loads. Repairs to the hull and a fresh coat of paint and new designation numbers topped off the transport's refit. I'd only caught a brief glimpse of Patricia, but that's all it'd taken. She was beaming with pride and I couldn't blame her.

"You awake, Commander?" Lamiraux asked. Given the choice between the open seat to my left and one beside Djordi, she'd strapped in right next to me. I hadn't realized my eyes were shut, but her question made me aware of the fact that I looked either like I was praying or asleep. Truth be told, it may have been a little of both. I was exhausted and nervous as hell. The excitement of the past twenty-four hours had taken a bigger toll on me than expected.

"Asleep? Naw. I'm just picturing all the ways to kill a Cerb," I said.

"I'd say we just blast it with the *Icarus*'s new ship-to-ship batteries. Seemed to handle that large asteroid pretty well. Doubt a Cerb ship would fare any better." There was a glint in her eye, a wolfish hunger for vengeance. As I looked about the *Border Mule's* hold, I saw it in every last one of us. Good. Channeled the right way, revenge could be a powerful motivator.

"I'm not talking about a Cerberus *ship*." I removed my '105 from the mag holster on my thigh and popped the battery out to check its charge. The metallic click echoed through the hold, drawing the eyes of half the extraction team. "I'm thinking something a little more *intimate*," I said.

Lamiraux's expression remained as blank as always. Nothing seemed to make her smile. I suppose it helped to keep her reputation intact. If push came to shove, and I had to choose only one Marine to have my back, it would have been her. She may have been short and petite, but damned if she wasn't a maelstrom of death when needed. "We don't even know what they really look like," she said, her French accent as thick as ever. "Rumor is we haven't found a single reference to them in the artifacts."

Djordi looked up from his meditation, or whatever it was he did with his head bowed like that. "Some people are saying the Cerbs aren't even related to the Builders. Two distinct species."

"Doesn't matter," I said, returning my sidearm to its holster. "I see one up close, I'm gonna cram my barrel down its throat and see how it likes the taste of superheated slugs." That elicited a smattering of 'ooo-rahs' from the Marines.

"What if it likes the taste?" inquired Djordi with a smirk.

"Then maybe they'll hurt on the way out the other end." The others laughed at that and the tensions eased a bit. The cargo bay's intercom chirped to life with Patricia's voice, interrupting us. "Prepare for landfall," she said.

I tugged at my harness and closed my helmet's visor per protocol. Sixty seconds later the landing thrusters kicked on and again, my stomach was in my throat. I clenched my jaw against the sensation and tried to think of something else. Dezzie had looked quite stunning earlier that morning, and her good luck kiss still lingered on my lips.

Thud.

The cargo bay door folded down into its loading ramp position, spilling bright orange light into the compartment. We rechecked our ammo, batteries, and helmet seals one last time before filing down the ramp and onto the surface of yet another dying planet. The air was dusty, but breathable, so we popped our visors and donned simple paper face masks. Always best to save your suit's air supply for an emergency.

Patricia had dropped us *inside* the compound's outer wall right on top of what looked like a courtyard. Well-worn tan and brown stone pavers of differing shades made a mosaic on the ground, and a portico with arching columns ran along three sides of the square. Private Tanaka had drawn the short straw and been assigned to run point. "Hey FNG," said Sergeant Lamiraux, looking at scans from her wrist com. "Go scout up to the northeast. Find us a door."

"*FNG?*" I asked.

Djordi leaned down toward my head and whispered, "*Fucking New Guy.*"

"Oh," I said.

Our replacement engineer, Lieutenant Williams, scraped some stone fragments from one of the columns into a small receptacle in her handheld. An LED flashed red then yellow, and finally green. "Scan indicates the structure is between three and five thousand years old."

That didn't make sense. There were gleaming metal spires towards the center of the compound, and the metal door Tanaka had found us was powered by electricity.

"How could the buildings be that old? You'd think the lights would have gone out ages ago," I said.

Major Chan had fallen in beside me as we made our way across the courtyard. "Maybe they added the technology and more modern-looking parts of the facility later. Like building on older layers."

"Or," Lamiraux suggested, "perhaps the original structure wasn't built by the same species."

It was all possible. For all we knew, we'd stumbled upon the Hades Galaxy's version of Baghdad, which had been built and rebuilt a dozen times in its history. Regardless, we had a mission to do and archeology wasn't a part of it.

Ten minutes later, we'd made our way through snaking corridors, dusty streets, and several buildings until we found the lift that took us to the basement. Luckily, we'd managed to disable most of the automated turrets, and avoid those we couldn't. Advancing through the facility gave me an eerie feeling of déjà vu. Sure enough, we found a large chamber like the one on Auriven. The Builders were nothing if not consistent. Here, though, there was one notable difference. Instead of three artifacts, we found six. When we loaded them on the grav sleds, we discovered them to weigh twice as much as the previous artifacts. I opened the spring-loaded door on the side of the closest one and inspected the insides. It was purple, like the one we'd used to destroy the Cerberus ship that attacked us on the last mission. This tetrahedron though, had nearly twice the facets as that one. "What do you think makes it weigh so much more?" I asked. "Seems to be the same size as the others."

Williams caressed the artifact's egg-shaped power unit, lost in lustful admiration. Most engineers waited their whole lives for something like this, and now she was one of only two tech heads to have made a discovery of such importance. The dumb grin on her face suddenly seemed appropriate. "Fascinating," she managed between sharp breaths. She scanned the artifact with her handheld. "Power output is a little higher than the ones you recovered from Auriven," she said, pausing to scroll through the scanner's readings. "I think this one holds about twice as much data."

If that were true, and we had *six* of them to extract... The sheer volume of data was staggering. I tried imagining that much storage in terms of petabytes, but I don't think I truly fathomed the number. I simply didn't have a good frame of reference.

"Get them loaded quickly," I ordered. Something was bothering me about this place. Maybe it was the alien look and feel, or maybe it was the fact that it was deserted—a ghost town of sorts. All I knew was I wanted to get out as quickly as possible.

But just as Tanaka and Lamiraux tugged on the handle of first grav sled, there was a sharp clanking noise from the other end of the chamber, from behind one of the large junction boxes where conduits from the artifacts snaked along the wall and out the ceiling.

Lamiraux deftly rolled behind the artifact to her right, drawing her service rifle from the mag holster on her back with the fluidity of a ballet dancer. She was deadly grace incarnate. Tanaka was a different story. He dropped the sled's handle without ceremony and leveled his '105, snapping off six rounds before I could give the order to stand down.

"That's enough!" I yelled. But it was too late. I saw a flash of white armor as someone—or something—scurried through a door at the end of the chamber. By then we'd all drawn our weapons. I don't know why I'd chosen my grandpa's Beretta over the service pistol on my other thigh, but it's cross-hatched wooden grip felt hard and familiar in my bare hand. I signaled for Tanaka and Lamiraux to advance toward the spot where the target had been seconds before, while Djordi and Chan fell in beside me, squatting low for cover. We crept along the east wall of the room to help flank the target area to provide any needed cover fire while Lamiraux and Tanaka investigated. The remaining Marines took up positions wherever they could.

While Lamiraux kept low to the ground, Tanaka bull-rushed the spot where the enemy had been. The muscular Marine pulled up just short of the door and leveled his pistol at some unseen target behind the junction box.

"Don't kill it!" I ordered.

"Yes, sir," he replied through clenched teeth.

Lamiraux secured the doorway while Chan, Djordi and I sprinted to Private Tanaka's position. That's when I saw what he'd trained his gun on. Sitting on the ground, hands extended to its sides was a humanoid creature. It was hard to say how big it was, but the proportions were right for something a little less than two meters tall. Whatever it was wore cream-colored body armor and had been carrying some kind of firearm, which lay a half dozen meters away on the floor. Its head was oval and featureless but seemed to be tracking my movements. I motioned for it to stand, which it did without hesitation.

"Obedient bastard," said Chan. "Can't wait to kill me my first Cerb."

I looked on the floor and noted a trail of crimson splotches leading through the doorway. At least we knew they could be hurt.

"Looks like you nailed the other one, Private," I said to Tanaka.

"All due respect, sir," he replied, "but I don't miss." At that, the alien raised its hands above its head, which I found strange. Either it did so out of instinct, or the thing knew exactly what we wanted. I pulled off my disposable breathing mask —the air inside the building wasn't as dusty anyway—and was about to ask our captive some questions when I heard a string of curses from behind me. I turned just in time to see Lamiraux drag the second alien by the arm back into the artifact chamber. It limped noticeably, and sure enough, blood seeped from an entry wound and trickled down its leg. That armor had to be tough. Really tough. The '105 could tear the limb off an unsuited target and punch a hole in steel plate an inch thick.

When Lamiraux got closer, I noticed she wasn't the one cursing, and then it hit me. "Pop your visor," I ordered as I brandished my pistol toward the other captive's face. It reached slowly for a nearly-invisible release on the side of its otherwise smooth helmet, and with a click and hissing of pressurized air, the faceplate split in half to reveal a woman's face. A *human* woman.

Chan seemed to lead the entire team in a shared sigh of disappointment. Lamiraux shoved the wounded man to a spot next to his partner and tapped his helmet release while keeping her rifle trained on him with her free hand.

"Okay, okay," he said in perfect Terran Standard. "No need to kill us! We just came for the artifacts." If I had my accents straight, I'd say our injured friend was from New York. There were plenty of freaks in a city that big, but not exactly the kind of *alien* we were hoping for. Definitely *not* Cerberus.

"Artifacts?" I asked, playing dumb. I needed to see what they knew.

"You know," he responded gruffly, "the big eggs you just loaded onto those mag sleds over there."

I ignored him. "Who are you?"

"Depends who's asking," replied the man. "You Galaxia?"

I nodded and the man sneered.

"Who are you?" I repeated. "Who sent you here?"

"The merry queen of fucking England, that's who," he replied defiantly.

Tanaka kicked the guy in the injured leg, sending him to the ground screaming profanities I'd never heard. But from tone alone I guessed they would have made even my drill instructor blush. After a few seconds of heavy breathing and grimaces, the man quieted down. His leg had to hurt, but damned if he didn't just sit there, glaring.

"Stubborn son of a bitch," said Chan in his Texas drawl.

I pulled Chan aside, out of earshot. "It doesn't much matter what their names are. We know they're from a rival corporation, but which one?"

He shrugged. "Galaxia provided us all the intel they had. None of the other outfits had the resources or manpower to make it through the Rift. Or so they say."

It was true. Galaxia was the biggest, most well-staffed, well-funded, and well-equipped corporation in the whole of human history if you believed the propaganda. Hell, they'd *bought* the Navy lock, stock, and barrel. Something didn't add up. Either Simms had exaggerated Galaxian dominance, or something else was happening here. I turned toward the others. "Sergeant Lamiraux?"

"Yes, Commander Johnson?"

"Collect some DNA samples from our guests," I said. Then I motioned for Lieutenant Williams to bring me her handheld. There was a part of me that knew I should have asked Djordi to do it, but another part of me—a bigger part than I cared to admit—just wanted to see what Lamiraux would do. She didn't disappoint. Peeling off her gloves and holstering her service rifle on her back, Lamiraux balled her fists and punched our male captive with her right hand, and the female with her left. Right in the mouth, both times. Then she sauntered over to us and scraped her knuckles on the edge of the scanning receptacle. After repeating it with her other hand, she wiped the blood on the thigh plates of her armored suit.

I tapped in a couple commands and scanned my thumb for verification, then waited for the response from the *Icarus*. If we were right, the DNA would match corporate contract records and we'd have our answer. Ten seconds later, Stohl responded with a secure text to my wrist com.

Let them go. Leave the artifacts. This isn't a fight we want.

When I protested, Captain Zhao himself raised me over voice.

"Release the detainees, Commander. That's an order," he said in an icy tone.

"Yes, sir," I said, nodding to Chan and the others. Our *guests* were released and sent on their way.

"What about my leg?" protested the man from Queens. "You can't just leave me all torn up like this!"

Sergeant Lamiraux and I made eye contact briefly before she returned to the injured man's side. It was all we'd needed. No verbal order, no 'yes sir, no sir,' just a single look. "Hold still," she ordered. "I'll repair the hole with suit sealant." After spraying the foam into the ruptured armor, she grabbed something from her thigh pocket and turned to walk away.

"That's it?" the man complained. "Nothin' for the pain?"

Lamiraux turned on her heel and held her hand out as if she were going to give him something, a pain pill perhaps. The instant he reached out with his bare hand, the sergeant stabbed his palm with a morphine stick. "Take two aspirin and call me in the morning," she said. The man let out a string of expletives and shook his hand angrily before heading out the door with his partner.

As Lamiraux caught up to the group an almost imperceptible smile turning up the corners of her mouth. But it was her eyes that said it all. They were smiling as widely as a kid on Christmas morning. We'd probably broken a dozen Navy regulations and corporate policies, and I'm sure I'd have to account for it all later. But I didn't care. We may not have captured a Cerberus soldier, or a big haul of artifacts, but I'd gotten the next best thing: the secret of how to make Jeanne Lamiraux smile.

10

RIVAL

Three may keep a secret, if two of them are dead.

— *Benjamin Franklin in* Poor Richard's Almanack

Patricia seemed intent on pushing the *Mule* to its new limits. She kicked on the modified afterburners before we'd even cleared the atmosphere. Lucky for us the new jump seats had good harnesses that held us fast against the bulkhead and our new battle suits had been fitted with improved circulation gear. I'd never been swallowed by a python—hell, I'd never even see a real one—but my suit's arm and leg constrictors made me feel like a baby mouse fed to some kid's pet snake.

I struggled against inertia but managed to tap a few commands into my wrist com, bringing up a holo display of the *Mule's* forward view cameras just when the final wisps of clouds and gas glided by as we entered the vacuum of space. Patricia had done well: we were pointed directly at the *Icarus*. But as we drew closer, something wasn't quite right. Yes, the shape was familiar—long with a blunt nose and bridge platform and engine housings in the back—but the newly painted call letters and name were missing from her hull.

I tapped into the *Mule's* com feed to listen in as Patricia brought us in on a standard docking approach. "*Icarus*," she said. "This is *Border Mule* requesting permission to dock."

Strangely, the lights of the battleship's aft docking bay were off, and the bay doors were shut. Patricia slowed the *Mule* to a crawl, which sent blood to the back of my head. Her request to dock remained unanswered for several seconds.

"Captain Simms," I said, choosing formality this time rather than her first name, "I don't believe this is the *Icarus*. It may look like our battleship, but it's not. Suggest you scan and send a message on encrypted channels to Zhao. Find out where they are."

I half expected her to protest or throw around her rank with some pithy, British remark, but she didn't. "I think you're right, Commander Johnson." A second or two later, her message went out to the *Icarus*. "Command, please respond with orders on emergency protocol four-nine-seven." Four-nine-seven was the naval code for rotating encrypted frequencies every two-and-a-half seconds. Very tough to home in on a frequency-hopping data stream.

It should have worked, but there was no answer—at least not from the *Icarus*.

"*Border Mule*?" came a female voice none of us recognize. There was a muffled snicker in the background, and a barely audible voice questioning our transport's name. Though the mocking hadn't been intended for our ears, we heard it nonetheless. The woman continued. "Permission denied. You'll have to find another way to get that sorry ass home."

Patricia brought the *Mule* about ninety degrees and tapped the thrusters. Within seconds we were clear of the larger ship and making our way into a higher orbit where we sat while deciding what to do.

"That's the other corporation's ship," Major Chan said. "They could just blast us outta the sky if they wanted to."

That caused several people to shift uncomfortably in their seats. "No," I replied. "They won't do that. The *Icarus* is around here somewhere, and I'd be willing to bet she's faster and better armed than this copy-cat ship.

"She's called the *SS Profit*," Patricia said. "That's what the transponder says.

"Why couldn't you see it before," I asked. "the transponder?"

Just then our encrypted com channel crackled to life, at first with static, then with intermittent blasts of frantic voices.

"...coming in hot...stay clear...new Cerberus ship."

It was Dezzie, and she didn't sound happy. "The *Profit* must have been jammin' us somehow," Chan said. "We couldn't see their transponder, but we couldn't punch a message through to the *Icarus* either."

Lieutenant Williams shook her head, her strawberry blond bangs flopping back and forth as she did. "No. If they were jamming us, we wouldn't have been able to speak with anyone on the *Profit*. More likely they just turned off their transponder until they knew our intentions."

"She's right," Patricia said over the ship-wide channel. "The *Icarus* was just on the other side of the planet. We don't have any satellites in orbit to relay messages, and the *Mule* doesn't have one of those fancy Entangled Particle Arrays for FTL coms."

It all made sense, but it didn't explain why Dezzie was so upset. I hit my wrist com. "Repeat last, over."

"We're coming in hot and taking damage" Dezzie repeated, a little more professionally than before. "The Cerb ship is pursuing. We took out the smaller one, but this one's bigger, and it's hull is a lot tougher."

Just then a large blue dot representing the *Icarus* crept around from the dark side of the planet, followed closely by a large red dot. The friendly ship had plotted a waypoint that crossed our orbit in less than two minutes.

"What is that thing?" Lamiraux asked.

"I don't know," Patricia said, "but I'm not sticking around to find out. Hang on." She punched the thrusters so hard the *Mule* moved like it had been shot out of a rail gun. Ten seconds later, we were on a trajectory taking us safely out of harm's way. In the meantime, she pumped the *Mule's* external optical feed to my com, which I displayed for all to see.

"What do you make of it?" she asked.

The unidentified Cerberus ship was big, almost as big as the *Icarus*. It was halfway between a triangle and an oval, with a dark brown and black mottled hull making it look old and worn out. Like the smaller variety of Cerbs we were used to seeing, this ship didn't have any portholes or windows. In fact, there was no light coming from it at all. How did it move? What was its propulsion system? It was a question that had baffled SciCorp about the smaller ships too. Unfortunately, we'd never been able to scoop up any debris for examination. Kind of hard to think about a salvage operation when you've got a giant red star about to vaporize you.

"Not much we can do from here but watch," Chan lamented. I could tell not being in the thick of the fight rubbed him the wrong way. Being a Marine was not a spectator sport. But while we'd all been watching the new Cerb chase the *Icarus*, none of us had noticed the *SS Profit* power up her rail guns and move in to assist. By the time she got there, though, our own battleship had arrived at its waypoint and sat in a face-off, trading blows with the large Cerb like two ancient sailing ships pulling up for a broadside with cannons. Neither ship was lobbing iron balls, though. And while the *Icarus*'s new weapons were dishing out plenty of damage, the Cerb ship was dealing its own measure of hurt. The *Mule* was close enough that at maximum magnification, the optical feed showed rending of armor plates and tearing of bulkheads. Where the enemy fire didn't hit solidly, it still left pits and pockmarks in the *Icarus*'s hull.

Nobody was surprised when the *Profit* unleashed its batteries on the Cerb ship. But none of us could have predicted what happened next, especially after our run-in down on the planet's surface. Just as the other corporate battleship got within firing range of the enemy, it pulsed with some kind of blue-white energy that engulfed it and the Cerberus ship, freezing them on the spot. Somehow, the *Icarus* remained outside the blast radius.

I hit my com. "What the hell was that, Dezzie?"

She responded, apparently as baffled as me. "I have no idea, Commander. But we're not going to stick around to find out. Let's finish this."

With both the Cerberus and the *Profit* dead in the water, the *Icarus* easily dispatched the alien ship. I'd never seen such an enormous explosion in space. The violet-colored flames burned brightly, dissipating quickly as their fuel source—likely tainted with potassium chloride if my college chemistry knowledge could be trusted—was expelled into the void. I'm sure someone was recording this and SciCorp would analyze what it could. It was a spectacular explosion to be sure. A little *too* spectacular. I turned to Chan. "I think that Cerb just self-destructed right before the *Icarus* finished it off."

"Now why would they do that?" he asked, consternation thick in his voice.

"Maybe they don't want us getting our hands on their tech?" I offered. But there was no time for idle speculation. Our red star counter was down to single digits, so there would be no answers today.

The instant the *Icarus* was free from enemy fire, Patricia plotted an intercept course that had the *Mule* docking with the bigger ship in less than three minutes. But before I could so much as unfasten my harness, Captain Zhao's voice rang loudly over the com channel. "Commander Johnson," he said, not waiting for a response, "bring your extraction team onto the *Icarus* immediately. Captain Simms will be taking the artifacts through the transit gate back to Eden without us."

If confusion were as valuable as gold, we'd all have been rich. From the looks of astonishment on everyone's faces, it abounded in the transport's cargo hold. "*Without* us, sir?" I asked.

"That's an order, Commander." I frowned. It wasn't so much that his voice had such finality to it that bothered me, but the fact that the reason behind the order was clearly something he didn't want to share with the team at large. I hated not knowing what was going on, and knew that it bothered my men, too. Regardless, I corralled B Company and hurried them through the airlock. They'd all been practicing zero-G moves with Djordi, so it went a lot smoother than in the past—

not that it had been bad before—but now it was a thing of precision and beauty.

I sprinted to the command deck and arrived, slightly winded, but at attention in front of the captain's chair. Zhao saluted me absent-mindedly and I found my spot on the deck behind him. "Lieutenant Stohl," he said calmly. "As soon as the *Border Mule* is free of her moorings, punch in the coordinates to the Rift.

My heart shot through my throat. The *Icarus* was damaged from the fight. Why were we headed to the Rift? Were we going home? Back to the Milky Way Galaxy? Or was it something else? There were just too many possibilities. I'm sure Zhao would let us know when it was right, but that was always much later than I liked. This time was different though. He brought up an image of the Rift on the main view screen.

The Rift wasn't like the Red Star Gates at all. We'd built the one in the Eden system, but it was compatible with the existing network of gates that connected all the dying stars in the Hades Galaxy. The Rift was something altogether different. There was no metallic ring, no artificial construct at all. In fact, it couldn't even be seen with human eyes. But rendered in full spectrum on our main display, it looked like a swirling vortex with erratic tendrils of energy spiking out randomly into space.

"Half an hour ago, Corporate Command sent word that something happened to the Rift. They didn't elaborate, but indicated a team of our best scientists and engineers have been dispatched on the *Andromeda* and the *Wall Street* to investigate.

I played with the numbers in my head. Even at .7C, it would take us nearly eighty thousand years to get back to that quadrant of space, which was such a large number it made the thought completely absurd. I assumed we'd be heading back through the gate to Eden, then by conventional means the two months it would take to get from there to the rift.

"They also informed us," continued Zhao, "that a sister gate has been built near the mouth of the Rift."

Well, there went that theory. I almost smiled because I hated long stints at speed.

"So, we can jump there from here?" I asked. "Through the Builder's gate?"

"Yes, Commander," said Zhao. "And the *Icarus* is to join and provide escort to the *Andromeda* and the *Wall Street*."

My eyes widened. Three ships made a flotilla. And a flotilla was usually run by one of the captains who would be temporarily elevated to the rank of admiral. Would it be Zhao, or one of the other captains? The two frigates were both originally Galaxian. My preference was for Zhao to assume command of the group. I'd already had enough corporate leadership, especially when that leadership had forbidden me from seeing my girlfriend and then tried stealing her right out from under my nose. I didn't have to worry about that with Zhao.

Captain Zhao nodded to Stohl, who seemed to have been permanently reassigned to the helm. In turn, Stohl slid his fingers across the console, bringing the ship's thrusters to one quarter power. We lurched forward, almost overtaking the *Mule*, which headed toward the gate. Seconds later, the smaller ship disappeared into the shimmering space at the center of the ring without fanfare. It was simply like watching a heavy object slowly sink into a cobalt ocean. I don't know why, but I was a little disappointed. I'd half expected a flash of light, or some strange optical effect as the ship traversed the threshold, but there simply wasn't one. Looks like the sci-fi shows got something wrong after all.

Not twenty seconds later, the *Icarus* followed through the gate. In that time, it had somehow been reset to a new destination, instantly sending us across the Hades Galaxy to the emergence point of the Rift. I shook my head and swallowed to wet my throat. Don't know if I'll ever get used to traversing a ring like that.

Sure enough, the moment we snapped to normal space on the other side of the destination gate, the *Andromeda* and *Wall Street* were there to greet us. Behind them, the normally invisible Rift glowed a very visible red, like the crimson maw of some demon from a horror film. We all stared in awe for several seconds before the yeoman looked up from her console. "Captain? They're hailing us." Her soft Irish accent was pleasant, and for the first time I noticed how pretty her face was. I glanced guiltily at Dezzie, but she didn't seem to have noticed.

"This is Captain Zhao of the *Galaxia Ship Icarus*."

The com crackled with static, likely from the Rift. I glanced at several spiking indicators on the lower left of the tactical display. But it quickly cleared up.

"Ah, Wang," came a familiar voice. It was Fleet Admiral Simms. The yeoman switched to visual now that we were in range. The admiral stood in front of the captain's chair on the *Andromeda's* bridge, peering back at us with his narrow face, dark eyes, and salt and pepper hair. I hated to admit it, but he was in great shape for a man approaching sixty. "It's good to see you."

"Yes, sir," Zhao replied. I'd never heard anyone use the captain's first name. Were he and Simms really on such personal terms? I found the notion hard to believe, especially after the way the admiral had summarily dismissed Zhao and taken command of the *Icarus* at the rendezvous so many months ago. Guess that was all water under the bridge now. Or was it?

"Captain," Simms continued, "assemble your command staff and shuttle over to the *Andromeda*."

What? Simms wanted to meet with the officers? This had to be important. And with the strange, ghost-like effects spewing out of the Rift, it couldn't be good.

"We have a corporate spy to uncover," Simms sighed, "and we have every reason to believe that that person is one of your crew."

Zhao's expression mirrored the shock we all felt. "Sir?" he questioned.

Simms arched an eyebrow. "Captain, the *Icarus* has been compromised. You have a *mole*." At that the main viewer cycled to a static image of the Galaxia corporate logo; two galaxies interconnected by the contrail of a rocket ship. I frowned. No matter how much we'd wanted to start anew in the Hades Galaxy, it seems we'd brought humanity's lesser qualities with us. Then my mind began to race. If Simms was right, and there *was* a mole amongst us, who could it be? More importantly, what methods would Galaxia use to find out? I shuddered and followed the rest of the command crew to the shuttle. I'd know soon enough.

11

MOLE

Why, sometimes I've believed as many as six impossible things before breakfast.

— Lewis Carroll in The Adventures of Alice in Wonderland

The look in the sergeant's eyes before he punched me in the face again said it all. He thought I was the mole. Or, maybe he had to tell himself that to do his job. Either way, taking a beating while tied to a folding chair in a maintenance closet didn't agree with me.

"How did you manage to get the Hades Class blueprints?" he asked between a punch to my jaw and one to my gut. The sergeant's nameplate had been disabled, but I could still see the faint outline of the nanoweave lettering: *Reynolds*. I filed that away for later use. He was a man with unremarkable features, average height, and a little overweight. He didn't carry it well. That didn't stop him from packing a mean punch though. Sweat trickled down his temples, and droplets formed on his upper lip. This was giving him quite the workout.

"How many times do I have to say it, Sergeant? It wasn't me." I licked the blood from my busted lip. "I'm *not* the mole."

He cracked his neck and pulled up a folding chair of his own, sitting in it backwards right in front of me. "Then how'd the Consortium get their hands on them? You saw that ship. It was identical in almost every way to the *Icarus* and the *London*."

"Maybe they stole the prints from the Navy, before the Hades mission? Or maybe they got them from the contractor who built the ships?" I exhaled in frustration. "This is ridiculous."

The sergeant sprang to his feet, flinging his chair into the wall of the small room. "Ridiculous? Ridiculous is what we do to corporate spies. The Geneva Convention don't apply in this case, Commander." In his anger, Reynolds's Rhode Island accent came out stronger than before. I suspect he tried to hide it as best he could. Especially after the attempted secession of '51. People across the North American Coalition were still smarting from that conflict.

His reference to the Geneva Convention was expected. It wasn't much, but the insinuation still filled my head with a dozen images of torture, none of which were particularly pleasant.

"Ever hear of vacuum cycling?" he continued.

I shook my head. Didn't sound bad, but if the sergeant was bringing it up in this context, it had to be.

"You spacers had to take EV training, right?" He didn't wait for me to answer. "Well, then you know what exposure to vacuum does to the human body." He retrieved a strange-looking glove and gauntlet from a duffle bag in the corner. It looked like most EV suit gloves with one small exception. The wrist joint was missing its clasps. He pointed to the rubber gasket just inside the end of the gauntlet. "This little thing here," he said, "seals to your skin. Anything below it, like, say, a hand…" he wiggled his fingers for effect. "…anything below it that might *accidentally* be exposed to vacuum wouldn't kill ya." He cocked his head to one side. "Wouldn't feel good but wouldn't kill ya." He picked his chair back up and sat down in front of me again. "Course we'd bring ya back in after a few seconds. Thaw that hand right out with some warm water."

The imagery was gruesome: a half-frozen hand, blood vessels popped, and capillaries ruptured. Then, the sound of crackling as pouring warm water over it led to rapid thawing.

"My pops always told me to finish a job though," Reynolds continued, a wicked smile playing at the corners of his mouth. "So, I'd make sure you got a couple more strolls on the hull."

The thought of freezing and thawing my hand repeatedly was almost more than I could bear. But I couldn't crack. I couldn't show this guy anything. So, I leaned forward as much as I could and arched an eyebrow in a conspiratorial way. "Tell you what," I whispered. "I know you're just doing your job." I nodded approvingly. "And a fine job it is. So, when we're done with this little charade, I'll make sure Admiral Simms knows how good you are at these things. I'm sure we could use this kind of...*gusto*...on an extraction team. Like, say, *B Company*?"

It wasn't likely that Simms would transfer Reynolds to a unit under my command after allowing him to beat the snot out of me, but the threat of it was enough to give him pause. Fear flickered in his eyes. It had been fleeting, but it had been there nonetheless. When he overcame his momentary indecision, Reynolds stood up and folded his arms across his chest, right above his beer belly. "OK. So, you didn't give 'em the blueprints. All you did was tell 'em where our next mission was. You sent them the coordinates."

I smiled and shook my head. "Sergeant," I said, trying not to sound too condescending, but condescending enough to make my point, "they don't tell you anything, do they? And you're just not smart enough to put it together for yourself."

He glowered and made as if to hit me but stopped at the last moment.

"They were *shooting* at us down there. Shooting at *me*," I said. "Now why would I tell the...what did you call them, the *Consortium*, where to find me, just so they could shoot at me and steal the artifacts out from under us?"

I could see the wheels turning in his head. I'd given him something to think about, something that probably hadn't occurred to him yet. "However, they managed to get the blueprints to the battleships, they had to have a facility to build one, either back in the Milky Way or here in Hades. A ship that big wouldn't go unnoticed by all the sensors studying the other end of the Rift near Jupiter Station. So," I paused, hoping he'd put it together.

"So, you're sayin' the Consortium's got a shipyard here on this side of the Rift?" asked Reynolds.

"And if they can pop into our Red Star Missions, using coordinates a mole gave them, the Consortium must have built their own transit gate somewhere." I paused to let that sink in. I knew there were others watching. At a minimum I was being recorded, so there would be someone smarter than the sergeant to test my theories. He furrowed his brow and squinted as he thought, but it wasn't coming together for him. So, I spelled it out for him.

"Do you think *I* know how to build a transit gate?"

He seemed to contemplate the notion. "No."

"Is there *anyone* on the *Icarus* who knows how to build one? Or has access to the plans for one?"

"If I had to guess I'd say no," he said.

Clearly, I had to lead a little more. "And who *would* have access to all that?"

"SciCorp," he answered. "But that don't explain how the Consortium knew which planet we were going to. How do you explain that one?"

Just then, the door opened with a swish and Admiral Simms stepped into the confines of the small room, leaving his personal guards just outside. "He can't explain it," said Simms. "Not yet anyway."

Sergeant Reynolds jumped to attention and saluted sharply until Simms released him. "Dismissed, Sergeant."

"But I ain't done, Sir. I still gotta..." he reached for the duffle bag.

"I said *dismissed*. Commander Johnson isn't the mole."

Reynolds saluted again and left the room.

"All due respect, Admiral," I said, relieved to be talking to someone with more than two brain cells sparking at the same time, "you're going about this the wrong..."

"That'll be enough, Commander." He nodded at my bindings and untied me. "We had to be sure."

"And now that your goon beat the shit out of me, you're sure I'm not the mole?" I said, rubbing the soreness out of my wrists.

"Nothing is sure in Hades," responded Simms. "Take the Rift for example. We thought it was natural. Even after learning how to build the transit gates, the Rift seemed too...organic, too random to be manufactured. And none of the transit gates can even come close to reaching the Milky Way."

That had been the party line since the beginning. The Rift is natural. But after we learned of the gate network, and how to build our own node, the first question I'd asked was who'd built the Rift. Nobody had a good answer.

"But something's changed," he said.

"You mean the visible energy radiating from the Rift?"

The admiral nodded. "We've brought nearly the whole bloody SciCorp here to figure it out."

It made sense. The Rift was our way back home. If something happened to it, if it became unstable or worse, if it closed, we'd be stranded in Hades. "It's not part of the gate network, is it?" I asked.

Simms shook his head. "Not that we can tell. It's a unique anomaly."

I could tell he was hiding something from me. "What aren't you telling me, Sir?

"Paul," he said, a little more informally than I was expecting. "We aren't the only corporation to come through the Rift. As soon as word got back about what we discovered, about Eden, about the hyper cells and abundant hydrogen in Hades, hundreds of other corporations flooded through. The competition for resources has begun in earnest. And the person...the corporation that controls those resources will have the biggest say in the future of humanity in this galaxy."

I think I saw where this was going, and the realization left me quite unsettled. "You think someone sabotaged the Rift? To keep others from coming through?"

"It's one of the working theories," Simms replied. "But there are those in SciCorp who think otherwise. They say there's evidence that whatever is causing the acceleration of supernovae in red stars and crumbling of their planets is the same force that's causing the Rift to...act up."

"So," I said, running my fingers through my hair, "we have a mole feeding sensitive company information and ship schematics to another corporation..."

"Consortium of corporations. Joining forces is the only way they could move against us so brazenly," Simms said, correcting me.

"The Consortium is stealing and copying our technology, trying to steal our artifacts, and some unknown power is trying to destroy our way home?"

Then it hit me. Like a ton of bricks, it hit me. "The *Cerberus*?" I asked. "They've been trying to keep us from the ruins, from salvaging any artifacts. They've even self-destructed just to keep us from their own technology. You think they're doing this to the Rift?"

Simms nodded his head gravely. "That's the other working theory."

Shit.

Shit, shit, shit, shit, shit!

"I still don't understand why the heavy hand with a guy like Reynolds," I said. "Why not ask me directly, sir? I'd have told you everything you wanted. You could've used a lie detector."

Simms smiled. "We have a certain way of doing things, Commander. This isn't the same Navy you're used to." He folded the two chairs and leaned them against the wall. "Besides, you're a Marine now, Commander. And Marines are like diamonds. They sometimes need a little vigorous buffeting to truly shine."

At that, Admiral Simms opened the door and left me standing there alone in the utility closet. My lip was swollen, and I'm sure I had a black eye. The most serious injury I'd sustained, though, was to my ego. I grimaced. I knew I had because the recently sealed cut on my lip cracked open as I did, and I tasted the familiar iron of my own blood again. My heart sank at the lack of trust I'd been shown, at how quickly Simms had turned on me, on *us*. That moment was the first time that I really regretted my career choice. What had I gotten myself into? And what kind of man was leading the Hades Mission?

My wrist com vibrated, signaling a priority message. It was from Captain Zhao. He'd ordered the *Icarus* command crew back to the shuttle. I washed up in the nearest sink I could find and headed to the launch bay. The *Andromeda* was about a third the size of the *Icarus*, but it still took me several minutes to make my way down the length of the ship. Of course, Galaxia had installed graviton plates on every deck. I wouldn't have expected anything less on the admiral's personal frigate.

When I made it to the launch bay, I almost ran into the others as they huddled together near the airlock door, waiting for it to cycle before boarding the shuttle. Dezzie saw me and gasped. Zhao and Stohl didn't say a word, but looked at me with wide eyes.

"What the hell did they do to you Paul?"

Dezzie asked as she broke decorum and ran to embrace me. Hugging her was always exhilarating, but there was an extra measure of relief and electricity this time. I held her longer than I should have, perhaps, smelling her hair and feeling her warmth in my arms. I looked at her beautiful, perfect face.

But something was wrong. Rather, *nothing* was wrong. Dezzie didn't have a scratch on her. Looking from one to the next, I discovered none of the others did. Was I the only one who'd received a beating?

"We'll talk about it on the *Icarus*," said Captain Zhao, who looked around us warily. "Right now, we need to focus on the Rift." He brought up a holo vid of the anomaly in the air in front of us. The tendrils of red energy had grown larger, and the readings from our sensors were going crazy. "It's gotten worse. A lot worse."

12

RIFT

Someone asked me, if I were stranded on a desert island what book would I bring... 'How to Build a Boat.'

— STEVEN WRIGHT

The war room on the *Icarus* wasn't much more than a rectangle with a central holo screen projected from an emitter in the top of an oval console about waist height. It was large enough for the six of us—Captain Zhao, me, Dezzie, Stohl, Djordi, and Major Chan—to huddle around while reviewing mission specs. My lip still hurt, and I could feel the swelling in my left eye getting worse, but it hadn't gotten so bad I couldn't open it. In hindsight, I should have stopped off at the infirmary for an analgesic and a cold pack. But Zhao had whisked us up to the command deck from the shuttle bay without so much as a word, and we'd dutifully followed close behind him. He didn't even look at me, much less ask what had happened.

Dezzie, on the other hand, couldn't get over how Simms had treated me. Even now, as we waited for Marine guards to take up position outside the war room doors, she complained. "All they did to us was ask questions," she said.

"Sergeant Reynolds asked me questions too," I said flatly. "With his *fists*."

Dezzie reached up to caress my bruised cheek, then lightly traced my bottom lip with her finger. There was a sudden heat in my stomach, and I wished we were alone. Unfortunately, this wasn't the time for that. The doors shut and Zhao produced a handheld with which he proceeded to thoroughly scan the room.

"Making sure nobody made unreported *changes* to the war room during the ship's refit," he said.

"You think somebody bugged it?" asked Chan in disbelief.

"Wouldn't surprise me," responded Dezzie, a look of worry etched on her face. She let go of my hand and took her spot to the right of Captain Zhao.

The captain then brought up a secure briefing screen and raised an EM shroud around us to ensure no transmission or sound waves could leave the room. It was like an invisible bubble of silence in which only the intended participants could hear and be heard. The floor and walls even began to vibrate to provide interference against anyone using sonic snooping lasers. I'd seen one of those in a spy movie back on Jupiter Station. The guy had listened in on the conversation from across the street by pointing the laser device at the shut window of the room the target conversation was in. Pretty neat stuff, actually.

By then, Zhao had keyed in his security code and scanned his thumb to access his personal files. A secure video feed from the *Icarus*'s sensor array snapped to life above the holo emitter. The image it displayed of the Rift was startling. Not only had the vortex of red energy grown, but the tendrils spiking from the center of the anomaly had noticeably intensified. I wondered if I was the only one with growing unease. The *Icarus* was pretty close to the Rift, and we had no way of knowing what it might do to us if it exploded or *imploded*. Or whatever strange wormhole anomalies do when they go on the fritz.

"This is what the Rift looks like now," Zhao explained, "and this is what it looked like six days ago." The image faded to a more docile version of the giant wormhole's terminus. "And then, there is this." He tapped a command on his console and fast-forwarded the video several frames.

"What the hell is that?" Chan asked, his Texas drawl adding to our bewilderment.

It started out as a small, black dot—maybe the size of a single pixel—in the middle of the Rift, but soon grew to fill nearly a third of the Rift's gaping maw.

"Those are ships," Zhao said. "Thousands of corporate ships."

"Whose?" I asked.

"Everyone's," he replied.

When Simms told me that the other corporations had sent ships from Jupiter Station through the Rift, and that the competition for resources in the Hades Galaxy had started *in earnest*, I hadn't expected it to be like *this*. The ships were so numerous, they nearly blotted out the entire wormhole, like a swarm of angry bees spewing out of a hole in defense of their hive. The ships were of all sizes and makes: colony vessels, freighters, transports, frigates, and yes, even several Hades Class battleships, which were easily recognized by their distinctive profile.

We were all holding our breath in awe, it seemed. "Ho-ly shit," Chan exhaled.

As he voiced our shared amazement, the swarm of spacecraft fanned out and headed in every direction imaginable. Some of them even made use of the transit gate Galaxia had built. How had they even known the access codes to sync it with their nav computers? Who'd given them the schema for gate destinations? The addresses?

"Holy shit, indeed," Zhao replied.

"When did this happen? Where are they going?" asked Djordi, a look of consternation on his gaunt face.

"Just a few days ago," Zhao said. "We checked, and it doesn't look like they're headed to any of the systems we scouted and claimed for Galaxia. I doubt they'd want to risk a conflict right out of the gate. There are corporate treaties to consider."

"That's all well and good," I said, trying not to be too much of a Debbie downer, "but someone's already stolen our technical specs. What's to keep them from stealing our uncolonized systems too? We can't possibly patrol them all. We only have two battleships and a couple frigates."

"*Had*," Zhao replied, the faintest hint of a smirk on his face. "We only *had* a few ships. Things have changed."

He scrolled through his encrypted files and pulled up a briefing labelled "*Project Diaspora*."

"Diaspora?" Dezzie asked. "What's that?"

Djordi rubbed his chin as he recited the definition of the word. "It means when a people travel great distances from their home to populate other lands…"

"I know what the *word* means," Dezzie retorted. "What is the *project* about?" She shot Zhao a questioning look.

"The corporate executives call it 'land and expand.' It basically means we need to spread out and occupy those other systems. Right now, we have roughly fifty registered to our name."

"We can't possibly build that many colonies," I said. "Each system might have as many as eight planets. Maybe more. That's more than a million people just to get started. Where are they going to come from? How are they getting here? Who's going to protect them from the Cerbs?"

Stohl nodded. "I heard the *London* had to chase down a Cerb ship right in our own star system a few days ago. Somewhere out past Nineveh." He sighed. "We still haven't been able to capture one though. SciCorp has confirmed our suspicions. They're fitted with self-destruct systems to prevent them from falling into enemy hands." The thought of Cerb ships loose in our home system, especially near our transit gate, was unsettling to say the least. Everyone was frustrated that we were dealing with an enemy we still knew so little about.

Zhao scrolled through the report and tapped the console when he found what he was looking for. The holo screen snapped to life again, this time rendering the schematics of several new ship designs. The old Mako Class hydrogen miners had been replaced with the Mako Mark II, a larger, apparently more capable version of the original. It made sense to invest in better miners if Galaxia were really contemplating such a massive territorial expansion. We'd need a lot more fuel.

Zhao swiped his finger across the holo screen to flip through a dozen other schematics, pausing at one called 'Battleship Mark II'. It looked a lot like the Hades Class battleship but was longer and had several more gun emplacements. A brief skim of the data sheet revealed it to have a crew of almost four hundred, and what looked like modular technology bays utilizing modified power plants—the giant egg-shaped units—salvaged from the artifacts we'd retrieved during our red star runs. It hadn't taken long for SciCorp to graft the Cerberus artifacts into our own technology tree.

"Four more battleships are scheduled for completion; the *Amazon*, *Pegasus*, *New Delhi*, and the *Orion*."

I groaned. "Who's in charge of naming planets and ships around here?" I said with as much disdain as I could muster. The names really *were* bad, a fact which nobody chimed in to dispute. Zhao just looked up from his console and shrugged. "Not me."

Despite the ships' names, it was exhilarating to find out that our little fleet had grown. Then again, it would be much harder to keep security tight on so many vessels. If there were an information leak, it just got infinitely harder to find its source.

"Where'd they build them? Jupiter Station?" Djordi asked.

Zhao shook his head. "No. These four are Hades born and bred. The Board of Directors built a secret shipyard in orbit around one of the outer planets. Had the fleet of freight haulers designed so that their hulls could be disassembled and quickly reassembled into a space dock."

I couldn't help but smile. The thought of repurposed freighters turning into a shipyard made me think of the old series of Transformer movies I'd watched as a kid. Grandpa talked about them while we practiced shooting plastic cups off fence posts, so I'd scarfed them down from the net and binge watched them in one night. All eleven of them. With Simms at Galaxia's helm, though, I wondered if we were more like Transformers or Deceptacons.

The thought occurred to me that with so many new ships, Galaxia would need a lot of new crewmen. "Who's gonna fly those things? Don't tell me they're splitting up our crew?" I cast an involuntary glance at Dezzie. She'd certainly be up for a captain's spot now. My heart sank like a cement life jacket.

"No orders yet," Zhao said, "but you can count on some of us getting new duty assignments."

We all exchanged looks, looks that said everything without saying anything. The crew of the *Icarus* had started to gel. We were a team. Breaking us up was inevitable, but it was something none of us looked forward to.

"So, what's the plan?" I asked, trying to draw everyone's attention back to the matters at hand. "Hades just got a whole lot more complicated." I rubbed my swollen eye. I knew this better than most. Nobody else seemed to have the fleet admiral personally gunning for them. No, that was my privileged position.

"Well," Zhao replied, "we have orders to escort the *Andromeda* and *Wall Street* for as long as they need to figure out what's happening to the Rift."

Chan arched an eyebrow and nodded my direction. "Looks to me like they want us close so they can keep an eye on us. The two frigates can take care of themselves," he said. "The mistrust around here is thicker than flies on a cow patty." I smirked. The imagery took me back to my grandpa's ranch in Montana. I knew exactly how many flies could congregate on a piece of cow shit. I'd counted them once as a kid.

"Indeed," replied Zhao. "For now, though, I need everyone to keep an eye out for anything unusual. Don't discuss tactical matters in the corridors, or even in here without one of these." He tossed a portable, self-adhesive EM shroud emitter to each of us. I caught mine and stuck it to the back of my left hand. They'd cleverly been disguised as adhesive bandages. Unless someone was overly nosy, the shrouds wouldn't raise suspicions.

Captain Zhao switched off the screen. "Dismissed."

I placed my hand on the small of Dezzie's back and gestured toward the door. "After you, Commander," I said, with growing anticipation. The look in her eye left no doubt in my mind that she'd soon be helping me *convalesce* from my beating at Sargent Reynolds's hands. The thought of those beautiful, full lips kissing my bruised…

"Not you two," Zhao said, at the last possible second. I was inches from the door and a part of me wanted nothing more than to grab Dezzie's hand and make a break for it. What would the captain do? Demote us? But no, I dutifully turned and stood at attention, as did Dezzie.

"Sir?" she asked. Strands of long, black hair had wriggled free of her bun and fallen loosely on either side of her face. Her emerald eyes darted from the captain to me, and back again. "Just us?"

Zhao nodded. "Yes, Commander Pearson." He waited for the war room door to whoosh closed, then motioned for us to come closer. "EM shroud works better within three feet." He leaned in. If he'd eaten onions for lunch, we'd have known it. "Simms is right," he said. "About the mole."

I raised my hands, palms forward in a defensive gesture. "You don't think I'm…"

Zhao shook his head and cut me off with a

wave of his hand. "Not you, Paul." Then he looked at Dezzie. "And certainly not you."

"So, you actually think one of the command crew is a corporate spy?" I said with eyes wide as saucers.

Again, Zhao shook his head. "Not one of the command crew. But information is indeed being leaked from the *Icarus*." He reached in his thigh pocket and retrieved a small electronic device with a couple of wires hanging from it. I took it for a closer inspection.

"Looks like a broken transmitter," I said.

"Yes. Third shift yeoman said that he heard some strange static and traced it to this 'faulty' transmitter in the coms console on the bridge, which maintenance promptly removed."

"Bad parts? Makes you wonder what else they messed up during the refit," I said, my mind still distracted by the thought of some healing time with Dezzie.

Zhao shook his head impatiently. "No, you don't get my meaning. This *wasn't supposed* to be there."

My eyes widened as the gravity of what he was saying finally sank in. "*Surveillance equipment?*"

Zhao nodded. "Disguised as a *new* redundant system," he said. "Pretty clever."

I handed the transmitter back to him. All I could think of was that now it had *my* fingerprints on it, and I certainly didn't want that brought as evidence against me.

"I did some investigation," continued Zhao, "and discovered records of a faint electromagnetic burst about an hour before we entered the transit gate for our last red star mission."

Dezzie pulled up the operations schedule on her wrist com. "Lieutenant Vargas was the yeoman on duty at that time. Have you questioned her?"

Zhao nodded. "Discretely. And without her catching on, I think. But I'm not sure anyone on the ship had anything to do with this."

I furrowed my brow. "What did you find?"

Zhao looked around warily and lowered his voice almost to the point of whispering. "That the transmission was sent while we were still in the Eden system, and it was sent to the *Andromeda*. So, I leveraged one of my contacts there to snoop around for me. He pulled the logs. They indicated that a tight beam transmission targeted the frigate's hull on deck one, section one."

It was my turn to swear, though I didn't have Chan's Texas accent. "Holy shit!"

Dezzie's face said it all, though. A look of utter surprise followed by a mixture of duress and worry clouded her countenance. "That's the admiral's personal quarters…"

Zhao shot Dezzie a strange look. I'd never seen that expression on his face before. "We can't trust Simms." He pointed at my black eye and busted lip. "Look what he did to you. There was no need for that. Why do it then?"

I shrugged. "I was hoping *you'd* be able to answer that. Seems to me he doesn't trust us. Me least of all." I wondered if my quarters were bugged too? Hell, was there *any* place on the ship I could feel safe?

"I don't think it's a matter of trust, Paul. He's just jealous," Dezzie said. She looked conflicted, like she didn't want to believe the evidence Zhao had presented us. But how could she argue with it? I wanted her to denounce the admiral. Nothing would have made me happier. To say that I was still a little hurt over their tryst—one that she vehemently denied—was an understatement. But she didn't denounce him. Not at first, and her reluctance to do so cut me deeper than I would have thought.

The captain didn't look convinced. He drew in a long, deep breath. "It's a matter of trust for *me*," he said, at last. "I don't believe half of what the admiral says anymore. He's up to something, and we need to know what it is." From the sounds of it, asking Simms directly wasn't an option Zhao would consider. I can't say I blamed him.

"What do you have in mind?" I asked. "He's president of the corporation and the admiral of the goddamn fleet! We can't just tail him like some trench-coated gumshoe."

Zhao nodded in agreement, then sighed. "You're not going to like it Paul. But it has to be done," he responded.

"What are you saying, Captain?" asked Dezzie. Then her brow furrowed deeply, and she frowned. "No," she protested. "Paul's not cut out for that kind of mission. He's too…" She looked at me apologetically. "Too *good*."

What the hell was she talking about? "Too good for *what*?" I asked.

Zhao leaned in closer and spoke in an even

more conspiratorial tone. The EM shroud made it so no one could hear us, which made his caution even more curious. "We need someone to keep an eye on Admiral Simms. And the easiest way to do that is through..." Dezzie and the Captain turned their gaze straight at me. What they meant for me to do hit me like a ton of bricks. No. I wouldn't. I *couldn't*. It was out of the question. But no matter how I squirmed, how strongly I shook my head, they stared, Dezzie with eyes of compassion and understanding, Zhao with an expression of stern resolve.

"...through his daughter? You want me to use Patricia to keep tabs on the admiral?" I said, completing the captain's sentence.

A smile on Zhao's face was as rare as a snowstorm in the Sahara. But I'll be damned if he wasn't grinning ear to ear. "That's right," he said.

This was crazy. I was with Dezzie. Everyone knew that. But she was nodding too, though her cheeks were streaked with tears. "It's our best option," she said. "Patricia likes you. We should... take advantage of that."

It had never occurred to me that Patricia Simms, daughter of our CEO and arguably the most powerful man in the entire Hades Galaxy, would have any interest in someone like *me*. Our first meeting on Auriven had been, well, less than ideal, to say the least. On top of that, back on Eden Prime, while waiting for the *Icarus* to be repaired, she'd avoided me like a leper. But now, it made sense. At the time, I'd just gotten back together with Dezzie. If Patricia truly had been interested in me...well, it would explain why she'd been keeping her distance. But I couldn't bring myself to believe it. If someone like her had any romantic inclination towards me, I would have known by now.

Still, what Zhao was asking me to do? What Dezzie was *allowing* him to ask me to do? I wasn't one of those Cold War Russian seduction spies. What were they called? Sparrows?

"We'll have to break up," Dezzie whispered, her eyes on the floor between us.

"You'll have to do it quite publicly," Zhao added.

Under different circumstances I would have smirked. No matter how we tried to keep it to ourselves, *everything* about my relationship with Dezzie was public.

Captain Zhao continued. "For this to work, we need Patricia to believe it's real."

"It won't matter if Patricia thinks our breakup is real. She's used to money and power. And have you looked at her?" I glanced sheepishly at Dezzie. "She could have any guy she wants."

Zhao made a strange face. "I think you underestimate yourself, Paul. You may not be Lieutenant Stohl, but you're a fine man with a bright future."

Great. He *had* to compare me to Mr. Perfect?

"Besides," continued Zhao, nodding toward Dezzie, "even a blind squirrel occasionally finds a nut."

I looked to Dezzie for help. She tried to play her part. "Just be yourself, Paul." She looked sideways. "All you have to do is get her... well, just do that thing you do."

I couldn't believe what I was hearing. "What *thing*?" I protested, though I had an idea what she was referring to.

"*THE* thing," she replied sheepishly.

"See," said Zhao. "You are not without recourse in this endeavor, Commander Johnson. Besides," he continued, "this is just a mission. Not real. It could save lives, even the ship."

I knew what the captain meant, but part of me worried that if I did what he was asking, that if Dezzie and I pretended to break up, it *would* be real. We'd only been back together for a few months, and now this? I was beginning to think we just weren't meant to be. My heart sank all the way to deck fourteen.

"You're right," I said. "I *don't* like it. In fact, I *hate* it." I turned to Dezzie, hoping she'd put an end to this nonsense. But all she did was stare back at me expectantly. "No," I said flatly. "I won't do it."

I locked eyes with her, saw the mixture of hurt and fear and pride in them. Saw their emerald fire turn to placid resignation. "It's OK, Paul. There are things in the universe bigger than the two of us."

Damnit. How could I argue with that? But I tried. "Why not ask Lieutenant Stohl to do it. You said it yourself, Captain. He can't walk down the corridor without every female heart skipping a beat."

Zhao just stared, expressionless. Dezzie shook her head and placed her hand on my arm reassuringly. "Paul, we both knew this was short-lived. I'll be promoted to captain soon, and you'll..." She looked at the floor again before gathering herself and smiling. "You'll be *here*, doing what you do best."

I'd never been a fan of boxing or MMA, but I knew those guys could break bricks and boards thicker than my hand. I'd always wondered what it would feel like to be kicked in the gut by someone like them. Now I knew.

I soaked in those big green eyes, memorizing them. I etched the shape of Dezzie's face in my memory, searing the outline of her lips in my mind. I reached up and caressed the scar that ran down her neck. Would she ever tell me how she'd gotten it? I breathed in deeply, filling my lungs with the smell of her perfume. I stepped back from her, out of arms reach, and straightened my uniform. Then, I turned to my right and snapped off a sharp salute to the captain.

Zhao's stoic expression had returned. "Dismissed," he said, and switched off the EM shroud.

13

TERMINUS

They say all good things come to an end. This is always true in matters of love, but only sometimes true in war.

— Juan Mendoza in Preface to War Sonnets from Saturn

I closed my eyes and exhaled slowly, wrapping my hand around the wooden handle of my grandpa's Beretta 92. The feel of its worn crosshatch grip was comforting to me. It was neither good, nor bad. Neither happy, nor sad. It just was. I aspired to be like that, letting unwanted feelings wash over me like water passing over a stone in a river. But I wasn't a stone, and I did have feelings. And yes, they were unwanted. Especially right now.

"Get him a piss bag!" someone yelled from the

observation stands of the firing range. It had been reconfigured for a three-way match between the record-holder and two challengers. I glanced through the plexiglass partition to my left and saw Dezzie, hair up in a perfect regulation bun, florescent green plugs dangling from her ears, and protective, nano-reactive visor over her eyes. She held a BR 105 loaded with target rounds in an aggressive stance; her slender arms were nearly straight, only the slightest bend in her elbows to keep them from locking.

To my right stood Private Tanaka. He held his own '105 loosely and bounced up and down on the balls of his feet while rocking his head back and forth to crack his neck. He flexed the muscles in his chest and back. I don't know if it was part of his warm-up routine or if he was trying to intimidate me. Either way, it worked.

My preparations weren't quite so elaborate. I usually just made sure to eat a good breakfast and go to the bathroom before a match. I didn't need any bio distractions. As far as my equipment was concerned, I'd chosen old-school over-the-ear muffs instead of plugs. Despite the pill I'd taken to calm my nerves, my hand shook uncontrollably. I wasn't ready for this. Under normal circumstances, I'd have been hard-pressed to consistently beat either one of my opponents. Dezzie had the second-best score on the ship, and Tanaka? Well, I'd seen firsthand just how accurate he could be in live action during our last red star mission.

"Nice target, Commander Pearson!" came another voice from the crowd. I glanced back at the makeshift stands. There must have been thirty people there to watch in person. If that wasn't bad enough, the match was being holo-cast to similar-sized groups gathered in the mess hall, the exercise courts, and both shuttle bays. It left me wondering who was actually *flying* the ship.

The target Dezzie had chosen wasn't unusual: just a standard man outline made of steel coated in capacitive polyurethane. What made the crowd jeer, though, was the fact that its capacitive coating was projecting an image of me wearing nothing but boxer shorts. Of course, Dezzie had chosen the ones with the red smoochy lip design on them. She'd given them to me to celebrate our first anniversary. It was a little embarrassing, but what really bothered me was the memory of what she'd done to me the night I'd first worn them. It was deflating to be reminded that there'd be no more of that for us. I sighed heavily and tried to clear my mind.

An array of red LEDs in the front of the range flashed twice then turned yellow. The countdown had begun. I squeezed the handle of my pistol and widened my stance, raising my weapon as I did. I continued the countdown in my head.

Three. Two.

The yellow LEDs flashed twice before turning green.

One.

It's hard to describe the *zone* to anyone who's never been in it. Imagine doing something so perfectly, with such ease and fluidity, that it's like breathing air after a rainstorm. Nothing you do while in the zone is wrong. Everything is perfect. Coming out of the zone often feels like coming off a high—not that I knew anything about that, of course. But the feeling of disappointment can be overwhelming; the reality of normal life slaps you in the face like a wet blanket. A cold one at that. But what's worse than finding the zone and coming out again is realizing you were never in it to begin with.

It only took three shots to confirm that I was definitely *not* in the zone today. Yes, the bullets struck their mark, but not as surely as I'd intended. Things didn't get any easier. My target didn't stay still. This wasn't unexpected; targets always moved in a scored competition. It was the *way* it moved that caught me off guard. After my initial volley of shots hit, the target launched forward, then suddenly jerked to the left, disappearing behind Dezzie's target. Unfortunately, I hadn't seen hers until too late and fired off a couple rounds.

Fortunately, the first shot flew straight, hitting right in my target's chest. A direct heart shot. Unfortunately, my second shot hit Dezzie's target as it passed in front of mine. It lurched down and my bullet splatted through the polyurethane covering. It's hard to describe what it feels like to shoot yourself in the forehead. Good news was the shot didn't count against me since it hit a valid target. Bad news was, it counted for Dezzie, who now needed one shot less to fire before time ran out.

I glanced at the digital timer projected in my visor's heads up display: twenty-seven seconds left. By now, my target was too far away to risk a shot, so I waited for it to move a couple meters closer before squeezing off several more rounds, all direct hits. Then I heard the crowd let out a groan of disappointment. Dezzie had missed one of her shots. Hope surged in my chest. I could still win if I could find a way to score an extra point.

The crowd started counting down. "Three, two..."

I fired three more times in rapid succession, all with perfect placement, then right as I was about to deliver my last shot, the target flipped down backwards until it was flat. My last bullet sailed past the prone target, striking the safety fabric on the range's back wall. I'd missed.

"One!" the crowd yelled as the LED array flashed an angry red.

The results were displayed on a giant screen above our heads, but I didn't have to look at it to know who'd won. Dezzie yanked out her ear plugs and threw them down in disgust. Tanaka, on the other hand, was jumping up and down and pumping his fist wildly in the air. Reluctantly, I glanced up to confirm the outcome: *Pearson- 49/50, Johnson - 49/50, Tanaka - 50/50*.

The plexiglass partitions receded into the floor with a whoosh, and I reached out my hand to congratulate the winner. "You're a *machine*," I yelled over the din of the crowd behind me. The room had never been meant to be packed with so many people, and firing ranges weren't designed with acoustics in mind.

Tanaka's smile split his face like a hand puppet,

but quickly turned to a look of confusion. "I don't have any augments, Commander."

"No," I replied. "You aren't actually a machine, you just *shoot* like you are!" It was quite a compliment, actually; one that someone had once given to me.

"Thank you, sir!" replied Tanaka, the smile returning to his face.

"In the range, you can call me Paul," I said.

He nodded and raised his fists over his head in a final gesture of triumph. I reached into my thigh pocket and retrieved the Olympic gold medal Simms had given me. "You deserve this," I said, handing it to Private Tanaka. "It belonged to Admiral Simms. He said to give it back to him once he matched my range score. Seems fitting for you to have it considering what you just did."

Tanaka saluted out of respect, then snatched the medal and waved it at the crowd. The move was met with more cheers. He placed the medal around his neck, holstered his weapon, and made for the exit.

I turned my attention to Dezzie. There was still a couple dozen observers in the crowd, so we kept our distance. We weren't *really* broken up, but the way she'd left things that day in the war room had me second guessing everything. Regardless, we had to look like a couple at odds with each other. Our eyes met. Her face was flat and expressionless, but her eyes told me everything I needed to know. She loved me, and I knew it. It wasn't much, but like a sip of water to a man wandering the desert, it would sustain me for a while.

I reached out with my hand to congratulate her on a fantastic display of shooting, but Dezzie just stood there. The crowd suddenly hushed. Everyone wanted to hear what she said next. I shrugged when my handshake wasn't accepted. "You beat your high score, Commander. Almost a perfect mark. If only you'd had time for one more shot," I said.

She sneered. "I was saving it for this." Without looking, she flipped the safety off and flung a bullet toward the Paul-shaped target, hitting it right in the groin. She'd had someone place a pack of engine coolant on the target there, which gave it the appearance of bleeding. Red liquid splattered all over the range floor and walls. "I don't miss when it really counts, Commander."

I didn't know how to respond to that, so I popped the clip out of my Beretta and slid it into my pocket as if I didn't care that she'd just attacked an effigy of my manhood. Her act was so convincing, I couldn't help but feel like she'd just stabbed me in the heart. I wondered if that was public enough for Zhao?

Tanaka was surrounded by a cadre of enthusiastic fans, all of whom lifted their drinks in celebration of his victory earlier in the day. They'd been at it for the better part of three hours. I'd hoped to miss the crowds but couldn't wait any longer to pull up my favorite stool at the bar in the officer's lounge. After all, with a roughed-up face from my beating on the *Andromeda* and a bruised ego from losing the shooting match, I had *two* good reasons to drown my sorrows.

I ordered a long pour of my favorite Canadian whiskey, but before I could so much as take my first sip, my wrist com vibrated wildly, and the overhead speakers blared an angry klaxon in a call for general alert. I glanced around to make sure nobody was paying attention and guzzled my drink before joining the others in a mad dash to our duty stations.

By the time I made it to the bridge, most of the command crew had arrived to relieve the night watch. I took up my place behind the command dais just as Captain Zhao strode briskly through the door while pulling on his uniform top. "Status?" he barked.

Stohl started to relay his report but stopped abruptly, scrolling through readings and results. "It's gone, sir."

"What's gone, Lieutenant?" The irritation in the captain's voice was shared by everyone else in the room.

But instead of elaborating, Stohl just shook his head and flicked an image of black space to the main viewer.

"What are we looking at Mr. Stohl?" Zhao asked.

"The Rift, sir. Or the place in space where the Rift *used to be*."

Zhao had been buttoning his uniform, but stopped mid-stream, a patch of chest hair poking out for all to see. "Give me a visual of the anomaly's last known position, Lieutenant."

Stohl keyed in a command and played a thirty second recording on the viewer. The *Andromeda* and *Wall Street* were clearly visible, having taken up positions closer to the Rift so that SciCorp could more easily carry out their scans. While the *Andromeda* remained stationary, though, the *Wall Street* suddenly peeled away and into the maelstrom of red tendrils of energy emanating from the aperture. Then, the unthinkable happened. With no apparent indication as to why, the *Wall Street* began to list awkwardly to one side before exploding in a blinding ball of light. Even with the active filters afforded by the *Icarus*'s video system, the explosion was so bright we all had to cover our eyes. By the time we could see anything in the viewer, though, the frigate was gone, and so was the Rift. Nothing but the faint twinkle of distant stars remained.

My first thought was that we'd been lucky. Nobody knew what had been causing the Rift to act up, and nobody could predict what might happen if the giant wormhole were to suddenly snap shut. In my mind, I'd imagined the worst-case scenario to be something like falling into the clutches of a black hole: ripped apart, atom by atom on the side closest to the anomaly, while being stretched into a string of molecules a hundred thousand kilometers long. I suppose I could blame all the old science documentaries I'd watched as a kid for those somewhat gruesome images.

My second thought was a number: one hundred and twenty-four—the number of souls they'd crammed aboard each of the small frigates. The number of men and women who'd just lost their lives. A profound sadness swept over me like a wave crashing onto shore. But it quickly turned to panic. Where had Lieutenant Jimenez been stationed? I looked quickly at Dezzie, who'd been scouring readings and data on her console. Somehow, she'd known what I was thinking. I don't know how, but she did.

"He's still back at the Eden Research Station," she said. There was no coldness, no pretense for the benefit of others, just concern. Just the woman I loved making sure I knew my friend was safe.

My relief was short-lived though. The realization that our only way back to the Milky Way Galaxy had just been destroyed sucked all the wind out of my sails. Everyone was in a stupor as the gravity of our plight became more apparent with each passing tick of the clock.

"Search for RF beacons. We need to look for survivors," Zhao ordered.

Normally, my filter was better, but at that moment I blurted out the first thing that popped into my head. "Survivors? The *Wall Street* was just blown to bits! How could there be any survivors?"

Stohl shook his head. "That's not accurate, Commander. Normally, there'd be a debris field; remnants of the ship—bits as you so aptly called them. But there's nothing there. Take a look for yourself," he said, motioning toward his console,

"No debris, no fragments, not even residual electromagnetic static."

"What are you saying," asked Zhao, his Chinese accent growing thicker.

Stohl swiveled his seat around to face the Captain. "It's like the *Wall Street* was never even there, Sir. The same goes for the Rift."

Just then Yeoman Richards placed his hand over one ear. "Captain…Admiral Simms has a secure round robin set up and is asking for all remaining command crews to…"

"I'll take it in the war room," said Zhao, cutting Richards off mid-sentence. He stood and worked at the last three buttons of his uniform. Then, he looked my direction and nodded his head toward the door. "Commander, you're with me and the XO. Lieutenant Stohl, you have the bridge."

I followed Dezzie and the captain out the door, barely aware of where my legs were taking me. My mind was swimming with questions, and my chest was exploding with emotions. Why had the *Wall Street* flown into the terminus? What had caused it to list at the last second, like a boat taking on water in rough seas? I was hopeful that Simms would have some answers, but could we trust him to tell us the truth? I purposefully slowed my breathing and steeled myself against any unwanted emotions. But try as I might, I couldn't help but feel like the Universe had flipped us the bird. Not only had it told us to go to hell, but it seemed intent on making sure we stayed there.

14

DIAMONDS IN THE SKY

As your bright and tiny spark
Lights the traveller in the dark,
Though I know not what you are,
Twinkle, twinkle, little star.

— JANE TAYLOR

Admiral Simms bore a genuinely ashen countenance. Either he was the best poker player I'd ever seen, or the destruction of the *Wall Street* had come as a shock to him too. Of course, after Zhao had found the surveillance device in the bridge coms console, my mind had been working overtime devising a number of conspiracy theories to explain why the admiral would bug one of his own ships. So, while a part of me wouldn't have been surprised if he'd sent a ship full of scientists to their deaths in order to achieve some nefarious goal, I was relieved when the admiral's expression of dismay seemed in keeping with such an unexpected catastrophe.

"What the hell happened," Zhao blurted out the instant the war room doors were shut.

The holo screen displayed a grainy rendering of Simms as well as Santos and Okufur, the *Andromeda's* captain and XO. "We're still trying to figure that out, Captain. In the meantime, I'm sending you sensor readings of the explosion and the events leading up to it. We had four class V probes monitoring the Rift when it happened. Have your people see if they can find something we haven't."

"Very well," Zhao replied. "How many…"

"One hundred and eighty-one," Commander Okufur answered.

Zhao pounded his fist on the console. "Damnit!"

"While I appreciate your feelings for our lost team members, Captain, we must keep our composure. Santos is taking the *Andromeda* to a safer distance. Keep in formation off our stern."

Zhao saluted just as the transmission ended, then turned to Dezzie. "I want our best people sifting through that data like miners looking for iridium on Capula III. Cross-reference it to our own readings. I want answers as soon as you have them."

I glanced down at the plain gold band on his ring finger and wondered who he'd left behind in the Milky Way. Some had left behind loved ones to join the Navy. The Navy made us all record letters to our families in case something happened to us in the line of duty. But Hades was so far from home, it couldn't even be seen with Earth's best telescopes. Without the Rift, it would take those vidmails nearly seventy million years to get to Earth. For some reason I was glad my letter was a three-minute recording of an empty chair. It made it easier to accept, I suppose. The Rift had been an umbilical cord to the Milky Way. Well, it appeared that the cord had been cut, and for the time being, we were on our own.

THE *BORDER MULE* lurched forward as Patricia punched the thrusters to full power. There wasn't any reason to go so fast, which meant she was just showing off the new mods she'd made to the transport's engines. I'd never sat in the cockpit before and was surprised at the creature comforts she'd installed. The chairs were extremely comfortable—they sported brand new nanogel cushions—and the view of the stars visible through the front windows was expansive, almost like the view one gets when walking on the hull of a battleship. Certainly, a better view than the rest of my extraction team had. They were strapped into the jump seats in the hold with no windows at all. But, for some reason, Patricia had insisted I ride up front this time.

During mission prep, she'd been cordial, if not affable. Compared to her former coldness, though, just about anything would have been an improvement. So, I decided to break what remained of the ice with some small talk. "You don't expect me to salute you, do you?"

Patricia didn't look up from her console.

"I mean, you're a transport captain, but *technically* speaking, we're the same rank—*commander*."

Patricia's hands glided over the console's surface, making minor adjustments to our speed and trajectory with the deftness and ease of someone who'd done this thousands of times before. I made a mental note of some of them—never know when you might be faced with piloting an unfamiliar ship.

"Only while aboard the *Mule*," she said with a flash of fire in her eyes. She wasn't as beautiful as Dezzie, but she was attractive in her own right. Her platinum hair was cut in a short bob and shaved tight on the sides and back, with bangs died pink on the ends. She wore matching lipstick, which I though was probably pushing the limits of what was acceptable by the regs. Her uniform consisted of a pair of mechanics coveralls with the top half turned down and tied at the waste. Underneath, she wore a white tank top that, on most people, would be an undershirt. Her rank insignia was pinned to the thickest part of the tank top's strap right above her left breast.

"What?" I asked dumbly, distracted by her…

"You only have to salute me while aboard the *Mule*, Commander." She drew out the last word, emphasizing my rank.

"Yes, ma'am," I said, snapping off a petulant salute, which nearly caused the corner of her mouth to turn up in bemusement. *Nearly.*

A proximity alarm beeped from the nav computer, signaling that we'd arrived at the transit gate in orbit around Nineveh. Patricia punched in an address I'd seen before. It was one of the fifty systems to which Galaxia had staked a claim before even arriving in Hades. Long range scans indicated the system had a large ocean world with a viable atmosphere and temperate weather. A perfect place to build a system headquarters. Our mission to the new star wasn't the only effort to expand Galaxia's footprint in Hades. Over the last few weeks the Board of Directors had sent out missions to colonize the remaining six planets in the Eden system, bringing the total number there to eight. Shipping lanes had been set up, and a fleet of transports had been built to facilitate movement of resources from one colony to another. There were also a few more Mako Mark II miners out and about, chipping away at the hydrogen-rich asteroids that littered the system.

"What should we name it?" I asked. "The new star system?"

Patricia shot me a sideways glance. "SBD-1826 just doesn't do it for you?"

What? Was Patricia Simms actually capable of humor?

I didn't have time to answer her before the familiar-yet-unwelcome nausea of transit punched me in the gut as we passed through the gate. An instant later, we were in orbit around a purple gas giant with rings. Its atmosphere had the most incredible white and grey eddies swirling about in massive bands wider than most planets. After a few more moments of observation, I decided it looked like a giant ball of strawberry and vanilla ice cream. And just like that, my growling stomach reminded me it'd been several hours since I'd last eaten.

Patricia pointed the *Mule* toward our target, a planet closer to the star, and unlocked her chair so it could swivel toward the aisle between us. This was going to be the hardest part of the mission, if you asked me—twelve hours at full speed to get to the pre-arranged meeting coordinates. Good news was the *Mule* had been fitted with the same inertial dampening tech the *Icarus* had, so we didn't have to strap in for the acceleration burn.

"It must have been hard," Patricia said. It was the softest tone she'd ever taken with me. But I had no idea what she was talking about and was certain my face said as much. She continued. "Losing your parents and siblings at such a young age."

Oh. My. God. How did she know all that? I'd made sure all that stuff was buried so deeply in my personnel file that only the president of the Federation could read it. I hadn't even shared my past with Djordi, though he'd been trying to get me to do just that for as long as we'd known each other. But the fact that Patricia knew...well, I guess it wasn't all *that* surprising. Her father was the CEO and Fleet Admiral, after all. And, for better or worse, it confirmed what Zhao had suspected. Patricia was plugged in. There was a part of me that had hoped she was ignorant of her father's business, merely an estranged child kept at arm's length. It was looking like that wasn't the case, though.

"It was," I replied. "But on the bright side, I got to go live with my grandpa on his ranch in Montana where I learned all sorts of useful things." I tilted my head to one side and nodded. "Go ahead. Ask me how far you can throw a two-day-old cow patty. Or what coyotes sound like when they're mating."

Patricia snorted. Or was it a laugh? It was hard to believe. Here was this short, petite, hard-as-steel woman with ice-water coursing through her veins and she had both a sense of humor *and* a laugh worthy of a stand-up comedian! I couldn't help but smile.

She stood up and started toward the single-berth sleeping cabin above the cockpit door. "Good," she said. "I know where to turn to for help when I'm given a pile of shit to work with." As she climbed the ladder to the bunk above the cockpit door, my eyes were drawn to the swaying of her perfectly-shaped rear end.

I tried to look away, but I was a moth and Patricia was definitely a flame. My grandpa had always been quick to toss bits of wisdom my way in his efforts to be both mother and father to a mixed-up little boy like me. In that moment I could hear his voice ringing clearly in my head: "Play with fire, boy, and you're gonna get burned." Despite his warning from another time and galaxy, I allowed my gaze to linger.

Patricia looked back over her shoulder, her eyes ablaze with heat. "Wake me up when we get there, Commander. I've been burning both ends of the candle and am due some rest." She slid into the bunk and closed the sleeping cabin's door, leaving me alone in the cockpit wishing the *Border Mule* had somewhere to take a cold shower.

SBD-1826 WAS A COMPLETELY inadequate name for the yellow star it designated. It was about one-and-a-half times the size of our own sun, but not as dense. Amazingly, its solar output and gravity were almost identical to Sol. At a little less than .8 AU from the star, the ocean planet we were scouting out was just inside the habitable zone. As a result, less than two percent of its surface water was frozen in the form of giant icebergs at the poles. A single large continent in the temperate zone north of the equator was the only landmass we could find. Luckily, it was about twice the size of Australia, and judging from its green color, it had an abundance of flora.

"Is the other ship already there?" asked Major Chan over the *Mule's* ship-wide channel.

"We've got her on scope. She's a transport just like ours," I responded, trying to calm the team down. Despite assurances that they were our new allies and—how had Simms put it? *esteemed* trading partners—meeting with Mitsumi Corp in one of our own star systems felt awkward, if not invasive. To say that we were a little on edge was an understatement. But, after our run in with the

Consortium during the last red star mission, who could blame us?

"It's not 'just like' my ship, Commander," Patricia said in rebuke of my assertion. "No other transport can do what this one does. The *Mule* is…unique."

"Yes," I said, "yes, it is."

I glanced down at my console's map and saw the familiar blue dot of a friendly ship near the continent's northern coast. I tapped my wrist com. "Yes, Major. The welcome wagon's already there."

Within minutes we'd glided down to the surface without so much as a single bounce. Patricia moved the *Mule* through the planet's atmosphere as if it were gliding on silk. The ground was uneven, though, so there was a momentary lurch to one side while the landing struts adjusted.

"Out you go, Commander," Patricia said as she retrieved a large EM shroud emitter from a storage compartment beneath the weapons locker. I'd peeked inside the locker while Patricia slept. I don't know what weapons she was proficient with, but there was enough firepower there to win a land war on Ceridia.

"What's the shroud for?" I asked.

Patricia shot me a playful grimace. "Isn't the whole purpose of an EM shroud to keep secrets?"

"You expecting Mitsumi Corp to spy on you here in the *Mule*?" I asked.

Patricia shook her head. "Not if I can help it."

I finished donning my armor and headed out the hatch. The sun was bright, and even though

SBD-1826 was a yellow star, the planet's atmosphere and surface water gave it a bluish tint, which wasn't surprising. What did catch me off guard, though, was the vegetation. From orbit the continental landmass had appeared verdant and lush. But as we'd made our descent—and even more so now that I was boots on the ground—it became clear there wasn't a single tree on the entire planet. Instead, the ground was covered in a spongy green and yellow moss-like organism.

Djordi came bounding around the end of the transport, all length and no grace in the planet's 1.2Gs. "How are you *lichen* the native grass, Commander?"

Seven heads turned abruptly to shoot him looks of disgust. It wasn't a bad joke as far as puns go, but nobody seemed to be in the mood, myself included. Djordi didn't seem deterred and chuckled at his own humor as we approached the other transport.

"Don't tell Captain Simms, but their ship looks just like ours," Major Chan said.

"You heard that?" I said.

"Yeah. You left the com on. The whole team heard."

Patricia may have disagreed, but to my eyes, Chan was right. Just as the Consortium battleship looked identical to the *Icarus*, the Mitsumi transport seemed to share schematics with the *Mule*. The only discernible difference was that the other ship bore the Mitsumi Corp logo—a pair of interlocking gears—in place of Galaxia's. There was no name or call sign painted on it though.

"Wonder if they even name their transports," I said.

"It is called the *Eagle's Talon*," came a heavily-accented voice. While we'd been comparing ships, four women had emerged from the other side of the transport unnoticed. "Because like an eagle, it is swift and powerful, and able to carry much in its claws."

The woman was of average height with a slender-yet-feminine build and sported a black, bowl-style haircut which framed her oval-shaped face and big, almond eyes. Her jawline was soft, yet she had an air of strength, and she walked with the confidence of someone used to the respect of those around her. She wore a two-piece grey uniform with orange piping, knee-high leather riding boots, and carried a short sword on one hip and a pistol of some kind on the other. She was a striking figure to say the least.

"I am Major Fukumi Ito, and these are my *keigo*," she said, pointing to the white-clad women several steps behind her. Their armor harkened to a samurai heritage, as did the soldier's comportment.

"Your *what*?" Chan asked.

Major Ito looked him up and down, pausing only briefly to appraise the rank insignia on his collar. "Bodyguard," she replied. "You also have the rank of major, do you not have such an escort when you leave the ship?"

Chan looked side to side before answering. "Of course. See, these here are *my* bodyguard, and that one," he said, pointing to me, "is my manservant."

Djordi and Tanaka snickered, but Sergeant Lamiraux sighed. "Enough of this. I am no man's bodyguard," she said.

"What we mean," I interjected, trying to salvage the conversation, "is that we are pleased to meet you, Major. My name is Commander Paul Johnson, this is Major Chan, Lieutenant Djordi, Sergeant Lamiraux, and Private Hirishu Tanaka." She squared herself to me and bowed deeply. I returned the gesture, then the same was repeated for each of our party. When she came to Private Tanaka, though, she bowed a bit more shallowly, and exchanged a few words in Japanese with him.

Chan leaned in to whisper in my ear, trying to speak out of the side of his mouth while smiling and nodding towards the other party. "What d'ya think that was all about?"

"We'll find out later," I said curtly.

"Do you have the artifact?" Ito asked.

"Straight to the point," I replied. "Yes. Shall we begin loading it into your ship?"

Ito nodded and bowed again. "Do you not wish to inspect the items we have brought in trade?"

I hadn't expected to do QA on the technology Mitsumi Corp had offered us for the artifact but nodded my head in the affirmative, as if her request were routine. Ito stepped aside, and three more women streamed out of the transport's aft loading bay. Unlike Major Ito's armored pseudo-samurai guards, these women didn't appear to be wearing anything at all! I mean, they *were*, but their grey flight suits were so incredibly skin-tight, nothing was left to the imagination. They each carried a flat disc about a meter across, which they presented with a bow to Chan, Djordi, and Lamiraux.

The discs were accepted with awkward bows of our own, followed by expectant stares from our guests. Ito was handed a fourth disc, which she proceeded to flourish as she talked. "As you know, Mitsumi Corp is the leader in nano-reactive fibers. The flight suits you see here are the latest in nanoweave materials. Smart suits, if you will." She nodded to one of her guards, who proceeded to unsheathe her katana and swing it with all her might at the closest woman in grey, striking her in the middle of her thigh.

I half expected the woman's leg to be lopped off, but the katana bounced off as if it had struck a steel pillar. Chan whistled, and both Djordi and Tanaka grinned dumbly. Lamiraux granted the demonstration the respect of an arched eyebrow, which was a significant reaction from her.

"Nano-reactive kinetic armor," Ito said. "Impressive, no?"

Before I could even utter a single word in agreement, though, she spun back around and unloaded three slugs into the poor woman's chest. Amazingly, she was unfazed, the impact of the bullets hadn't even caused her to flinch.

I had to get me one of those.

"Now," Ito continued, "I will demonstrate how to apply the suit."

Apply? What a strange choice of words. But a couple seconds later, when Ito had removed her boots, pants, and shirt, I began to understand. She placed the disc on the ground and stepped onto it before removing her underwear and bra. I immediately looked away, which caused her significant consternation.

"Do you not wish to see the demonstration, Commander? Is the nanoweave not to your liking?" asked Ito.

I sheepishly returned my gaze to Ito's naked form and watched as she pressed a button on the disc with her bare foot. In a split second, a cylinder of tiny particles shot out from the holes in the disc, swirling around her like an opaque wall of smoke. Then, as soon as it had started, the *application* was finished. Ito now wore a skin-tight nanoweave flight suit just like the others.

I felt like I'd stumbled onto the set of a new sci-fi movie, and I hoped I wasn't as slack-jawed as the rest of my team. When I'd gathered my wits, I folded my arms across my chest and pretended to appraise the suit much in the same way my grandpa had the cattle he bought for his ranch. "Acceptable," I said.

Suddenly, there was a loud thud from somewhere on top of Ito's transport. One of our extraction techs shouted in surprise. "What the hell?" There was another thud, then a few more coming from the *Mule*. I glanced toward the sky and saw the flares of dozens of small meteorites. Ten seconds later the shower was over. We didn't even have time to take shelter from the hail-sized rocks. I bent to pick one up, turning it over in my gloved hand to inspect it. Was it what I thought it was? I held it up to the light, marveling at its half translucent properties. I tapped my wrist com for a quick composition scan, but Ito had already beat me to it.

"Diamonds," she said, admiring the one she'd picked up.

I tapped my com. "Captain Simms?"

"Go ahead, Commander," replied Patricia.

"Any chance you could use the *Mule's* scanners to look for fist sized diamonds in the area?

A few seconds later, her response came. I could hear her smiling. "You're standing on a layer several feet thick, commander. Even the ocean floor is covered with them."

It must have been raining diamonds on this planet for a million years. "Keep it," I said to Major Ito. "Think of it as a souvenir from your visit to the Prospera System." I didn't have authority to change SBD-1826's name, and I certainly didn't have permission to give Mitsumi Corp a giant diamond worth over a million credits, but I did. Besides, the name seemed to fit.

Ito smiled and bowed in gratitude. "Thank you, Commander Johnson. You are too kind." She nodded her head toward the *Mule* and the three women in nanoweave headed up the ramp after Tanaka and Lamiraux. I shot her a quizzical look. "They will go with you for a period of time sufficient to train your teams on the flight suits and help you tool your fabrication equipment for production."

"Help with fabrication?" I asked. I must have been making a dubious face because Ito seemed insulted.

"Yes. Drs. Yanagasawa, Nakamura, and Sato are the foremost scientists in nano technology."

I bowed deeply at the waist and thanked her before turning toward the *Mule*. Djordi stooped nonchalantly to scoop up one of the diamonds from the ground. He froze mid-movement when he saw my stern expression. I shook my head and he reluctantly dropped it to the ground. The guy looked like a kid who'd just broken his favorite toy.

"Captain?" I said through my wrist com. "Hope you have a spare bedroom. We've got guests."

15

NEW WORLD ORDER

In life, change is inevitable. In business, change is vital.

— Warren G. Bennis

The news of Zhao's departure came as a shock to everyone. We all knew there'd come a time when things would change, but a promotion to *vice admiral*? After the way Simms had treated him when they'd first met on the bridge of the *Icarus*?

"They want him nearby instead of off flying around," I said. "Simms must suspect Zhao of something." I leaned in closer to be sure my portable EM shroud was enveloping both me and Djordi. He barely nodded, his mind clearly elsewhere. I'd caught him and Dr. Nakamura 'practicing' zero-G maneuvers in a supply closet near cargo bay two a couple days ago. I'd made the mistake of assigning Djordi to the Mitsumi Corp delegation. I'd hoped he'd become an expert in our new nanoweave suits, maybe create a training program for Galaxia recruits. I *hadn't* expected him to...well, it just didn't seem right. He was so tall and awkward, and she was so short and graceful. Maybe it's true what they say: opposites *do* attract.

"You're overreacting Paul," Djordi said. "Too much cloak and dagger stuff. Do I need to remind you that Zhao and the *Icarus* were the victims here? Why would Admiral Simms promote someone he suspects of corporate espionage?" He shook his head. "You don't give the governorship of an entire solar system to someone you distrust."

He had a point. The Prospera system was a prize unlike any other, and since the Board of Directors had structured the compensation package for system heads to include commissions from trade exports, Zhao stood to become a very wealthy man.

"Maybe," I said warily.

Djordi looked up at me thoughtfully and changed the subject. "How are you taking the other...changes?"

He was referring to Dezzie being promoted to captain, and the subsequent move of Commander Greeley from the *London* to the *Icarus* as her XO. Greeley was probably more qualified than I was, but part of me had been disappointed when she didn't choose me as her first officer. I suppose promoting her ex-boyfriend to be her XO didn't really fit the false narrative we were going for though, but I wondered if this little farce had just cost me the fast track to captain.

When I didn't answer him, Djordi looked at his wrist com and headed for the door. "Meeting with the command crew in four minutes. We'd better get going."

I turned off the EM shroud as discretely as I could. I hated not being able to confide in Djordi the way he deserved, but Zhao's order for absolute secrecy was clear. And that was before he was a vice admiral. Now the order was *crystal* clear.

The war room was crowded when we got there, and I had to settle for a spot near the back behind several other officers. It didn't seem to bother Djordi, though. At his height, he could easily see over the heads of most people. That wasn't the case for me. So, I jockeyed for a spot that allowed me to see enough of the holo screen to follow along. Dezzie was sporting a brand-new uniform and a captain's insignia on her collar.

"Without the Rift, our only feasible way back to the Milky Way is gone. Luckily, SciCorp has made a discovery that may shed some light on what happened. I need not remind you, this isn't just some new fancy physics we've discovered. The more we learn about what happened to the Rift, the greater the chance we can potentially reverse it."

I was surprised by Dezzie's last assertion. Many of the crew were still struggling to deal with being cut off from the rest of humanity. Why dangle a carrot of hope like that?

Dezzie continued. "I've asked Lieutenant

Jimenez, formerly of SciCorp, to provide additional details."

Formerly of SciCorp?

"Thank you, Captain Pearson. To cut to the chase, the last set of artifacts we exfiltrated from RS-1721 significantly elevated our understanding of the Builders and their technology. And, we discovered a reference to a new class of stars in the Hades Galaxy. As you know, a majority of them are either red or yellow." He flicked across his wrist com, which sent an image to the holo screen in the middle of the room. "We call them *white stars*. What makes them so different from yellow and red stars is still a mystery, but we do know this—the Builders were developing some valuable technology in these systems, technology that is somehow related to their system of transit gates." Hearing him talk like this reminded me how much I missed his accent. It was good to have someone as smart as him around again.

Dezzie stepped forward again and continued the briefing. Her command of the room was absolute, partly because she was a natural leader, and partly because none of the men in the room could take their eyes off her. "The *Icarus* has been tasked with traveling to one of these so-called *white stars* and sussing out exactly what the builders were doing there. But there's a catch," she said. "White stars are nearly as unstable as red stars, so we won't be able to stay in the system very long."

I moved to my left so I could get a good look at Dezzie's face. She was beautiful as ever, but just below her calm veneer I sensed a roiling of worry.

What wasn't she telling us? Maybe it was the weight of command. She'd worked her whole career for this moment, so I couldn't bring myself to feel sorry for her. After all, in my mind, she'd chosen her career over me. As long as we were on the same ship, and had differing ranks, our former *entanglements* were off limits. Our break-up was no longer pretend. I'd lost her once before, and now I'd lost Dezzie for good.

"Commander Johnson?" Dezzie asked.

The crowd of officers in front of me parted like the Red Sea, and I stepped forward. "Yes, Captain?" I don't know if I'll ever get used to calling her that.

"Assemble your best extraction team. You'll be leading the landing party," she said.

"Yes, ma'am," I replied.

"But leave a spot open for Jimenez. He'll be going with you."

I glanced at the Lieutenant just in time to see him flash a grin before regaining his composure. It was good to know he missed being part of the team.

"Yes, ma'am," I said, and then Dezzie dismissed the room. Not once did she look me in the eyes.

PATRICIA EASED the *Border Mule* into the shadow of a large asteroid. "Damn Cerbs," she groused. "There's too many of them. It'll take us several days to reach our target if we have to asteroid hop like this."

She was right, but the cover offered by the largest asteroids was the only way to ensure we went undetected by the enemy ships: there were four in this sector alone.

"Maybe you should have installed mass batteries on the *Mule*," I offered. "I'd prefer taking the Cerbs on head first to all this sneaking around."

Patricia arched an eyebrow. "A single Sentinel? Perhaps. But three? And a Guardian to boot?" She shook her head, her pink-tipped bangs flopping side to side as she did. "You're dumber than you look."

I feigned offense. "That hurts. That *really* hurts. Does your father know how disrespectful you are to his officers?"

The smile faded from her face. "We don't talk much anymore."

"Really?" I inquired. "If I had relatives in Hades, I'd…" I thought better of it and didn't finish my sentence. If things between Patricia and the admiral were strained, the last thing she needed was for me to lecture her. "I'm sorry."

"It's fine, Paul. He's just been distant recently. More distant than usual, anyway. Between the scrutiny of the Board and the destruction of the Rift, I'm sure he's got plenty on his mind."

For whatever reason, Patricia seemed to have warmed up to me a bit. I wanted to keep pressing, to dig a little deeper on the subject. It was part of my off-the-books mission, after all. But I didn't get the chance. The com beeped loudly, interrupting us with a message from the *Icarus*. Patricia nodded and I tapped the channel open. "This the *Border Mule*," she responded.

"The captain wants you to know we don't have much time left. Need to get a move on," Stohl said.

I glanced at the data streaming in from the solar probe we'd launched after transiting through the system's gate. From the looks of things, we had about eighteen hours left, which to Stohl's point, wasn't a lot of time.

"Things would go a lot quicker if we didn't have those pesky Sentinels in the way," I said.

"Captain's got a plan for that. We're gonna try to draw them to the far side of the sector. Hopefully we can distract them long enough for you to shoot the gap to the planet."

While it didn't address what would happen if the Cerbs returned to their patrols around the planet, it was as good a plan as any I could think of. Patricia seemed to agree. "Acknowledged, Lieutenant. We'll let you know when we get to the surface," she said.

It didn't take more than a few seconds for the Sentinels to react. Their aggressive nature made them nothing, if not predictable. We'd had little experience with the Guardian-class Cerbs, but it seemed equally intent on chasing down the *Icarus*, which left us a wide travel lane to our destination.

THE TARGET WAS AN INHOSPITABLE, heavy gravity

steppe planet just on the edge of the habitable zone. By all rights, we should have landed on a frozen tundra, but the system's star, which glowed a bright white in the sky, had been hyperactive long enough to burn off most of the surface water. It must've released a billion tons of carbon dioxide from the polar ice too, since the atmosphere was twice as thick as we'd expected. Luckily, our new nanoweave flight suits far surpassed anything we were used to. No more bulky EV suits, no more clunky armor. Just sleek, skin-tight nano-reactive fabric. The freedom of movement was unparalleled, and the fully transparent helmets gave us an unencumbered field of view. The suits left little to the imagination though. I looked down at my waistline and immediately regretted all those donuts I'd eaten during the past year. Even though Tanaka was built like a Greek statue, he refused to wear the new suit and kept to his old Marine armor. Said he didn't like the way the suits showed off his man parts. To each his own, I suppose. I thought about ordering him to wear the nanoweave, but figured he'd see how much better it was than conventional armor and change his mind.

As soon as we were all suited up, we headed out. I didn't need Jimenez or anyone else to point us toward our destination. The ancient facility we'd spotted from orbit was massive: a giant ring about three kilometers across with spokes that led to a central tower dwarfing any structure we'd managed to build on Earth. It was quite a feat of engineering on a world with enough gravity to topple most skyscrapers.

"What do you suppose it is?" Lamiraux asked. Even she couldn't hide her amazement.

I turned to Jimenez expectantly. He shrugged. "Reminds me of the old supercolliders back on Earth."

"You think it's an atom-smasher?" Chan asked. "That idea seems kinda low-tech compared to everything else we've seen from the Builders."

"I'll know more after I take a closer look," Jimenez replied.

Ten minutes later, after dealing with half a dozen sentry turrets, we'd gained access to the central tower. The Builders were fond of using a titanium alloy someone had nicknamed 'hadanium.' But the surface of the buildings here seemed to be made of something entirely different. The material was both reflective and iridescent at the same time. And, perhaps more importantly, all but indestructible. While the rest of us had removed our gloves to examine it with our bare hands, feeling its cool, smooth surface, Tanaka unholstered his BR-105 and blasted it with three superheated slugs to no effect. But it was Chan who made the obvious connection. "Imagine lining your flight suit with armor made from this stuff. Or even your ship. You'd be like an indestructible space armadillo!" The image made me smile.

While this expedition was similar in many ways to our first red star mission, where we discovered the alien artifacts left by the Builders, there was something very different here. The buildings were less artistic, less expressive than the architecture found before. Things here had a more *industrial* feel to them.

Jimenez scrolled through the readings on his handheld. "Commander Johnson, I think we'll want to head to the third level on the north-east side of the tower. If I'm reading this right, that'll be the best place for us to start looking."

I nodded and we did as he suggested. If there was ever any doubt that the Builders were humanoid, the presence of stairs and benches, as well as the size of doors and entryways erased it. Jimenez led us up a couple levels and onto a balcony that looked down onto a circular landing platform. I knew what it was the minute I saw the charring and blast marks on the floor. Surrounding the edge of the platform, was a trough-like structure that had some kind of conveyer belt leading into the bowels of the facility.

"Looks like a refinery of some kind," said Jimenez. He motioned his handheld around in a one-hundred-and-eighty-degree arc as he scanned. "And I'm picking up traces of hydrogen carbonate. Lots of it."

"Hydrogen *what*?" asked Djordi.

"It's the stuff we mine from asteroids with the Mako Class miners," answered Jimenez. "Looks like the Builders did the same. I bet they used the same dissolution and electrolysis methods we do to isolate the hydrogen for use in fuel cells. But I wonder how they sequestered the carbon particulates. That would be the challenge. Without burning them, you'd have a pretty big mess on your hands."

"Right," I said, trying not to make a face. "So, this was an energy factory of some kind?"

"I'm leaning toward that hypothesis, Commander," Jimenez said. "But I need to follow these conveyor belts to the processing chambers to be sure."

I gestured broadly with my hand. "Lead the way, Lieutenant."

Again, we followed him as he picked his way through winding corridors and stairs. Unlike the ruins on Auriven, the power didn't just snap on when we entered the buildings. But after a few minutes playing with some kind of junction box, Jimenez had the lights up.

When Tanaka signaled the way was clear, we descended into a large chamber with a wall of machinery and conduits. The conveyor belts from above all met here, feeding into a hopper in the top of the machine. A giant lazy Susan littered with oval-shaped objects rotated around a central axis to bring each one to the end of the machinery's conveyor. Robotic arms and graspers hung from the ceiling like a giant automobile factory.

"Those look a lot like the artifacts we found on Auriven," I said.

"Yes," Jimenez replied, his eyes glued to the display of his handheld, "but these are different."

"How so," I asked.

"Well, for starters, they're about twice as heavy as the two-ton artifacts but roughly the same size, which leads me to believe exotic dark matter is at play here. If you…"

He stepped around the closest egg and suddenly disappeared. Like a hologram turning off, he was gone. We scanned the room for signs of danger, a half dozen weapons suddenly drawn and cocked. Then, on the other side of the room, Jimenez suddenly flashed into existence, still walking in the same direction he was when he disappeared. "…imagine a more powerful version of the egg's battery pack…" He stopped abruptly and looked around, confused. "What just happened to me?"

"You tell us, Lieutenant," I said. "You just disappeared, then reappeared about twenty-five meters away without skipping a beat."

Jimenez strode back to the object and calculated how long it would take him to walk that distance, counting out loud as he did. "Twelve seconds," he said at last. "That's about a twenty percent compression rate."

Chan sighed heavily. "Lieutenant, you're gonna need to explain this in a way us jarheads can understand it. Most of us haven't seen the inside of a physics book since AIT."

He was right, but I thought I knew what was happening. "He's saying there's some kind of anomaly in the room compressing time and space."

"Like warp drives from Star Trek?" Djordi asked.

"Something like that," Jimenez said absentmindedly. He'd returned his attention to the computer scanner in his hand, fascinated by the readings it was feeding him.

"So, let's load one of these bad boys up on the *Mule* and take it back for your friends at SciCorp to tinker with," said Chan. "I'm done playing hide and seek with ancient alien relics when we've got real live aliens up there waiting for me to kick their asses. And I'm dying to take a can opener to one of those ships to see what's inside."

Jimenez started to respond but stopped abruptly as a cacophony of clicks echoed throughout the chamber. It sounded like a dozen or more gun safeties being flipped off at the same time. It sounded that way, because it *was*. Like cockroaches coming out after the lights are dimmed, nearly thirty white-clad Consortium soldiers appeared out of nowhere and leveled their service rifles at our party. Stepping forward from among them, a helmeted man limped over to us, pausing in front of Lamiraux. He removed his helmet and tossed it to her. "Remember me, sweetheart?" came his thick Brooklyn accent. When neither Lamiraux nor any of the rest of us responded, the man raised his right hand, palm toward us and wiggled his fingers. "This ring a bell?"

Even from several paces away, I could make out the small round scar Lamiraux had given him during our first encounter with the Consortium. I stepped forward cautiously, hands up at shoulder height, squinting to see the name on his chest armor. "Major De Luca?"

He broke his stare with Sergeant Lamiraux and

glanced my way. I stretched out my hand. "Sure!" I said. "We remember you guys. We left you some artifacts at that planet a while back. I think you still have our mag sleds. You didn't come all this way to return them, did you?" De Luca glared at me. "'Cuz that would have been super thoughtful," I continued. "and frankly, would go a long way toward repairing relations between our two organizations."

"See," he said, "You guys do such a good job finding them, we thought we'd tag along to see what you have for us this time."

Djordi clenched his fists. "You stole them from us!"

"You left them," De Luca said. "And your equipment." He motioned toward two helmeted soldiers pulling a familiar-looking mag sled behind them. They dropped it right in front of the relic Jimenez had been investigating when he…

Wait. If that thing could produce a spacial-temporal anomaly, we might be able use it to our advantage. But it didn't seem to be causing any strange effects at the moment. Maybe our scanning had triggered it? I clasped my hands behind my back and began pacing as if giving a lecture. At least that's what I hoped they'd think. What I *didn't* want them to see was the message I was typing into my wrist com. A message to Jimenez telling him to get another scan queued up.

"Well," I said, smiling. "We've found some interesting items here for sure." I pointed at the 'lazy Susan' filled with relics. "And there's plenty to go around."

By then several Consortium soldiers had begun loading a relic onto the mag sled, which whined under the weight until one of them adjusted the field beneath it to compensate.

De Luca shook his head and wagged his finger. "Mighty nice of you, Commander. But you wanna know what I think?" He stepped closer and motioned for me to lean in to hear him, as if he were about to share some grand secret. I begrudgingly obliged, hoping it would serve as the distraction Jimenez needed to carry out the order I'd just sent him.

"I think we'll just take the whole lot of them," De Luca gloated. His expression was like that of any bully: smug, self-assured, and full of hate. I started to protest, but his eyes flashed wide with anger and he punched me in the gut so hard, had I not been wearing my nanoweave suit, I would have doubled over in pain. But it was important the enemy didn't know about our little surprises, thinking fast, I coughed loudly and inhaled as if I'd been kicked by a mule. My acting job seemed to have worked. Tanaka and Lamiraux lunged forward in my defense, but De Luca was ready. It was exactly the response he'd been hoping for. He smiled widely as he produced a knife from a sheath on his boot and slammed it into Lamiraux's hand, pinning it to his helmet like a toothpick in an olive from one of those fancy martini drinks. The move didn't deter Tanaka, though. He managed to take another step before De Luca squeezed off a well-placed round in the Private's thigh, right in the seam between armor plates. "What was it you said when you shot me, Private?" He holstered his sidearm and turned his back to walk away. "You never miss? Well, now, you'll never *forget*." I wondered if Tanaka regretted not wearing his new Mitsumi Corp flight suit. In a way, though, it was quite fortunate he hadn't. By bleeding, the fact that the rest of us wore kinetic-response nanoweave armor was an advantage I didn't want De Luca knowing about. Not yet anyway.

When I'd finally caught my breath and my vision had returned to normal, I waited until De Luca was within arm's reach of the relic, then dipped my chin to Jimenez. He tapped a command into his handheld, and before De Luca's foot hit the floor for his next step, he vanished, along with the three soldiers who'd been loading the relic.

That's when all hell broke loose. That's when the war for Hades began in earnest.

16

HANGING BY A THREAD

A horse is half broken twice in its life: once right at the beginning, and once right before the end.

— JEFFRY JOHNSON, MONTANA RANCHER

Sergeant Lamiraux was like a boulder in a raging stream. She stood motionless as bullets whistled by and the chaos of battle swirled around her. I couldn't get over how serene she looked. Even her muscles—which were quite visible through the millimeter-thick nanoweave of her flight suit—seemed relaxed. To top it off, her eyes were closed, and there was a rare look of bemusement on her face. But she wasn't completely still. As I tumbled forward to take cover behind a discarded relic housing, I spotted her lips moving. I'd never seen her pray, but then again, I'd only ever seen her in one real skirmish. Maybe this was her way of finding center before unleashing a whirlwind of death on her enemies? Well, that's what I was *hoping* she'd do. Lord knows we needed it, especially outnumbered four to one.

It's not as if we weren't holding our own, though. Chan had managed to roll to his left, unholster his '105, and silence four enemy soldiers before coming to rest behind the main chases of the relic machine. Djordi and Jimenez had somehow made it to cover amidst the pods scattered near the closest wall. They both crouched low, weapons drawn at the ready. They weren't the most assertive soldiers in our party, but I'd watched them in the shooting range aboard the *Icarus* and knew them to be more than adequate with a gun.

My gaze, though, kept returning to Lamiraux, and it suddenly dawned on me that she wasn't praying at all. She was *counting*. When she reached eleven, she yanked De Luca's grappling knife out of the back of her hand and, after a brief pause, cocked her arm and threw it across the room—at what I couldn't say. Sure, there were bound to be Consortium soldiers in that general direction, but... Without warning, De Luca and the three soldiers who'd disappeared into the relic's spacial anomaly rematerialized some twenty-five meters away. De Luca had just enough time to take another step before the knife struck him in the back of the knee, sending him tumbling to the ground amidst a stream of colorful Brooklyn expressions.

Chan acted quickly, and put down the three other soldiers, who probably didn't deserve it since they weren't actively threatening us. But it was swift, and I hoped painless. I met Chan's gaze. He motioned for me and Tanaka—who was holding his wounded leg tightly to stanch the bleeding—to head to the door. I answered his suggestion with a curt nod. We may have been dealing the enemy a good bit of damage, but there was no reason to press our luck and endanger ourselves unnecessarily.

Even with Tanaka's injury, it took us less than eight minutes to sprint through the winding halls and across the open fields between the facility's spokes. After clearing the ring, itself, we saw Patricia standing in the *Mule's* loading ramp, waving us in. She was still wearing her mechanic's coveralls and tank top, and held a modified AR-899 service rifle—the kind with the optional explosive grenade launcher. The choice of weapon seemed strange for someone as short and petite as her, but I wasn't complaining.

The LZ wasn't enemy free. Just to the north of our position sat the Consortium transport with its loading ramp down. It bore a strong resemblance to the *Mule*. Maybe that's what prompted Patricia to train her weapon on it and fire a single explosive round into the dorsal exhaust manifold. She knew *exactly* where to hit it, and the results were *spectacular*.

Unfortunately, Patricia had stirred up the hornet's nest. No sooner had she fired than a dozen Consortium soldiers began raining down super-heated slugs on the *Mule's* position, forcing her to retreat inside.

I tapped my wrist com. "*Icarus*? This is Johnson. We're gonna need armored extraction. The LZ is hot. Repeat the LZ is *hot*." A greasy plume of black smoke meandered skyward from the *Mule's* port engine pod. "And we may have just lost our ride," I quickly added.

The com crackled with static, then I heard Lieutenant Stohl's terse response. "Acknowledged, Commander. I sent along a dropship as soon as the fighting broke out." The noise in the background told me the *Icarus* had its own hands full with the Cerbs or the Consortium, or *both*.

I turned to the team hunkered in the entryway to the courtyard. "Captain's sending us an armored dropship for extraction. Should be here any second."

Right on time, and just as I finished my sentence, an explosion rocked the *Mule*, and another one of her engine pods burst into flames. The blast sent white sand and chunks of titanium hull plating into the air in a ball of purple flames like a giant firecracker set off too close to the ground. The concussion of the explosion reverberated in my chest and was so loud in the planet's heavy atmosphere that it set my ears ringing. I rubbed at my temples and shook my head to clear the cobwebs. But before the ringing subsided, a half dozen Consortium soldiers converged on the crippled transport. Patricia was in trouble.

I glanced back to Chan and pointed toward the sky. Off in the distance, we could see the contrail of our dropship as it approached at a shallow angle, its hull an angry orange as the thick atmosphere created more friction than expected. Or maybe it was expected, but the dropship pilot had elected for speed of descent over safety. Regardless, by the looks of it, our troop carrier would be at the LZ in thirty seconds. I had to hand it to Stohl. For a pompous, stuck-up, holier-than-thou Ken doll, he had a knack for coming through in a pinch. Ok, maybe he wasn't pompous or stuck-up. Or even holier-than-thou. But old habits die hard, and I was having trouble letting go of my disdain for the guy. He *was* a Ken doll though.

"Chan! Get the team to the dropship!" I looked back at Tanaka, who was leaning on Djordi and Lamiraux as he walked. My thoughts were drawn to the man I'd lost on my first mission as leader of B Company. And to the v-mail I'd had to record and send Patel's parents back in India. I pointed at Tanaka. "You got this, Major?" Chan nodded.

Then, I unholstered my Beretta, gripping it tightly in my right hand while I raised my '105 in the other. Chan's eyes went wide as saucers. "What are you doin', Commander?!"

I clenched my jaw with determination. "Nobody gets left behind, Major. Especially the admiral's daughter."

Before he could protest, I sprinted toward the *Border Mule*, guns blazing. The BR-105 carries a firing capacity of thirty-five. Tiny pieces get lopped off its bar of specialized heavy metal until the material is completely spent. My Beretta held fifteen 9mm rounds for a total of fifty shots between the two guns. It took me probably twenty seconds to close the distance between me and the

Mule, and in that time, I emptied both weapons. The enemy soldiers weren't expecting me to go all Han Solo on their stormtrooper asses, but it wouldn't have mattered if they had: fifty shots, fifty hits on four targets. Yes, they'd managed to tag me twice, but the kinetic nano-reactive armor of my flight suit held up, and the slugs bounced off like rocks flung by a child's slingshot. The Consortium had definitely gotten the raw end of the deal. I leaped over the bodies littering the ground near the transport's cargo ramp, mortified at my own lethal efficiency. I'd never fired on live targets before, much less killed a living person. *Enemy combatants*, I told myself. *Enemy combatants*. Calling them that didn't really help, though, especially when I made the mistake of letting my gaze wander to the face of one of the fallen men. His eyes seemed frozen in place, wide with what could only be a mixture of surprise and fear. Or pain.

Again, I shook my head to regain focus, pausing only briefly to assess the situation before making for the ramp. The *Mule* was in bad shape. The small arms fire had hit a coolant line next to an electrical conduit, sparking a fire and causing the first plume of smoke we'd seen. But the second hit —the one that'd shaken the ground—had done some *serious* damage. If the other three engines pods remained operational, the *Mule* might stand a chance of achieving escape velocity. But if one of the remaining engines gave out, any attempt to get away in the *Mule* would be short-lived. To make matters worse, at least two enemy soldiers made it aboard the transport before I could take them out. I knew Patricia was tough, but feared she might not be able to handle two combat-trained troopers at the same time. My fears were alleviated to a degree, though, when I saw another fallen enemy on the cargo bay floor near the secondary airlock. Someone had given him a red smile right below his jaw. I'm glad his helmet visor was still down so I couldn't see his eyes, especially since he was lying in a pool of his own blood. Or *was* it his? A trail of red splatters led right up to the closed cockpit door. I tapped my wrist com. "Patricia, you there?"

Static.

"*Mule*. Come in. This is Commander Johnson, over."

Nothing.

Then, the deck began to vibrate as the main drive kicked on. The transport was preparing for takeoff, and I had no way of knowing if Patricia was the one flying it, or if the Consortium soldier had managed to commandeer it. It wasn't the proudest moment of my life, and maybe I could blame it on the adrenaline of combat, but...I panicked. I pounded repeatedly with both fists on the cockpit door, yelling into my com. "Patricia! Open the door. It's Paul."

My efforts were only met with the sound of the hydraulic struts closing the loading ramp as the *Mule* lifted awkwardly to the sky. If Patricia was in control, she'd have responded by now. I spent the next thirty seconds running through a dozen scenarios that would have her still alive but unable to let me know. I spent only two seconds thinking of the scenarios where she was... I didn't have time to finish that thought. My wrist com vibrated with an incoming message, and my heart leaped out of my chest.

"Commander? This is Chan. We saw you take a couple slugs to the chest before makin' it inside the *Mule* as it dusted off. What's your status? Over."

My heart sank again. Don't get me wrong, I was happy that Chan and the others were still alive, but I was hoping to hear Patricia's voice on my com channel. "I'm fine, Major. Mitsumi Corp has made a nice fashion statement with these new suits. You keeping an eye on B Company for me?"

"All due respect, Commander, I've been with B Company longer than you've been shaving. They're all here and accounted for. What about Captain Simms? Is she with you?"

I didn't really know what to say. "Maybe," I replied. "I mean, she might be. I'm locked in the cargo hold. Patricia managed to fight off one of the intruders, but the other one made it into the cockpit with her."

"Acknowledged," Chan said. "Our ride's about to lift off. I know you'll clean up that mess and meet us back at the *Icarus*. Over."

"Good luck, Major," I said. And I meant it. Even in an armored dropship, the return trip to the *Icarus* was fraught with peril. I keyed up a holo display of the battle. It was worse than I'd expected; a dozen red dots buzzed around our battleship's blue dot. But I had more pressing matters at hand. I had to find a way to override the locks on the cockpit door and rid ourselves of an unwanted stowaway. But how?

I scanned the wall with my wrist com and found the power conduits snaking from a junction at the top to the servos in the door's locking mechanism. I'd watched enough sci-fi and spy vids to know that when you cut the power to a locked door, it magically opened. But for the life of me I couldn't remember if the cockpit door was built with a fail-closed or fail-open mechanism. It was worth a try, so I pulled a cutting torch from the emergency extraction kit on the wall and began cutting through the panels right over the conduit. Once through, I proceeded to torch through the wires in a flash of sparks and smoke. There was a part of me that'd been hoping for a movie moment, but I wasn't terribly surprised when the door didn't open. I banged on it in frustration. That seemed to have caught someone's attention, and, in an instant, they switched off the grav plates, sending my cutting torch floating off behind me. I managed to grab hold of one of the bar grips on the wall near the hatch to anchor myself while I thought things through. How could I get into the cockpit?

Then it hit me. The *Mule* wasn't big enough to have two air filtration systems, and since we'd pressurized the cargo hold in the last refit, a nice big vent above the cockpit door led straight to the compressor unit. With a little cutting and nudging I might be able to make my way through the bulkhead and into the cockpit through its air feed vent. I'd need some tools though, so I pointed myself towards the port-side bulkhead and pushed off with my legs. It was a poorly thought-out move though, as I almost missed the grip bar on the wall. But I snagged it at the last second and righted myself so I could…

Suddenly an alarm echoed in the cargo hold, accompanied by flashing red lights: an alert that the bay doors were opening, and they were opening to the vacuum of space! I had just enough time to tighten my grip on the bar as three hundred cubic meters of air rushed past me. If you've ever wondered if the force of fifty thousand kilos of atmosphere feels like being sucked into a giant vacuum cleaner, well, it does. And, it was more than I could handle. But right before I was blown out into space, I managed to grab the end of the utility cable inside the tool locker and clip it to my belt. I imagined the sound it made as it was violently stripped off its winding pulley. I say *imagined* because if it did make any noise, it was drowned out by the roaring of the air being sucked out the door. Funny what goes through your mind right before you die.

Luckily, though—or unluckily—the utility cable held, and I came to a back-cracking halt when I reached its limit. I wasn't dead, but I was certain my belt had just crushed the vertebrae in my lower back. And, to add to my dilemma, I watched helplessly as the *Mule's* cargo bay doors began to close shut. I had about ten seconds to figure something out, or my cable would be snapped in two, and I'd be left tumbling helplessly in the wake of the transport's engines. Sure, I'd probably survive. Until I ran out of air. Mitsumi Corp had been pretty thorough and included micro pockets for air absorption throughout the nanoweave that would fill with breathable air while in atmosphere. If I remembered the specs correctly, I had about a two-hour supply—plenty of time for Search and Rescue to find me. But if the *Icarus* were destroyed by the Cerb fleet or the Consortium, there'd be no SAR efforts. And with all my heavy breathing, the amount of O2 I had was bound to be less than what the specs suggested. There were no two ways about it—I was fucked.

17

TYING THE KNOT

Which is the better strategy: fleeing the fire, or becoming fireproof? Neither. Snuff it out before the flame grows too hot.

— NIKOLAY SOKOLOV IN BATTLES AND
TACTICS FROM THE MARTIAN SKIRMISHES:
THIRTY YEARS OF REFLECTION

The next ten seconds were at the same time the longest and the shortest of my life. I didn't have time to think of *what* to do, but an eternity to think of why I shouldn't have done it. I'd never been the kid to reach the top first in the rope climb during P.E. class, but I wasn't going to let that stop me now. I just pretended the back of the *Mule* had one of those velcro flags attached to it and Peter Bernhardt was climbing the rope beside me. No way was I going to let that jerk beat me. And, before I knew it, my hand landed on the charred exhaust manifold of the *Mule's* busted engine. It's a good thing it wasn't working; taking the plasma exhaust from a fully lit thruster in the face didn't sound like any fun. I quickly tapped a command into my wrist com, sending the signal to my nanoweave suit to magnetize the palms, knees, and feet, and in an instant, I was like a bug on a windshield. Good news was there were no windshield wipers to contend with. Bad news? Well, here I was, in a spacesuit, walking on the hull of a ship, again.

The first order Admiral Simms had given after taking command of the *Icarus* was for me to paint the new corporate logo on the ship's hull. It was somewhat ironic that I was spacewalking again, but this time, it was to save more than corporate pride. His daughter's life was at stake. Fortune had smiled on us both today, but I had to think fast; we were approaching the transit gate, and if there were anything worse than walking on the hull of a ship, nothing but the weak forces of magnetism to keep you from flying off into the void, it had to be transiting a gate while clinging to the wrong side of a ship's hull.

But, as luck would have it, I was only twelve meters away from an access panel on the ship's communication array. The nanoweave suit had a smart circuit in it that sensed when to magnetize one boot and demagnetize the other, freeing me from having to deal with manually inputting alternating commands. It wasn't nearly as bad as I'd expected, though, and in a few seconds, I'd twisted the release mechanism and removed the hatch. The utility cable was still attached at my waist, so I tied its frayed end to the hatch's handle so it wouldn't float away. Then, I took a look inside.

The space between the outer hull and the inner bulkheads was tight, but there was enough room to move around if I cleared some things out. It wasn't hard to choose which items to remove—the biggest one was a large, insulated hose feeding air to the cargo hold from the compressor unit not far away. I knew that as soon as I cut the hose, alarms would go off, but counted on whoever was in there with Patricia thinking something had gone wrong with the cargo bay doors. So, I grabbed my grappling knife from my boot and sawed through the tough insulation and into the hose. I cut a section away big enough to allow me into the space, and I fished the hatch back toward me with the cable, sealing it shut from the inside. I like to say it was all part of my plan, but I'd just been lucky. As soon as I sealed the hatch shut, the air bleeding from the hose filled the between-decks and pressurized the space. Now, when I popped the interior access panel, the cockpit wouldn't depressurize. My grandpa always used to tell me even a broken clock is right twice a day. Well, that meant I had one more thing to be right about before tomorrow.

I studied the conduits and wiring that ran along the interior wall, taking note of where they went and where they came from. If my guess was right, the large bundle to my left led to the life support console, which meant the panel right in front of me was somewhere on top of the aisle between the cockpit door and the captain's chairs at the front. I took my knife and carefully peeled back the plastic insulation, then turned the locking mechanism from the inside. I drew in a deep breath, grasped my knife tightly in my hand, and coiled my legs up to my chest, which wasn't easy to do in such a tight space. Then, I slammed the hatch open and burst through to the cabin, dropping to the deck in a crouch, knife at the ready.

What I saw wasn't exactly what I expected. Patricia was in the pilot's seat, looking over her shoulder at me with wide eyes. Her bewilderment soon turned to laughter, though, and I followed her gaze to the floor beside me. Laying dazed on the deck, with a sizable dent in his helmet, was a Consortium soldier. I returned Patricia's smile and quickly snatched the man's weapon from his hands, leveling it at his head while waiting for him to sit up. If I were truly a broken clock, there would be no more being right today.

"Get up," I ordered firmly. "Keep your hands where I can see them."

The soldier stood slowly, raising his hands near his head. "How did you..." he asked, but I threatened him with the assault rifle, and he stopped abruptly.

"Take off your helmet," I said. The other man did as I ordered. The collar of his inner suit hissing as the pressure in the cabin and his helmet equalized. Then he twisted it off to reveal a thin, craggy, face. "How much are they paying you?" I asked.

"Not enough for this," the man said, rubbing the back of his head.

"Insurance policy?"

He nodded.

"Hazard pay?"

He nodded again.

"Family?"

He shook his head. "Just my mates back on the surface."

"Someplace to send the body?" I asked.

The look of understanding in the man's eyes will never leave me. He knew what had to be done. I motioned with the rifle for him to open the inner door to the cargo bay and get in the airlock. I punched the panel next to the door and watched it shut with a whoosh. Then, I opened the second airlock door. The soldier turned his back and floated through the hatch and into the hold, flipping me the bird as he went. I couldn't blame him. I'd have done the same thing. I removed my helmet and turned back toward Patricia, who looked at me expectantly. When I smiled, she arched an eyebrow. "I didn't think you had the stomach to space him," she said.

"But you thought I was going to there for a second or two, didn't you?"

She grimaced before answering reluctantly. "Yes." Then, she grimaced again, this time in pain. That's when I saw the crimson stain in the torso of her overalls.

"You've been hit!" I yelled, rushing to the front of the cockpit. I grabbed her wrist and lifted her tank top to get a good look at the gunshot. A light blue glob of gel had sealed the wound but was trickling blood each time she moved.

"You trying to sneak a peek, Commander?" She was using humor to deal with her pain. That's when I realized the pool of blood back in the hold wasn't from the dead Consortium Marine. Patricia suddenly looked whiter than before. "Who patched you up?" I asked.

"Leather face back there couldn't fly the ship, so it was in his best interests to keep the pilot alive. Knew exactly who I was. Even called me by name. I think he was hoping to bargain for safe passage back to his battleship."

"Well," I said, "he can have safe passage back to *our*s instead." I glanced down at the nav computer and reset our waypoint to bring us to a small asteroid about halfway between the transit gate and the *Icarus*. "And we have to move fas…"

There was a muffled pop in the ceiling above us, followed by a high-pitched hissing sound. I grabbed a flashlight and shined it into the darkness of the hole I'd just dropped through. The access panel on the outer hull had warped and was leaking air out of its seam. I guessed the silicon gasket had doubled up or gotten out of alignment when I closed it. I turned to Patricia. "You have an EV suit somewhere?"

She looked at me in horror. "Yes. But it's in the starboard-side locker back in the hold."

Shit. Shit, shit, shit! This was *not* the way Patricia Simms was going to die. Not if I could help it. But I was out of ideas, and the cockpit's meager supplies offered nothing that could be used as a suit…

Wait. A suit! That was the answer! I reached

around the co-pilot's chair and retrieved a large, flat, metallic disc and tossed it to the deck behind us. "It's a nanoweave flight suit like mine. Just take off your clothes and step on the disc, it'll do the rest."

Patricia shot me a dubious look. "I will *not* be getting naked in front of you, Commander."

I grabbed her arm and pulled her to her feet. "You will if you wanna live, Captain Simms." I shoved her onto the disc. She peeled off her tank top, moving gingerly as she did. The bullet hole in her side looked painful. There was no exit wound, so the slug was still in there. The good thing about super-heated projectiles is that sometimes they can cauterize the blood vessels. But the dark, purple discoloration surrounding her wound meant that wasn't likely to be the case here. Another popping sound and a louder hissing hastened her effort. Patricia tossed her shirt to the floor and began working feverishly at her boots. She had no bra—a fact no man on the *Mule* had failed to notice—and the rest of her clothes came off with ease. She stepped onto the disc and looked me in the eye. "What now?"

"Tap that button with your toe," I said, pointing to a flat, red circle near the edge of the disc. Patricia did as I said, sending a smoky column of nanobots into action. Moments later, she wore a second skin of grey nanoweave, and the disc had been transformed into a clear helmet at her feet. "Put it on," I said, pointing to the headgear.

"What about him?" she asked, testing the suit's com unit.

I knew she was talking about our Consortium prisoner in back, but I chose to ignore her. There wasn't time to deal with him now. "He's sealed in back there with at least twelve hours of O2, maybe more if he doesn't get too excited or breathe too fast." I glanced at the soldier's dented helmet on the deck. It may have been damaged, but there was a chance it was still airtight. I wished there were time to toss it back to him. "Besides, if we open the airlock now, there might be just enough pressure difference to blow that hull maintenance hatch off its hinges. If there's an explosive decompression, that hole isn't big enough or the right shape to make it easy for us to…" I tried to force images of the two of us being sucked through the small hatch at awkward angles. If we didn't die, there'd be more broken bones than a dinosaur museum after an earthquake.

Patricia shot me a worried glance. "How do you suggest we get out?"

Truth is, I hadn't really thought my plan through all the way. I'd been so concerned about getting Patricia suited up that I hadn't really come up with steps two, three, and four. But I was nothing if not quick on my feet. I stepped closer to Patricia, our helmets bumping as I reached an arm around her…and opened the weapons locker on the wall.

"This'll do nicely," I said, eyeing a BR-405. It was a distant cousin to the '105 but packed about five times the punch. The Marines had recently swapped out their close-quarters shotguns for the '405's ballistic slugs. May have been low tech, but damned if it wasn't more effective. I stepped back from Patricia, cocked the weapon, and pointed it at the cockpit's wrap-around canopy. I handed her the end of the frayed cable dangling at my feet. "Tie this around your waist and use the best knot you know." Her look said it all; fear, pain, gratitude, and defiance. "I'll be the one writing up the mission report," she said in her most imperious tone. "No way am I going down in the records as a damsel in distress, saved by a Prince Charming."

I chuckled. "So, you're admitting I'm a Prince Charming then?"

She glared and tugged at the cable around her waist. I did the same and turned my back to shield her from the blast. Then, I pulled the trigger, sending us tumbling into the void. A thought occurred to me in that moment. Patricia and I weren't...well, I don't know what we were. Enemies? No. Friends, perhaps? I'd never really been afraid of death. But as long as that utility cable was holding us together, no matter what else happened, no matter what we were to each other in that moment, neither of us would die alone.

18

WAR GAMES

War is a game that is played with a smile. If you can't smile, grin. If you can't grin, keep out of the way till you can.

— WINSTON CHURCHILL

Space battles are nothing like the movies. No roaring ion engines. No *pew pew* of laser fire. No rocking explosions reverberating through the void. Space battles are more like a cross between a silent movie and a distant firework show. This one was no different, except that Patricia and I had a front row seat as we drifted helplessly through space. The explosive decompression caused by blowing a fist-sized hole in the *Mule's* cockpit window had sent us both tumbling into vacuum, connected only by the thin utility cable and service knots we'd both used to secure it around our waists. The service knot was the first one any pilot learned and could be used for anything from securing a thousand kilos inside a cargo hold to climbing a wall in a basic training obstacle course. But I never could have guessed it would be the tenuous link holding me to the fleet admiral's daughter. Life's full of surprises.

We'd survived the decompression, but that's where the good news ended. Seconds after being blown free from the *Mule*, which continued its course toward the battle, things got worse. As my grandpa used to say, it went to hell in a handbasket, whatever that was. Patricia was in worse shape than either of us had realized. Besides losing too much blood, she was running out of air. There hadn't been enough time for her nanoweave suit to completely fill its air pockets with oxygen. The scant seconds between donning the suit and our hasty exit from the cockpit had garnered her a meager ten-minute supply of air. Luckily, she'd passed out from the loss of blood, and her shallow breathing had stretched those ten minutes into twenty. I racked my brain for a way to connect our two suits, to set up a buddy-breathing system, but there wasn't anything to work with; no tubing, no materials, nothing. As if that weren't bad enough, we were floating in a spot right in front of the transit gate. If any ships decided to make a run for it, we'd be bugs on a windshield before they knew what had happened. It reminded me of the time that guy tried kayaking the St. Lawrence Seaway and got sucked into the shipping lanes by the riptide. They'd tried to save him, but it'd been too late. We wouldn't have to contend with super tankers or cargo carrier ships, but I hoped a similar fate didn't await us. I tapped my com unit and tried to bring up the *Icarus*. We were well within coms range, but the electromagnetic interference from the battle was causing enough static to render our main channels useless.

At first, I was upset that they hadn't sent us help. But the more I watched the battle unfold, the more it made sense. Things weren't going well for the good guys. The *Icarus* was outnumbered seven to one. She'd managed to take out the first of the Cerb sentinels, but the others swarmed in like angry hornets. The space around the *Icarus* was filled with bright yellow battery fire which lit up her shields like a Christmas tree. I grimaced. Not three months ago, shields were something from a sci-fi movie. I can't imagine what would have happened had the battleship been without them.

"Commander Johnson?" came a scratchy voice over the com. "Paul? You there?" he insisted.

It was Lieutenant Stohl, and he sounded frazzled. At least the coms were starting to work again.

"Yeah, it's me," I said. "And I've got Patricia with me."

"I show your com signal coming from...what the hell? Where are you? The *Mule's* nearly twenty-thousand kilometers from your current position!" Stohl said, his voice a mixture of worry and fear.

"Long story," I replied. "Right now, all that matters is that Patricia's in bad shape. I don't know how long she'll last. Her suit's out of air." My voice trailed off involuntarily, as if the severity of our plight were just now sinking in.

"Acknowledged," Stohl replied. "I'll relay the details to our engineering team. Maybe we can think of something you haven't."

Almost before he'd finished his sentence, the *Icarus* was rocked by a large explosion that bathed its translucent shields in a bright orange ball of flame. What the hell was *that*? It wasn't the Cerbs. It seemed to have come from one of the Consortium battleships. I heard the explosion through the com almost the instant I saw it. Static hissed violently inside my helmet. Instinctively, I raised my hand to my head to cover my ears, but only managed to clank my helmet with the side of the large slug thrower I still held in my hand...

Wait a minute! The BR-405 had a CO_2-powered recoil reduction system in its plastic stock. If I could get the back plate off the butt... In an instant my hand was on the grip of my grappling knife, which I used to pry off the rifle's rubber butt and expose two slotted screws. Thank god they weren't Philip's head. Ten more seconds of twisting had the stock plate free and the recoil system exposed. And there it was...the most beautiful coil of plastic tubing I'd ever seen. Cut out and unraveled, the tube was probably half a meter long. I knew that the nanoweave suit was designed to repair itself, but I had no idea how long it would take. So, I spun Patricia several times, reducing the utility cable's slack by wrapping it around her waist as I did. I turned off her suit's reactive armor, then did the same to mine. With our faceplates touching, I cut a hole in the nanoweave, right at the suit's neck and shoved in one end of the tube while pinching the free end with my other hand. Once the nanobots made a seal around the tube, I repeated the process on Patricia, taking care not to stab her neck in the process. I hadn't realized it, but I'd been holding my breath the whole time. When I finally inhaled, I could tell there was a difference in pressure, and I almost panicked. But only a second later, Patricia's faceplate began to fog up from deep breathing. It had worked! But I had no way of knowing how long we had before both of us would use up my suit's emergency supply of air. It was better than the alternative, though, and I let out a long sigh of relief.

With nothing left to do but wait and watch, I tapped my com unit again, and brought up a three-dimensional rendering of the *Icarus*. I'd only spent a few minutes jury-rigging the buddy-breathing system for Patricia, but in that small amount of time Galaxia's flagship had taken significant damage. The shields were failing, and nearly seventy percent of the hull's armor plating had been blown off by the mystery projectile weapon. In fact, I counted at least four significant breaches before shaking my head and turning my attention to the state of the ship's weapons. That scene wasn't much better. Three of Icarus's four battery placements were inoperable, and the one that did work had already fired nearly ninety percent of its available ammunition.

It wasn't all bad news, though. The *Icarus*'s main thrusters were still working, and the helmsman was doing a good job keeping the ship out of the firing radius of several pursuing enemy craft. While the good guys were dealing with the four horsemen of the apocalypse, the Consortium was having a much easier go of things. Not only had they brought three battleships, but all the Cerberus ships had decided to chase the *Icarus*. While two of the big Hades class vessels stayed in formation, ready to engage any threat that might fly too close, the third ship swooped low into the atmosphere to provide escort to three transports which had set a course straight for the transit gate. I wondered how many of those relics they were carrying away. As if they needed another push to keep them ahead of Galaxia from a technology perspective. By all appearances, the Consortium had discovered several new modules for their ships.

"*Icarus*? This is Johnson, over."

Stohl replied in a harried voice. "Commander, this isn't a good time. If you haven't noticed, we're trying to shake four Cerbs who want nothing more than to inspect the inside of our exhaust ports with their guns."

Was that a joke? From Lieutenant Stohl? Maybe stress brought out the latent humor in his personality? I grinned, but quickly replaced it with a serious expression. I don't know why I did. It wasn't like they could see me. Force of habit, perhaps. "That's my point, Lieutenant. I'm tracking three transports filled with those relics from the surface headed straight for the transit gate. Would be a shame to let the Consortium get first crack at researching those things."

My suggestion was met with several seconds of silence before I heard Dezzie's voice on the com. "Confirmed. Each transport is carrying three of those...devices."

Nine relics? To our zero? This wasn't good. The only thing worse than Admiral Simms getting his hands on them was letting the Consortium make off with the prize. Better the devil you know than the devil you don't, I suppose.

"What do you suggest, Commander? We've only got one battery, and barely enough ammo left to take out a sensor drone." Dezzie seemed pessimistic, and I couldn't blame her. From her perspective, the view was just this side of dire.

"Those transports are stock. They haven't been upgraded with inertial dampening systems like the *Mule*," I said.

"What's your point, Paul? Get to it. We're running out of room to move up here."

She was referring to the two Consortium battleships that had suddenly broken orbit to flank the *Icarus* and prevent her from doing *exactly* what I had in mind. "I'm counting on everyone having a barf bucket nearby. This is gonna hurt." I punched a proposed maneuver into my wrist com and sent it over. I heard a gasp as Dezzie reviewed it.

"You can't be serious?" she said.

I'd plotted a course straight across the path of the fleeing Consortium transports. With any luck, the timing would put them within the firing radius of the Cerberus sentinels chasing the *Icarus*. But she was in no shape for a scrap with three Consortium battleships. So, I'd punched in a boomerang move at a large asteroid along its flight path.

"No time to debate, Captain. Either we do this and stop the Consortium from getting a jump on relic research, or we let them coast through the transit gate like a stroll on Sunday afternoon."

There was no hesitation. The *Icarus*'s engines flared bright blue as it surged forward toward the enemy escape route. I had to hand it to Dezzie. It was a gutsy move. Easy for me to suggest, harder for her to order. At that moment, I almost lost my appetite for command altogether. Captaining a battleship was dicey business. I wasn't sure I had the stomach for it.

I'd never felt so helpless. Watching from the relative safety of the transit gate with no way to render aid other than the occasional suggestion over our barely-working com channel. It was awful. But then, my attention was brought back to my own plight. Patricia had begun to stir. Perhaps the oxygen from my suit had roused her from unconsciousness.

"We still fucked?" she asked.

"More than ever," I said. "But we're wading through it together," I continued, pointing to the small tube connecting our suits' air supply. Her eyes were dilated, and she'd lost her color, but she managed a weak smile.

"Thanks for the air, but I gotta ask…when's the last time you took a bath?"

I could feel a smile splitting my face from ear to ear. "We may have a small problem, though," I said, pointing to a streaking *Icarus*. It didn't take her long to figure it out.

"That maneuver's gonna get them all killed," she said. "The asteroid doesn't have enough gravity to change the ship's trajectory."

I shook my head, though I doubt Patricia could see it; her eyes were fixed on the battle in front of her. "We aren't using the asteroid's gravity like that," I said. "Ever played tether ball?"

Her eyes flared wide with comprehension. "You've got to be kidding me! If you're saying what I think you are, it could rip the *Icarus* in half and kill everyone on board. They'll be cleaning human remains out of every crack and crevice in the bulkheads for months!"

She was right, several months ago anyway. But after researching those first few alien artifacts, we'd added some pretty nifty tech to our ships. "Guess we'll see if those new inertial nullifiers live up to their name," I said.

It wasn't just the nullifiers we were counting on either. SciCorp had recently fabricated a new kind of high-tensile nanotube material they'd spun into cables as thick as a man's arm. The idea was to use them in some kind of towing or netting. Harpooning an asteroid to swing a ship around in a boomerang maneuver was probably not on the list of intended applications. We didn't have to wait long to find out if it worked though.

Patricia gasped sharply and I stopped breathing as we watched the *Icarus* approach the target asteroid without slowing. She swung around it like a ball around a pole in a school playground. The move snapped the tow cable and practically disintegrated the asteroid, sending large chunks flying in every direction. But the *Icarus* didn't break in two, and while it didn't exactly reverse course, it had been enough to shake the Cerbs. Several seconds passed—an eternity it seemed—before our com crackled with Lieutenant Stohl's voice. "It worked," he said incredulously. "It fucking worked!"

In as long as I'd known him, I'd never heard Stohl utter a single profanity. Not once. It was one of the many reason's I hated the guy—he was just too perfect. But in that moment, I was giving him a virtual high-five, and caught myself smiling widely. "Is everyone ok?" I asked. I couldn't imagine there were no injuries. Maybe even a few fatal ones.

"No casualties reported so far, Commander." There was a chorus of cheers in the background, which made me wish I were there on the bridge to celebrate with them. "That's more than the enemy transports can say," he added.

I quickly zoomed our display to focus on the Cerberus ships. They maintained a straight-line course and plowed into the hapless Consortium vessels, raining battery fire on them. It was over before it even started. The escort ship changed course, intent on exacting revenge. Soon, all five alien vessels had engaged it in the familiar dance of space battle. With their sister ship suddenly in danger, the remaining Consortium battleships quickly moved in to render aid. That's when the *Icarus* made a break for the transit gate.

"You guys need a ride?" said Dezzie. I'd never been so happy to hear her voice.

"Sure," I said. "But these damn suits might get in the way. Suggest postponing the makeup sex."

She chuckled. The com was still acting up, but not enough to hinder us too much.

"We got a warm bed for you in the infirmary," she said.

"Was planning on sneaking aboard as stowaways, but with an invitation like that, how could we refuse?" I replied.

I switched to our local com channel and spun Patricia toward me again. "Looks like we've got our getaway car," I said. When she didn't answer with some pithy British comeback, I glanced down at her through fogged-up glass. She hadn't responded because she wasn't awake. She was unconscious again. *Unconscious*, I told myself. *Unconscious*. And then, the *Icarus* was upon us. We'd be safe soon enough.

Something was wrong, though. The embattled ship was moving too fast. "*Icarus*, you're coming in a little hot, don't ya think?"

"Commander," replied Stohl in a somber tone. "Check your display. We've got a missile about to climb up our..." He sighed so heavily I could hear it as if he were inside my helmet with me. "Well, we can't slow down Paul. We don't have shields, and the hull's a mess. We're already going as slow as we can. If we reduce speed any more than we already have, we won't make it to the gate."

I scrolled through pages of readings from my wrist com. He was right. The Consortium had fired a parting shot, probably more out of spite than any real hope of destroying the *Icarus*. But, in the state it was in, that's exactly what was going to happen if Dezzie didn't get them through the transit gate. And she had less than forty seconds to do it.

"Go ahead and increase speed, *Icarus*. I'll find a way to snag your hull as you pass by." I went through a dozen calculations and modeled four different approach velocities in the next few seconds before realizing the truth.

"Dezzie?" I whispered.

"Paul…" she said.

"Heavy is the head that wears the crown," I said with a chuckle.

"It wasn't an easy decision, Paul. But the numbers made the choice for me."

I understood what she meant. There were more than three hundred souls aboard the *Icarus*, and, though Patricia was Admiral Simms's daughter, and I was Dezzie's… Well, there really wasn't much of a debate. I'd have done the same thing.

By now the *Icarus* loomed large through my faceplate as it streaked by, trailing sparks and venting atmosphere out of several breaches in her hull. It came so close, in fact, I felt as if I could almost reach out and touch it…

Wait! That was it! I quickly tapped a command into my wrist com and magnetized my suit's boots. If I could time it just right… But my foot hit the non-metallic surface of a com panel instead of the hull, sending us spinning slowly away from the ship.

Shit! Shit, shit, shit!

To make matters worse, I'd lost my grip on the BR-405. Now what? My heart felt like a stone sinking to the bottom of an icy lake. Within seconds, the *Icarus* had dialed home and slipped into the transit gate's event horizon. I stared at its eerily translucent surface. I could see the stars in space behind it, but knew it was a lie. The whole notion of living through this was a *lie*. I closed my eyes and prepared to die.

But before I could even begin to watch the movie of my life, something hit the side of my helmet. I opened my eyes to find Patricia tapping my faceplate with the end of the tubing I'd used to rig up our buddy breathing system. She held it crimped in one hand and was point with the other. Her lips were moving, but no sound was coming from them. Something had happened to our coms. Before I ran out of air, I managed to figure out what she had in mind, and I smiled. Patricia extended her arm and released her grip on the hose, sending the last of our oxygen spewing into space. The effect was two-fold. We suddenly veered toward the plane of the gate. That, of course, was the good news. With any luck the burst of propulsion would send us through to the other side. The bad news? We'd both just taken our last breath of air. But, still, I smiled. In those last few seconds of life, I wasn't alone. *We* weren't alone. And then I lost consciousness to the void.

19

WELLSPRING

I believe that imagination is stronger than knowledge. That myth is more potent than history. That dreams are more powerful than facts. That hope always triumphs over experience...

— R̲O̲B̲E̲R̲T̲ F̲U̲L̲G̲H̲A̲M̲

Generally, when one thinks of waking up in a hospital, one imagines being greeted by family and friends. If not them, then at least an attractive nurse. So, I may have been slightly disappointed when I awoke in the Colonial Central Hospital on Prospera with Djordi towering over the foot of my bed. My vision was still blurry, and my skin tingled like your foot does when it falls asleep. But I was breathing, and, as far as I could tell, I was alive. Had to be, because there was no notion of heaven, for me, that included Djordi so close to my bed.

"Where's Patricia?" I asked as soon as my head cleared enough to remember what had happened. "Is she alright? Did she make it?" My voice carried a frantic tone that I wasn't used to, but given what we'd just been through, I gave myself a pass. It'd started with me trying to save her, but in the end, *I* was the one in need of saving. Somehow, Patricia had managed to rescue us both.

Djordi dipped his chin in a shallow nod. "She's going to be ok. Admiral Simms ordered her to sickbay on the *Andromeda*."

"Good," I replied, and I meant it. The highest paid position in Galaxia Corp, outside of the CEO, Board of Directors, and Joint Captains, was the fleet admiral's personal surgeon. If you wanted the best medical care in the Hades galaxy, the *Andromeda* was the place to go. Some people might have been upset Admiral Simms hadn't ordered both of us there. Not me. I was just happy to be alive. Colonial Central may not have been much more than a repurposed cargo module from a fleet freighter, but if New Eden were any indication of what was in store for a thriving new colony, it wouldn't be long before the fledgling hospital was a gleaming steel and glass spire of medical hope. It wasn't there yet, but, for now, it was more than enough for me.

I surveyed the room and wasn't surprised to find it a cramped jumble of medical equipment, power cords, and mismatched furnishings.

"Thanks for coming to keep an eye on me in this dump," I said.

"Doctors said you'd wake up any moment," Djordi replied. "That was over two hours ago. I've been waiting here the whole time."

"Well," I said, "coming back from the dead is tiring business. Besides, I needed my beauty sleep."

A giant grin split Djordi's face. "It would take more than a couple hours of rest to fix what's wrong with *your* face, Commander." He mocked me with a sloppy salute.

That's when I noticed that he was wearing civilian clothes, and that he had an overstuffed duffle bag which sat on the chair against the wall. I tried to make a gesture, but the move sent spikes of pain up my arm. "You're out of uniform, Lieutenant. You score some shore leave while I was out of it?"

Djordi's smile faded into a thin, straight line. "You might say that," he answered in a more serious tone.

"Djordi? What aren't you telling me?"

"After the battle of White Star Alpha—that's what they're calling it—Mitsumi Corp decided to annul their trade pact with us."

"*Annul?*" I asked incredulous.

He nodded. "They've severed all diplomatic ties with Galaxia."

I knew he'd been seeing Dr. Nakamura from Mitsumi Corp for several weeks, so he probably had the best intel of anyone regarding the matter. "Why on earth would they do that?" I asked.

Djordi ran his hand through his short, blond hair and sighed heavily. "There's no easy way to say this, Paul. After the beating we took back there at that white star system, Mitsumi Corp has decided to align with the Consortium."

My heart sank like an atmospheric probe with no thruster fuel, and the throbbing in my head increased two-fold. "Why?" was all I could manage to say.

"They're smart, Paul. They see the writing on the wall. Galaxia isn't the dominant power in Hades anymore. Smaller corporations stay viable because they know who to partner with," he glanced at the Galaxia insignia painted on the wall of my hospital room, "and who *not* to."

My head was spinning, but I was managing to put it all together: what Djordi was telling me... why he was out of uniform. "So that's it?" I asked, my voice surging louder with anger. "You're just leaving us?" I tried looking him in the eye, but Djordi refused to lift his gaze from the ground. "For a girl?"

That struck a nerve, and he jerked his head towards me. If looks could kill, I'd have been dead a dozen times over. "That coming from the guy who signed onto the Hades Mission because he liked the smell of some girl's cheap perfume?"

It was a low blow, but mine had been too. This wasn't the way I wanted to say goodbye to the man who'd become one of my closest friends. I was better than this. *We* were better than this. "I'm sorry, Djordi. That was...uncalled for. You're right. If your heart isn't here, you gotta follow it, wherever it goes." God, I sounded like a sappy greeting card, but it was true, I guess. No point in him sticking around if he was just going through the motions. I couldn't help but think this was all my fault. I'd been the one to assign him to work with the Mitsumi Corp engineering delegation.

His glare softened and the corners of his mouth turned up in a weak smile. "I resigned my commission this morning. Mitsumi Corp offered me an equivalent role with similar pay and benefits. Plus, I'll get to help test modifications to the nanoweave suits. They're actually incorporating some of my suggestions."

I understood a man's need to be appreciated, to feel useful. It just hurt that my best friend was joining a rival corporation, even if in an indirect way. It wasn't like this in the military. You didn't just quit the Navy. But corporations were different, and I was having a hard time wrapping my head around it all.

"Christina Nakamura isn't the only reason for my decision, Paul. I grew up on Ceridia Prime. The Drift Wars started the day after we moved there, and only ended a few months before I went to college. How do you think the war ended?"

"I'm not sure really," I said. "Only know what was reported on the Galactic Net. The Navy was pretty tight-lipped about it. Something about a truce?"

Djordi shook his head. "Ceridia knew there was no way to outlast the Fed. Even if they stopped the frontal assaults, the planetary blockade would have eventually crushed our will to fight. Ceridians are survivors, Paul. And that's all I'm doing here. Surviving."

"You know they'll peg you as the mole. In fact," I said, "I'm surprised you haven't been detained."

Djordi turned his head so I could see the barely-noticeable bruise around his left eye and cheek. "Let's just say the exit interview was very thorough," he said. "Besides, Galaxia thinks I'll be a marked man over at Mitsumi Corp. I just want to be useful in Hades. And to be with the woman I love. We're getting married." His eyes were silent apologies. "Does that make me a bad friend?"

"No," I said. "It makes you a good husband." I couldn't help but think of the choices Dezzie had repeatedly made; her career over our relationship, the mission over me. There was a part of me that was actually jealous of Djordi.

I fought back a tear and nodded my understanding. At that, my best friend turned his back and walked out of the room. I wondered if I'd ever see him again and vowed that as long as I was in command of B Company, none of us would fire a single shot at a lanky, white-clad Consortium soldier over two meters tall.

THE NEXT FEW days were uneventful, to say the least. I tried calling Patricia, but she wouldn't answer. I did manage to get a couple emails through to her, but she responded very briefly and to the point. The longest exchange included a cursory thank you and courteous well-wishes.

Something was up. The lack of communication didn't stop with Patricia, though. Neither Dezzie nor Jimenez would answer my calls. I'm not sure if there was an EM shroud around my hospital room, or if someone was actively jamming my wrist com, which only worked intermittently. When it did, the channels were quiet. That's what tipped me off that something big was about to go down. They were trying a little *too* hard to keep whatever it was from leaking. The lack of information was driving me crazy, but worse than that was the shit they tried passing off as food. I just don't get it. No matter the world—or the galaxy in this case—in which you found yourself, hospital food was inedible. This morning's breakfast had been sawdust and gelatin formed into sausage shapes served with a side of worm meal eggs and soy milk. How they expected me to get better was beyond me. So, when my com finally chirped alive with a crystal-clear signal from Dezzie, I nearly jumped out of my bed.

"Commander Johnson?"

"Yes, Captain, I'm here!"

"Your vacation on Prospera's over. So, put down your frilly drinks with little umbrellas, get suited up, and take a shuttle to the *Icarus*. You've been reactivated pending medical clearance." My wrist com dinged an alert that said, "Medical Clearance Granted." How convenient.

"Wait," I said, somewhat confused. "The *Icarus* is in orbit? Here?" Last I'd heard, after plucking me and Patricia right out of the transit gate, the *Icarus* had limped back to Eden for repairs. Or scuttling. Whichever was more cost effective, I'm sure.

"Yes, we're here. Made the trip just for you. So, get a move on. We'll debrief you in an hour."

An hour? That would be pushing it. I wondered why she was in such a hurry. "Yes Captain. And…Dezzie?"

"Yes, Paul?" she sounded a little irritated. Was I pushing things too much by being so informal?

"I…well, it's good to hear your voice is all." I sounded like a stammering teenager afraid to ask out his high school crush. I hated how Dezzie could still do that to me. We may not have been a couple anymore, but there probably wasn't anything short of death itself that would quell my feelings for her.

"We're glad you made it back to us alive, Commander Johnson." It was such a formal response, completely bereft of emotion. I was confused and hurt. At the end of her sentence, the channel went dead, and so did a part of my heart.

THE *ICARUS* WAS A MESS. I'd been led to believe she'd been in dry dock undergoing repairs. But from the looks of it—at least from the outside—she didn't even look space-worthy. Gaping holes in the hull had been quickly patched with resin and emergency polymer repair sheets, and three of the four battery installments remained mangled clumps of twisted steel. In a way, the *Icarus's* hull looked more like a patchwork quilt than a battleship. Maybe the enemy was afraid of needlepoint and would see her and quake in fear? Why had the Joint Captains pressed her into service so quickly? My stomach lurched at the thought of what could force them into making such a brash decision.

As our shuttle turned to make for the *Icarus*'s docking bay, I was surprised to see she wasn't alone. Four large vessels sat in high orbit around Prospera. I recognized the *Amazon, Pegasus, New Delhi,* and *Orion* from the blueprints I'd seen before. I knew they were bigger than the *Icarus* but seeing them first-hand helped me appreciate just how much bigger. They were the largest ships I'd ever seen. It was quite an imposing sight.

When I finally made it to the war room, I found the usual cast of characters: Dezzie, Chan, Stohl, Dezzie's XO Commander Greeley, Jimenez, and to my surprise, Vice Admiral Zhao. He was looking much better than the last time I'd seen him. His cheeks were fuller. His eyes were brighter. The beleaguered air about him had all but vanished. Governorship of a new system must have been agreeing with him. I remembered the diamonds we'd discovered when we first landed on Prospera. As Governor, he got a percentage of all trade profits. By my calculations, Zhao's bank account wasn't doing too bad either. He nodded my direction and returned my salute before smiling.

"Paul! It's good to see you. The two of you gave us quite a scare back there. Admiral Simms sends his regards and his thanks."

"I'm the one who should be thanking him. Patricia un-botched my attempt to save us," I said.

"Duly noted, Commander. But that's not exactly how she described it in her report. Regardless, we are lucky to have both of you still among us."

True to her word, Patricia had been the one to write the mission report describing our escape from the white star relic planet. I'd have to go back and read it when I got the chance. I can't imagine there were any damsels in distress described in the report and wondered how she characterized my mishandling of things. Would I be a Prince Charming, or a court jester?

Dezzie nodded to Commander Greeley to begin the briefing. I'd barely spoken five words to the man, but he seemed a capable officer. Average height and middle-aged, Greeley was the kind of man who'd worked twenty years to rise through the ranks. From all reports, he'd earned each star on his collar. He tapped a series of commands into the console and brought up a rendering of the Prospera system. Small avatars of the giant warships hovered around a holographic planet in the air above the console. They looked like grown-up versions of the snap-together plastic models I used to build as a kid.

"We are amassing the fleet in the Prospera system. As you can see," Greeley said, pointing to the ships orbiting the planet, "we recently christened four new Mark II battleships. Together with the *Icarus* and the *Andromeda*, we will form a flotilla of six ships: five battleships and one frigate." I arched an eyebrow. Calling the *Andromeda* a frigate was a stretch. She may have started out as a warship, but with all the modifications Admiral Simms had made to it, she was closer to a luxury cruise liner than anything else.

"Flotilla?" I asked. "Why do we need such a large force? Are we planning on storming a Cerberus stronghold? Or a hostile corporate takeover of the Consortium? And what about the *London*?"

Commander Greeley moved as if to speak, but was interrupted by Vice Admiral Zhao, who swiped at the holo image until he reached a molecular model. "While you were recovering, Commander Johnson, the *London* was destroyed on a mission to RS-1621."

I was shocked. Sure, we'd had some close calls in battle, but we'd never *lost* a battleship before.

"Now, regarding the mission at hand. The *Icarus* may not have made it back from White Star Alpha with an intact relic, but you did manage to bring back the next best thing: Lieutenant Jimenez's scans." Zhao stepped back and motioned for Jimenez to continue the briefing. Jimenez toggled the display to an image of some kind of exotic atomic model. There were protons and electrons and other subatomic particles I'd never seen before.

"What is that?" asked Chan. "Some kind of doomsday weapon?"

Jimenez shook his head, a hint of frustration surfacing as he did. I'm sure he was tired of Chan always trying to turn new discoveries into ways of killing the enemy. But the major was a Marine, and a damn good one at that. How else would he see the universe if not through a soldier's eyes? "No," said Jimenez. "It's the atomic structure of a new element. Right now, we're calling it Element X. The relic housings on the planet orbiting White Star Alpha were full of this stuff."

I remembered the landing platform and conveyor belts leading to the large machine room in the sub-basement of the facility. "Is that what those machines were making? From the hydrogen carbonate?"

Again, Jimenez shook his head. "No. We believe the hydrogen was being turned into fuel cells to power the containment fields in each of the relic pods."

"That's a lot of fuel cells," I said.

Jimenez nodded. "Secondary, tertiary, all the way down to ten sets of backup power cells. It was very important to the Builders to keep Element X contained."

I took a step closer to the holo display, appraising the molecular structure. "And I bet you guys have a theory about that too, right?"

"Yes," Jimenez continued. "Do you remember the spacial-temporal anomaly we experienced when scanning that first relic?"

How could I forget? Jimenez had disappeared and reappeared like some magician's assistant in a circus show. "Let me guess. Element X did that?"

"Correct, Commander. My scan disrupted the containment field long enough for Element X to distort space-time in the immediate vicinity of the relic."

Chan grimaced. "I thought you said those things had a dozen backup batteries."

"Ten," Jimenez said, correcting him. "But only one was functioning and even then, it was almost drained. That's how my scan was able to interfere with the containment field so easily."

"Why weren't the other batteries working?" I asked.

Jimenez grinned a knowing grin. "That's a good question, Commander. Our best guess is that those relics were nearly three thousand years old."

A hush fell over the room. This was all well and good, but so far SciCorp had managed to raise more questions than they answered. "What exactly is it for? What's its purpose? Where does it come from?" I asked.

"There's a lot of debate going on in SciCorp on that very subject. Nobody knows how the Builders got it, or how the relic machinery places it inside the containment fields. As to what it is for? Some believe it was being weaponized. Others, like me, believe it was being used to create the system of wormholes in Hades." I remembered them telling us our transit gates were just facades on the surface, doors to an existing network of wormholes and faster-than-light travel lanes. Then it hit me. I knew what the relics were really for.

"Lieutenant, what would happen if you amassed a large quantity of Element X in one place and turned off the containment field?" I asked.

"I like where you are going with that Commander Johnson. You sure you don't want to join SciCorp?" He grinned before continuing.

"Some of us believe enough Element X would punch a hole through space-time, warping it so thoroughly it would create a very large wormhole."

"Large? As big as, say, the *Rift*?" I inquired.

Chan's eyes grew wide, as did the others in the room as they realized the implications of my theory. Suddenly, there was a way back home to the Milky Way. Our hope was as tangible as anything in the room, and instantly filled our souls.

Vice Admiral Zhao waved his hand dismissively. "It's only a theory at this point. But either way, a weapon, or the way back home, we can't let the Consortium get their hands on it."

Now it made sense. Amassing such a large force in this sector, rushing the *Icarus* into service, and calling me up from the hospital early. "You've found another white star, haven't you?" I said.

"Yes," Zhao said. "Problem is, given our history with the mole, we can be certain the Consortium knows about it too."

"So, it's a race," Chan interjected. "First one to White Star Beta takes the prize?"

Dezzie shook her head and keyed in a command on the console, taking over the presentation. "It won't be that simple. Probes have reported a heavy Cerberus presence in this White Star system."

"How heavy?" I asked, bracing myself for the answer.

"About four times larger than any Cerberus force we've encountered." She swiped the display.

"And that's not all. There's half a dozen of *these* guarding the habitable planets in the system."

The holographic display rendered an image of a new class of Cerberus ship. It looked like a manta ray flying backwards, and if the spec sheet next to the image were correct, it was almost as big as a Mark II battleship but nearly twice as fast. Its primary weapon had been designated 'Mass Battery.'

"What're we calling it?" I asked.

"Interceptor. Nothing fancy," Zhao responded. "But the damn thing chased our probes across four sectors before catching up to them and destroying them. It fired at all four simultaneously. We're lucky to have gotten as much data as we did."

Damn. *Four* targets at one time? In space battles, that was the equivalent of… well, damn, there really was no equivalent. It was *impossible*.

Dezzie tapped another command and the hologram displayed personnel pictures for me, Chan, Jimenez, and Sargent Lamiraux, who wasn't even in the room. "We're splitting up B Company for this one. Need your experience in other units." I knew what she was really saying. If failure were imminent, spreading valuable assets across multiple teams in different physical locations ensured you could sustain some losses. It was as close to an admission of defeat as I'd ever seen before a fight. "Each of you will command an extraction team with three transports and thirty-six Marines." A line shot out from each photo to connect it with a ship in orbit. "Chan will transfer to the *Amazon*. Jimenez? You're with the *Pegasus*.

Lamiraux will lead our contingent from the *New Delhi*, and Lieutenant Stohl has volunteered to join the extraction team from the *Orion*."

Several sets of eyes turned to Stohl, wide with amazement. He smiled sheepishly. "What? I couldn't let you have all the fun," he said.

"What about me?" I asked.

"You'll be taking the XO spot on the *Pegasus*," responded Dezzie. She glanced at me, reading my expression like a cheap comic book. "Just for this mission," she added. "Their XO was recently promoted to captain of the *New Delhi*, so we're desperate." She smiled wanly.

I ignored the jab and interrupted. "What about Patricia? Will she be running with one of the extraction teams?"

It was Zhao that answered. "She has reluctantly agreed to pilot a transport for the *Orion*. After losing the *Mule*, she's been less… interested in running sorties."

"We'll meet up with the *Andromeda* and head through the gate," said Dezzie as she turned off the holo projector with a flick of her finger. "We leave immediately."

20

SURGING TIDE

Once woven into the fabric of time, you can no more stop an event than you can stay a tidal wave with a dam of paper.

— Dimitrius Lorenz in Essays on Fate

Space looks a little different from the command dais of a battleship, and while the cushion of my seat wasn't any thicker than what I was used to, it sure felt like I was sinking further in under the weight of my new position. I don't know how Dezzie did it, all that responsibility: the lives of three hundred people hanging on every decision, every *mistake*. Luckily for me, I was just the XO. Captain John Foster was actually in command of the *Pegasus*. But that fact gave little comfort, especially once subordinate officers began asking me for orders. How was I supposed to know what speed was appropriate to break orbit? Or who to put in charge of defense against boarding parties? My answer of "The guy with the biggest guns" was met with a mixture of smirks and sideways glances. Guess they weren't used to command humor on the *Pegasus*. Or maybe they were just used to an XO who knew what the hell he was doing. If they found it strange to have a new first officer, how do you think I felt? Not having Dezzie around, or Djordi? I was loathe to admit it, but I even missed Stohl. So yeah, the awkwardness went both ways.

"Captain," said the helmsman, a short man with a five-o-clock shadow and beady eyes. I still hadn't memorized the bridge crew's names. There just hadn't been enough time. "We've arrived at the transit gate." The main view screen flickered to life, displaying the gate and one of our sister ships, the *Amazon*. From our perspective nearly directly behind her, I was concerned the big ship wouldn't fit through the gate. But I'd studied the blueprints enough to know that the Mark II was only slightly wider than the Mark I. Most of the new ships' increased size came from added length, and the *Icarus* had no trouble with transit. So, it stood to reason that the new ships would fit just fine.

Within seconds the *New Delhi*, *Orion*, and the *Icarus* all arrived and took up positions near the *Amazon*. Seeing the *Icarus* beside the fleet's next gen battleships made me appreciate the upgrades sported by the Mark II. While the *Icarus* only had four battery placements—three of which weren't even working—the Mark II battleships had twice the firepower. Besides that, and the size difference, the newer ships had another advantage—an additional bay for the technology modules SciCorp had created from recovered Red Star artifacts. After mining them for data, the orbs, crystals, and tetrahedron were removed and the egg-shaped artifact modules were used to power the upgrades. The standard technology module fitted on all the newer ships was something we were calling EMP, or Electromagnetic Pulse. The Consortium had been the first to adapt that technology to an Earth ship, and I'd seen it firsthand. I was hoping that having it on our own ships would help to even the playing field for the good guys this go around.

Within a matter of minutes, our little flotilla was joined by a handful of transports and Makos to mine for hydrogen. If we were going to get the Element X back home safely, we'd need functioning relic containment fields. I just hoped the alien machinery that made them still worked after so long. We were taking a huge risk.

"Sir," said the tactical officer, "Admiral Simms and the *Andromeda* have arrived and signaled the green light for transit."

Captain Foster nodded. He was an older man, perhaps in his sixties, with craggy laugh lines and crow's feet. But his eyes were steel, and he looked as fit as anyone I'd seen in a uniform. Well, except for Stohl. "Take us through in sequence, Lieutenant," he ordered.

When we got to the other side, our consoles lit up like Times Square on New Year's. Alarms sounded, lights flashed, and the crew jumped into action like a hive of bees hit with a rock. Not sure why that image came to mind, I sure wasn't dumb enough as a kid to mess with a beehive like that. OK, maybe once. But I never poked one with a stick.

"Display up," Foster ordered. The view of the system on the main screen elicited gasps and dropped several jaws. The star was, of course, white, but it was pulsating visibly, clearly on its last leg. We'd have precious little time before it went nova. But that wasn't what had everyone's eyes bulging. A fleet of fifteen Consortium battleships held formation on the other side of the system, probably eight hours away. There were just as many support ships, including some upgraded miners. I say upgraded because they were larger than even our Mako Mark II. A thought ran through my mind—and everyone else's I'm sure. How was our flotilla going to contend with a force three times its size? A force with upgraded support ships? I wondered what kind of modifications and exotic tech the Consortium battleships came equipped with this time around. It was a sure bet that if we'd been improving our tech, they'd been busy doing the same.

The Consortium wasn't the only worry, though. The enemy fleet had two faces in this system—one of them human, the other one alien. Twenty-four Cerberus ships patrolled the three habitable planets orbiting the white star: twelve Sentinels, seven Guardians, and five of the newly-discovered Interceptors. It was by far the largest force of Cerberus ships we'd ever encountered. The news wasn't all bad, though. At least the Consortium fleet would have to contend with the Cerbs at the planet closest to their position. But then again, we'd have our own pack of wolves to deal with if we wanted to start collecting Element X. Nobody knew how much it would take to open the Rift again, or even if that were the correct use of Element X, but we knew one thing—it was better for Galaxia to find out than the Consortium.

The screen snapped to a view of Admiral Simms on the bridge of the *Andromeda*. He stood and clasped his hands behind his back. He looked eager, like a wolf circling a baby deer. Somehow, I didn't think his motives for this mission were as altruistic as the rest of us. We just wanted to get home to the Milky Way. I feared he wanted his corporation to play gatekeeper to the Hades Galaxy. For a man like him, control and money were the ultimate goals. How he'd raised a daughter like Patricia was a mystery to me.

Speaking of Patricia, I'd identified her transport the moment the viewscreen displayed our flotilla. Her ship was called the *Intrepid*, which made me smile. Though it accurately described Patricia, it was such a bland name compared to her previous transport.

"We have designated this white star with a name, rather than a number. It shall be called the Bountiful system. The closest planet to the gate is now Bountiful III. We will focus our mining efforts on the richest asteroids in that sector. This will reduce transport time to the relic factory on the surface."

I noted that the enemy miners were headed to an extremely hydrogen-rich sector a little further away from the other relic planet, and hoped that the admiral's strategy would give us an edge.

"The *Orion* and the *Amazon* will proceed to Bountiful III and remove the Cerberus threat in anticipation of the rest of the flotilla's arrival. Godspeed." At that, the transmission ended, and the screen displayed the corporate logo against a blue background.

Captain Foster turned my way and nodded. "Commander, you've fought these things. What should we expect when the *Orion* and *Amazon* engage the enemy?"

I studied my console for a few seconds before replying with a sigh. "Well, sir, I don't expect they'll have much trouble with the Sentinels. They have weak hulls and are easy to destroy if you can last long enough against their guns. I believe the new shields will keep our ships safe long enough to do the job. If we can isolate them away from the Guardians, that would be best. As far as the Guardians go, they have blast doors for hull plating, but weak weaponry. They're like the equivalent of an orbital phalanx. The Cerbs tend to use them for blocking moves since they can take a pounding. If we get sucked into engaging the Guardians too soon, the Sentinels will eat our lunch."

He nodded. "I see you've read the tactical report. But what about their behaviors? And these new *Interceptors*? Give us something we don't already know."

"Cerbs are aggressive," I said. "But we can use that to our advantage. The main thing to remember is they seem to have a patrol radius and don't stray from it very far. But the Interceptors?" I shook my head and shrugged. "Vice Admiral Zhao said they chased our probes all the way to the transit gate and destroyed several at the same time. They've got some fancy targeting systems that allow multiple kills at once."

"Four," added the tactical officer seated just below the command dais.

"That's what worries me," I said. "If one of those things gets loose behind our defenses it would tear up a transport convoy real fast."

"That's why we're holding back here," said Foster. "To protect the transports and miners. For now, we just sit back and watch." That's exactly what we did, and it was *awful*.

Bountiful III was classified as an L5 Terran planet. It was too bad the star would go nova and vaporize it soon. Terran planets were rare in the Milky Way and seemed to be just as rare here in Hades. The explorer in me desperately wanted to grab a transport and fly recon below the planet's ample clouds. After running my own extraction missions, being on the bridge of a starship in a completely different sector of the system left me aching for action, especially when it became clear that the *Orion* and *Amazon* were having their way with the Cerbs.

As the two battleships entered the sector, the four Sentinels rushed towards them. But the *Orion* veered off to an asteroid outside the *Amazon's* kill radius and waited. The Cerbs were committed, though, and without a gravity source between them and the *Amazon*, they couldn't give chase. Poor bastards. The second they were all inside the kill zone, the *Amazon's* captain ordered an EMP that instantly disabled the charging ships. It was a risky move, though, because the EMP also disabled the *Amazon*. But this had all been part of the plan. Before they were able to spin their power cores back up, the *Orion* swooped in and used the hapless enemy ships for target practice. I wondered if the Cerberus knew what sitting ducks were.

By then, the lone Interceptor in this sector had covered over half the distance to the *Amazon*, which was still disabled. Its multi-target mass battery began pounding the two ship's shields the second it got in range. The *Amazon* took the brunt of it. Still disabled, its shields were down, allowing the Cerb's superheated battery slugs to tear through her hull like a fork poking holes in a tinfoil dinner. Alone, though, the Interceptor seemed outmatched by the *Orion*, with her Mark II batteries, and within minutes the Interceptor had lost. But when it was clear defeat was imminent, the Cerberus's anti-capture tech kicked in. As usual, all that was left was a residual energy signature and fragments no larger than a thumbnail. Why they hadn't weaponized that capability was still a mystery, but I was glad they hadn't. Those batteries were already a handful.

The two Guardians finally lumbered onto the scene, pecking at the *Orion's* shields. Strangely, they weren't targeting the defenseless *Amazon*, and after a brief exchange of fire, the *Orion* dispatched them as well. Her shields were depleted now, and she too had taken hull damage, but she wasn't venting atmosphere like the *Amazon*. With the immediate threat gone, repair crews were already suited up and walking her hull to repair the worst of the damage.

The fleet-wide command channel rang out with the Admiral's voice. "If you haven't already been shot at, I want your asses in orbit around Bountiful III."

Captain Foster turned to his helmsman. "Set course, and don't spare the horses." The remaining Galaxian ships wasted no time setting waypoints to the relic planet. I turned to Foster. "Sir, I think we should send at least two of the battleships to the asteroids between Bountiful III and the enemy. Create a kind of defensive front. If any of them advance this far, we can EMP them." He nodded. "And next time we should hop asteroids to the destination. It gives us greater flexibility if we need to change course."

He nodded to the comms officer. "Relay as a tactical suggestion to all ships."

By the time the rest of the flotilla made it to Bountiful III, two Makos had dumped their loads and headed off to mine more hydrogen. Jimenez's team was the first on the ground, probably by design. There were few, if any, Marines more qualified than him to ensure the facility could still produce relics. Captain Foster piped the extraction team's com feed into our ship-wide channel to listen while we waited.

I was so focused on keeping an eye on the Cerbs and the Consortium, though. It was hard to pay attention to our own activities. The Consortium had sent half of their fleet to deal with Cerbs while the other half protected a tight convoy of miners and transports. Their efficient maneuvers made our efforts look unprofessional and downright haphazard. It quickly became clear to me that we would never produce more relics than them. The heavy stream of hydrogen they were sending to their relic planet would be too much for us to keep up with.

"Everything seems to be working down here," said Jimenez. "Alpha Team has secured the facility and production has begun, but we're going to need more hydrogen carbonate."

One of the Mako pilots must have been listening on the same channel. She set a waypoint for a juicy-looking asteroid on the far side of an adjacent sector. Mining that area hadn't been part of the plan, but until just now, we hadn't had any way of knowing how much hydrogen would be needed. I heard the pilot's scratchy voice over the tactical channel. "Have…that…mined out in… snap." I only hoped she was right. The waypoint she'd set was long and her destination unprotected and exposed to both Cerb and Consortium ships alike. It made me more than a little nervous. So nervous, I suggested to Foster that one of the Mark II battleships match her waypoint to arrive with the miner and provide cover.

"Admiral Simms has ordered all battleships to stay in formation around Bountiful III, Commander. If we stretch ourselves too thin, the enemy could pick us off," he replied. "We can't afford to lose a battleship so early in a campaign."

But even as we spoke, it became a moot point. A Consortium battleship set an extremely long waypoint to the asteroid our Mako was heading to. My tactical display indicated the ship was called the *CSS Avenger*. This was bad. *Really bad.* At this point, there was no way for our miner to change course. It was already beyond the gravity well of its initial asteroid and wouldn't pass by another gravity source before reaching the target waypoint. In less than three hours, the miner would be easy pickings for the *Avenger*. But then something incredible happened.

As the *Avenger's* flight path took it through a pack of Cerberus ships, it opened fire first on a Sentinel, then an Interceptor. The Sentinel responded in kind, but the *Avenger* was too much, and the smaller Cerb ship was destroyed in minutes. The Interceptor was a different story. Like the smaller ship, it had returned fire. But, unlike the Sentinel, which had set a waypoint to an asteroid closest to the flight path of the *Avenger*, the Interceptor set a waypoint to *match* the *Avenger's* destination.

"You seeing this?" Captain Foster asked.

"Yes, sir," I said.

He hit a command on his console. "Admiral Simms?"

"I'm quite busy at the moment, Captain Foster. This better be important," replied the admiral. Just when I thought his tone couldn't get any more arrogant, it did.

"Sir, are you seeing this? The *Avenger* and that Interceptor have parallel flight paths. They're going to destroy each other before reaching our miner!"

It was true. The two large ships pulled within firing range on route to the same asteroid as our miner. The exchange of fire was brief though. The *Avenger* slowed briefly—how it did that without a gravity source is a mystery—and then disappeared.

"What the?" someone on the fleet-wide channel said. It was exactly how we all felt though. The Consortium battleship simply disappeared. The last few rounds from the Interceptor's mass batteries sailed unimpeded through empty space, as it streaked toward our miner's asteroid.

"Report!" barked Captain Foster. "Was the *Avenger* destroyed?"

The tactical officer shook his head. "No, sir. I'm not showing any debris or residual energy echoes. It's as if it disappeared, sir."

Foster snorted in disgust. "An entire ship doesn't up and disappear, Lieutenant. Maybe the Cerbs have a new kind of weapon?"

"No," I said. I'd noticed the enemy ship suddenly appear a sector and a half away. "It *did* disappear. The *Avenger* teleported."

There was good news in this revelation. The enemy had shown its hand. This tricky little secret had been divulged when only a solitary miner was at stake. At least now we knew what we were up against. But our miner was toast, and any chance we had of gaining the upper hand in this conflict was about to go up in smoke. Outmanned, outgunned, what hope did Galaxia have? A dark thought crossed my mind. Galaxia had lost its place at the head of the table. We were now playing second fiddle to the Consortium. I hated to admit it, but maybe Djordi and Mitsumi Corp had been right.

21

CRASHING WAVES

Rocks are hard, water slack,
But drip enough, the rock will
crack.

— *Ancient Brazilian Saying*

The pilot of our Mako miner was in luck. Galaxia was a corporation that placed tremendous value on skilled pilots. Unlike Marines, they were prized assets worth saving. I just hoped she had the sense to wait until she was closer to the destination asteroid before ditching her ride. Search and Rescue ships were fast, some of the fastest available, since they doubled as scouts. But even with the highest thrust-to-weight ratio of any model in the fleet, if the pilot ejected too far away from a gravity source, her rescue could take days. It was things like this that reminded me just how vast space really is.

"I know this one," Captain Foster said. "She's a

smart pilot. Saw her name on the list for promotion recently. She knows what to do. She'll be fine."

Part of me wondered if Foster was trying to reassure the bridge crew or *himself*. In the meantime, reports from the surface were coming at regular intervals. Jimenez had gotten the relic machinery up and running, and our remaining miners were making quick work of the nearby asteroids. The first delivery of hydrogen would be enough for three relics. "You're cooking with gas down there, Lieutenant!" I texted to Jimenez. He must have been busy because he didn't acknowledge my note.

We weren't the only ones making significant progress, though. The Consortium miners had just dumped five huge loads at their own alien facility, which meant they'd soon have a little over twice as many relics as us. There really was no way for us to keep up with that level of production. Our only hope was to disrupt them somehow, and with only six offensive ships—two of which were damaged from the earlier skirmish with the Cerbs—the odds of successfully doing so were not in our favor. We didn't have to come up with a plan for that though. The Consortium seemed eager to bring the fight to us.

"Captain," the tactical officer said. What was his name? Lieutenant…Athos? "Ten Consortium battleships have broken orbit around Bountiful II and plotted waypoints to asteroids in Sector E4." E4 was filled with Cerbs and stood between our relic operation and the enemy planet. "ETA is two hours."

Captain Foster nodded, then stood and made for the door. "I'll be in the war room. Lieutenant Athos, you have the bridge." He looked back over his shoulder and nodded for me to follow him. The war room on the *Pegasus* was like the one on the *Icarus*, but it was bigger and, in addition to the central holo projector, sported several tactical displays on the wall. Foster called up a three-dimensional holo rendering of the star system. Ten red dots converged on three asteroids within easy striking distance of Bountiful III. "We're going to have to be smart about this," he said, keying on the command channel. A visual of each ship captain as well as Admiral Simms popped up, accompanied by a heated conversation that was already in progress.

"We should cut our losses," said Captain Yanagasawa of the *Orion*. "Finish production of those three relics and beat a hasty retreat." She shook her head. "We've clearly got some catching up to do in the technology department."

"Agreed," Ma'afala said. When he spoke, the blue dot representing the *Amazon* grew larger and pulsed. "Meeting the Consortium armada head on is suicide. They've essentially blockaded us from their relic planet, so any attempts to disrupt their operations would have to go through ten Mark II battleships armed to the teeth with god knows what!" Several heads nodded amidst a murmur of agreement.

Admiral Simms's expression remained flat, almost unreadable. I knew it was his 'thinking face' though, and he tilted his head before responding several long seconds later. "What are your thoughts, Captain Pearson?"

It seemed unfair to put the most junior captain of the group on the spot like that. Dezzie cleared her throat and stood tall though. "We've never let the odds stand in our way before, Admiral. Just the fact that humanity is here in Hades to begin with defies explanation. By all rights, we should be squabbling over mining claims in the Milky Way, not battling over alien technology in another galaxy." She paused briefly and exhaled. "But we are. In my mind, cut-and-run is not an option."

Captain Ma'afala snorted loudly, his Pacific Islander face was as emotive as any I'd ever seen. "That's easy for you to say. You've only been captain for a few weeks. What experience do you have that…?"

Dezzie cut him off. "I know someone from each extraction team. They're my friends down there, Captain. Any plan we come up with puts their lives in danger. Besides," she added, "I may not have been her captain, but the *Icarus* was fighting the Cerbs and the Consortium before your ship even had its toilet seats installed."

Admiral Simms smiled, and everyone but Ma'afala nodded their agreement. "I have an idea," I interjected. "But some of you won't like it."

Foster made a face of surprise. "Spill the beans, Commander Johnson."

"We're outgunned, outnumbered, and their uniforms are prettier than ours. But I think there's a way to come away from this with the upper hand," I said.

Captain Yanagasawa chimed in from the bridge of the *Orion*. "Disruption's out of the question now. They've already unloaded over twice as much hydrogen, and that's just the beginning. The disparity can only get worse."

I nodded. "That's why we're gonna let them generate as many relics as they can, then hit their loaded convoy on its way to the transit gate."

Wary looks abounded. I could tell I wasn't winning them over. "There's only one gate. They have to come across our bow, so to speak, to make off with their relics. They will almost assuredly provide a stout escort for their convoy. Ten, maybe twelve battleships. One for each transport."

"No way we could strafe that many ships, Commander. Not with our weapons." protested Vice Admiral Zhao, whose image appeared next to Captain Miller of the *New Delhi*.

"I agree, sir. I'm not suggesting we do. How many of you read my report from our first red star mission? The one to Auriven?"

"We all did, Commander. What's your point?" Asked Ma'afala.

"Well, we didn't have any weapons on the *Border Mule*, but we managed to vaporize a Cerb Sentinel."

A smile split Dezzie's face. "With a jury-rigged artifact," she said. "You're suggesting we use a relic the same way? Will it even work?"

I shrugged. "Relics use the same kind of hydrogen fuel cells as artifacts, only ten times as many. If anything, they'll make an even bigger light show. And with that much Element X, we may just take out the entire fleet."

"Or punch a hole in reality," Ma'afala fired back.

"If there's a mole in Galaxia feeding the Consortium our intel," said Dezzie, "we have to assume the enemy has read your mission report too, Commander. That rules out the element of surprise."

"True," I admitted, "but it won't counter their overconfidence. Frankly, at this point, the Consortium has little reason to fear us. We'll use that to our advantage."

The plan had started as an idea but was rapidly taking shape in my head. I'd need help though. Lots of help. "Admiral," I said, "we can do this. We have to try, at least."

He nodded and tapped orders into his console. "I'm placing you in command of the operation, Paul. We'll only have one shot at this, so make it count."

"Yes, sir," I said with a salute. What had I gotten myself into? If I thought the weight of temporary promotion to XO was a lot, it paled in comparison to leading a mission like this. People would die because of me. Win or lose, good people would die.

THE IDEA WAS simple in theory—wait until the Consortium transport convoy was en route to the transit gate, intercept it with our own transport, and detonate a makeshift bomb. Nothing could go wrong with such a *hastily-devised* plan, right? I mean, if I'd had the back of a napkin to draw it up on, I wouldn't have even had time to do *that*. When others suggested sending a single battleship with EMP to disable the convoy first, I simply pointed out that not even our best shields could keep it alive long enough to do that against so many enemy ships firing simultaneously. So, it was back to my original plan.

"You know, this probably won't work," said Dezzie over the mission channel. Her voice was commanding yet familiar. I don't know if anyone else could hear her worry, but I could.

"You know me," I said. "Going for the impossible is in my nature." I wondered if she caught my double meaning, but the awkward silence that filled the air left little doubt. "Too bad we don't have a halfway-decent pilot to execute this crazy plan," I said at last.

"Execute isn't exactly the word I would have chosen, Commander," said Patricia over the com. I watched as the blue dot representing the *Intrepid* plotted a course across the flight path of the Consortium convoy.

"And I asked for a halfway-decent pilot. Guess you'll have to do. These are desperate times." Admiral Simms had initially refused to allow Patricia to join the mission. But after some earnest father-daughter debate, he eventually relented.

Chan joined the banter. "If she don't cut it, Commander, I can fly this tub. Been flight certified for twenty-two years. I'll manage if needed." That both Patricia and Chan were on the transport intended to *blow up* the enemy convoy was both comforting *and* frightening. On the one hand, we needed the best we had if we expected to succeed. You simply don't send in players off the bench when the game is on the line. You needed players with ice water in their veins. Chan was the consummate soldier, and Patricia was nothing if not steely cold. We really couldn't have asked for better.

"You done testing the remote for our little package, Major?" We'd installed a make-shift control unit in the relic housing to remotely disable the hydrogen battery powering the relic's containment field. With the nine backup batteries disengaged, disrupting the field at the right time would only take one push of a button. We'd also strapped a small tactical nuke to the relic. Mixing that much explosive power with ten hydrogen cells would produce an explosion big enough to vaporize a dozen ships. Or so we *hoped.*

"Done, sir. But blowin' this thing is gonna be the easy part. It's deliverin' the package that I'm worried about," said Chan. That made two of us. Or two-thousand. Delivery was definitely the weak link in our plan. With such a well-armed escort, getting the relic bomb in effective range before the enemy battleships shot it down would be the tricky part. And by tricky, I mean damned near impossible. Luckily for us, I'd only been right once today, and, like a broken clock, I had one more success left in the day. It had to be this.

The next two hours were excruciating for both

sides of the battle. The convoy was en route and unable to change directions at speed. They saw the *Intrepid* approaching but could do nothing to stop it. They saw our battleships fire at her as the transport 'escaped', but it was too late. They were, no doubt, wondering what we were up to. So, their response when Patricia hailed them on all channels wasn't unexpected.

"What are your intentions, *Intrepid*?" they demanded.

Patricia was a better actress than I expected. She managed to lace her voice with fear so palpable, I could almost see it. "I...we...we want to speak with Svet Djordjijevski."

"Who?" came the reply.

"Djordi. He resigned his commission and joined Mitsumi Corp. Is he in-system?"

There was a brief pause. "No, *Intrepid*. He's not. But his wife is."

A new voice crackled over our com. "This is Dr. Nakamura," she said.

"I'll cut to the chase, Christina," said Patricia, using Nakamura's first name. "We want to defect. And we've brought a relic as an offering of good will."

Again, there was a long moment of silence. "This is Fleet Admiral Gordon." His voice was deep and scratchy, like someone who'd spent years smoking flash. "Are you requesting corporate asylum?" he asked.

"Yes, Admiral. Will you have us?" said Patricia. By now the *Intrepid* was about three minutes from the firing radius of the closest Consortium battleship. "It wasn't an easy decision," she added. "But we know where the tides are rising."

I could almost see the smile on Admiral Gordon's face. "That may be the smartest decision you've ever made. Welcome to the Consortium, soldier."

If there were twelve people on the bridge of the *Pegasus*, there were twelve deep sighs of relief. Somehow, it had worked. I'd bet on the Consortium's pride, and it seemed to have paid off in spades. Accepting defectors in the middle of a battle with your rival was just the thing they'd use to recruit new corporations. If the mighty Galaxia couldn't stand against the Consortium, then nobody could.

The next phase of the plan was almost as crucial. Now that it seemed likely the enemy wouldn't fire on the *Intrepid*, Patricia was supposed to turn the ship on its axis, so the cargo doors faced forward. SciCorp had hastily strapped directional thrusters to the relic bomb. At precisely the right moment, Chan was to open the doors, reverse the polarity on the grav plate in the cargo hold, and engage those makeshift thrusters, sending the relic toward the approaching convoy. Then, he and Patricia, both of whom were suited up and equipped with several days' worth of O2 and thruster packs, were supposed to ditch the *Intrepid* and detonate the bomb. At least that's how we drew it up. But that's not how it happened. Not by a long shot.

22

PAYING THE PIPER

Far better is it to dare mighty things, to win glorious triumphs, even though checked by failure...than to rank with those poor spirits who neither enjoy much nor suffer much, because they live in a gray twilight that knows not victory nor defeat.

— THEODORE ROOSEVELT

Before Patricia could flip the *Intrepid* around, our sensors picked up several Consortium battleships powering up their batteries.

"They're onto us!" I yelled over the com. "Get out of there ASAP!" In about forty-five seconds, my friends were going to die, and I felt helpless to do anything about it. But I knew someone who could. Then, the unthinkable happened. They opened fire, even though the *Intrepid* was outside the kill zone. In a way, the enemy's impatience was what saved the mission. A bevy of superheated battery slugs rained down on the transport, peppering its path. Only one struck, and, even then, it was just a glancing blow. However, it had done just enough damage to disable the thruster control systems. "I can't get us into position," Patricia said. This was bad. *Really bad.* If we couldn't fling the relic bomb out the back of the *Intrepid*'s cargo hold, we'd have to devise a different way to deliver the payload. I opened a channel to one of the transports heading back to the safety of our flotilla. "Jimenez? You there, over?"

"Yes, Commander. Things look grim," he said.

"Any bright ideas?"

"Maybe," he said, "but it's gonna be hard to do."

"Relay your instructions to Chan. We've only got a few seconds left," I said.

I knew the instant he'd done it because Chan signaled me his acknowledgment via text over a private channel. We both knew what had to be done, and we both knew that Patricia wouldn't be a willing participant. Minutes passed. Too many minutes. Somehow, though, the little ship survived the initial wave of enemy fire. And now Jimenez's plan was in full effect. From our perspective a couple sectors away, all we saw was the *Intrepid* disappear as battery fire flew unimpeded through the space where it had been an instant before. A couple seconds later the transport reappeared right in the middle of the Consortium convoy.

Some events forever change your life, and some become turning points in wars gone wrong. This moment was both. The flash of light from our makeshift bomb was bright and lingered for what felt like an eternity before finally ceding to the darkness of space. Just as theorized, the explosion was so powerful, it vaporized not only the twelve fully-loaded transports, but the miners and battleships that accompanied them. The entire Consortium fleet was gone. And so was the *Intrepid*.

The bridge of the *Pegasus* was a mixed bag of emotions—elation that comes with victory against seemingly insurmountable odds mingled with the gut-wrenching loss that accompanied losing comrades and friends. "I don't know how you did it, son, but you did," Captain Foster said through a smile that split his face ear to ear.

I could barely speak. The shock was just too much to handle. "I wasn't the one who pulled the trigger, Captain. Chan and Pat..." I couldn't even finish the sentence.

"They were among the finest soldiers I've ever met," Foster said. "I'm sure the admiral's proud of her." I didn't care how Admiral Simms felt. All I knew was that I'd just lost...well, I'd just lost more than anyone else in the fleet.

An hour later, after collecting as many post-battle scans as possible, we lined up at the gate for transit back to the Prospera system. I turned to our tactical officer, Lieutenant Athos. He shook his head. "Nothing sir. No debris. No escape pods. No...bodies."

The moment we arrived in orbit around Prospera, Captain Foster summoned me to the war room where he erected an EM shroud and hailed the Joint Captains for a classified debriefing. I noted the conspicuous absence of Admiral Simms.

"What the *hell* happened back there, Paul?" asked Vice Admiral Zhao.

"We completed the mission, Admiral. That's what happened." I don't think I'd ever talked to a superior officer like that in my entire career, but I was in no mood to be challenged or questioned.

"How *exactly* did we win?" Captain Ma'afala asked, a trace of suspicion in his voice. Was that guy always so pleasant to deal with?

"When enemy fire disabled the *Intrepid*'s maneuvering thrusters, we could no longer deliver the payload as planned. And we didn't have much time before the transport was close enough for enemy fire to be more effective. So, I had Lieutenant Jimenez text Major Chan his best idea."

"And?" Ma'afala urged.

"And Jimenez instructed Chan to disable the containment field of the relic. Just like on our first white star mission, the Element X inside the relic created a spacial-temporal anomaly. It teleported the transport into the convoy at exactly the right moment. They didn't have time to ditch before the bomb was detonated. And if they did, the blast radius was so large, it probably wouldn't have mattered."

"The timing had to be perfect for that to work. Who could have done that without any preparation or training?" asked Captain Yanagasawa of the *Orion*.

I was about to answer her, but Dezzie beat me to the punch. "Major Chan, that's who," she said. "Best damn soldier in all of Hades."

There was a chorus of agreement from the Joint Captains, and then Zhao called the meeting to an end. "Commander Johnson, report to my office at System HQ. And bring your belongings. Your assignment on the *Pegasus* is over."

"Yes, Admiral Zhao," I replied, saluting him sharply. Normally, I'd have been curious about my next assignment. Would I go back to leading B Company? What would it even be like without Chan? And how could I ever look Admiral Simms in the eye again after sending his daughter to her death? But these thoughts were only like rain drops on a windshield. I noticed them, but they failed to capture my full attention. No, I was too busy wrapping my head around the events of the past few hours. Zhao had assigned me to *seduce* Patricia as a way of keeping an eye on Admiral Simms. Zhao was convinced—with good reason— that Simms was connected to the mole that had infiltrated Galaxia's command structure. I'd never get to complete that mission now, and we were right back where we were that day in the *Icarus*'s war room, speaking in hushed tones beneath a shroud. Except this time something was different. Whether it was my desire to get over Dezzie, or my zeal to complete my mission, I'd broken the cardinal rule of the spy business. I'd allowed myself to develop feelings for my mark. I'd fallen for Patricia, and for a second time, the Hades Galaxy had seen fit to crush my soul.

The next sixteen days crawled by at a snail's pace. SciCorp had confirmed our suspicions about Element X. At least in theory. They were able to warp space a couple times before running out. This meant there'd be a concerted effort to retrieve as many relic units as possible from white stars. It also meant that, if we had an active mole, Galaxia wouldn't be the only corporation after them. Chances are the Consortium—or some other rival corporation—would be there to greet us every time. Given the urgency of our situation, I was itching to get back out there. Instead, I'd been temporarily assigned as Vice Admiral Zhao's executive secretary, attending his briefings, offering my opinion on matters of military strategy and public policy. There are those who work their entire careers for an opportunity to build a society, and few ever hold a position to make half the impact I did. But I was bored. It wasn't that the work was unfulfilling—it was satisfying in its own right—but it wasn't what I wanted. Life on a starship, exploring the universe, the thrill of battle, the pain of loss. I wanted it. All of it. The good *and* the bad.

Instead, Command had decided my experience and skills were better used elsewhere. I'd been assigned ancillary duties on a subcommittee working to discover who the Cerberus really were. Where they came from. What drove them. And more importantly, how to defeat them. All of which was crucial work. Still, it wasn't duty on a ship, and I soon grew tired of brainstorming sessions and science reports. So, when my wrist com vibrated with a priority one message from Fleet Command, I could barely contain my excitement.

"Report to the *Icarus* for assignment," it said. Strange that the order didn't include any details. But things were evolving in Hades. Galaxia was evolving. Changes to protocol and procedures no longer came as a surprise. So, I gathered my things into a single over-stuffed duffle bag and caught a shuttle to Prospera's space dock.

My pilot was a young woman with brown eyes and short, curly black hair. She saluted me nervously as I boarded through the port-side doors. I was the only passenger, so I took the co-pilot's chair, eager to feel the hum of a console's capacitive surface beneath my hands. This, of course, made my pilot even more nervous. But about ten minutes into our preflight checks, she got up the courage to ask me what was on her mind. "Commander Johnson," she said sheepishly. "Is it true what they say about you?"

I arched an eyebrow. "And what exactly do they say about me, Ensign…" I glanced at her name tag. "…Adebayo?"

"That you discovered the first alien artifacts, the first relics, that you destroyed the first Cerberus ship, and that you won the battle of White Star Beta. They're calling you the Hero of Hades at the academy on New Eden."

What a mouthful. There was so much wrong with her question, I didn't even know where to begin, but I felt compelled to disabuse her of the notion that I was some kind of war hero. I wasn't.

"I'm not," I responded with a sigh. "I'm just some guy from the prairies of eastern Montana who followed his heart one too many times. A guy who's been lucky in his assignments, and luckier in the company he's kept."

She blushed with embarrassment. I hadn't meant my response as a rebuke, but it was clear she'd taken it that way. I clapped her on the shoulder and smiled. "No real hero believes that he is."

It was just what she needed to hear, and a look of immense pride returned to her face. "I can't wait to tell my mates from the Academy" she said, her voice a little glibber than she wanted. Her gaze shot to the console in shame. One of her com indicators flashed and she read the message before returning her attention to the flight plan. "Let's get you back in the saddle," she said.

The ascent was smooth and uneventful. But the instant I laid eyes on the *Icarus*, my heart began pounding like an African drum. Scaffoldings encircled her fuselage and worker drones buzzed about her hull like bees around their hive. Not only was the *Icarus* being repaired, but she was being refit, upgraded to a Mark II battleship. Palettes of titanium beams and prefabricated bulkheads floated nearby, tethered by construction moorings for later use. They'd made a great deal of progress in two weeks, but the *Icarus* was far from ready. By my reckoning, she'd be in space dock for at least another month. Despite the relative disarray of her hull, the ship's core was intact and operational. I could tell if for no other reason than the lights were on, spilling out of portholes and windows.

A thought occurred to me as my pilot swung us around to the opposite side of the ship. Would they assign me a new bunkmate now that Djordi was no longer with Galaxia? Or would I have my quarters to myself again?

Just then, I noticed our angle of approach seemed a little off. "Where are you going, Ensign? Your vector's too wide." Maybe she was nervous, or maybe she'd just made a rookie mistake. Either way, it was correctable. "You should adjust our heading to point three two mark seven. That'll bring us in even with the port-side docking bay."

Ensign Adebayo shook her head. "No, sir. My orders are to take you somewhere else." Our shuttle veered off to the left and lurched forward with a burst of thrust that left the *Icarus* and the space dock in our wake.

"Where are you taking me?" I asked, more curious than upset.

She didn't answer, but smiled broadly, her bright white teeth shining in the dim light of the shuttle's cockpit. A moment later, we arrived at Prospera's moon and swung around it. Blood rushed to the back of my head and my flight suit's compression bands kicked in to keep me conscious. Adebayo giggled as we broke the plane of darkness on the far side of the moon. There, floating gracefully in orbit, bathed in her full running lights was one of our Mark II Battleships. I couldn't quite make out the call letters on the aft engine housings, but as soon as we pulled even with the main fuselage, I saw the drones had just begun painting the ship's name in bright Galaxia red: *GSS...*

I was confused. Was this yet another surprise ship the Board of Directors had built and hidden away until now?

"You're sure our orders are to come here?" I asked.

"Yes, sir," Adebayo responded. She keyed up the communique she'd received at the beginning of our trip. Sure enough, it had changed our destination to the ship described only as *[under refit around Prospera II]*. We docked at the nearest collar and I breezed through decon protocols. For some reason, they hadn't required the spray-down. Maybe the ship would be sterilized after the refit was done. At any rate, I made my way to the command deck, enjoying the stroll along corridors fitted with full-G grav plates. I only ran into a handful of people along the way, all of them dressed in heavy-duty construction suits or coveralls. Perhaps the full-time crew wasn't aboard yet.

My wrist com buzzed. It was a text from Dezzie: *You coming, Paul?*

I didn't bother with a reply since I was only a few paces from the doors to the bridge. Two Marine guards flanked the entrance and saluted me eagerly as I entered.

"There you are," Vice Admiral Zhao said. He stood at the front of a large gathering of officers and Marines, each of whom I knew. To his left, Admiral Simms stared at me with a look of boredom. To his right, Dezzie. On the other side of the command dais I found Gunnery Sergeant Lamiraux, Lieutenants Jimenez and Stohl. Private Tanaka stood at parade rest in the final position. There was a gap between him and the others, and I couldn't help but imagine it as a tribute to our missing comrades, Captain Patricia Simms and Major Chan.

I saluted the Admirals and Dezzie and was quickly released from attention. "Paul, I want to give you something," Simms said. He handed me a rectangular case covered in plush, black velvet. I accepted it and opened the lid, which was held shut by strong magnets. Inside I found several lapel stars, a set of lieutenant's pips, and a handheld pad with thumb scanner.

"Your orders," Simms said, nodding toward the pad. I thumbed it on and read the single line of text it contained: *Hand out the promotions and grab a bucket of paint.*

Promotions? Paint? I must have looked lost, because Dezzie broke decorum and snickered. Simms extended his hand and dropped a metallic diamond shape with five stars in its center in to mine. "*Captain* Johnson, your orders are to assemble a crew. Vice Admiral Zhao and I took the liberty of assembling several likely candidates here on the bridge. Forgive us any oversights."

"Wha...?" was all I could manage to say in response.

Zhao smiled broadly. "Choose your crew, son. The ship is yours. You may be the 'Hero of Hades', but you'll still need help flying this thing."

Wait. Ship? *This* ship? A Mark II Battleship? Choose a crew?

Zhao shook his head and snatched the captain's pin from my hand, removed my commander's stars, and pinned the new rank insignia to my collar. "Now give these folks what they deserve, Paul."

I looked at the ranks on the collars of the group standing on the other side of the dais. They each saluted me heartily. I released them from attention and snagged the commander's stars from the velvet box. "Admirals," I said, "I may have to skip a rank here or grade there..."

"Captain's prerogative," Simms replied.

I nodded my thanks and turned back to the others. "This may come as a surprise to some of you, but I don't really like Lieutenant Stohl. Hell, he was my ex-girlfriend's ex-boyfriend...that's a lot of ex's...and, I may have been a little jealous of him. I mean, look at him. He's practically perfect. But it's not his straight teeth and manly physique that makes him perfect as my XO. It's his unwavering loyalty, his intelligence, and his ability to see what needs to be done before I do."

I turned to Stohl and extended my hand. "Will you accept this posting, *Commander* Stohl?"

He flashed us his pearly whites and shook my hand vigorously. "Thank you, Captain Johnson. I won't let you down."

"No, you won't. And that's precisely why you're my Number One," I said.

Then I turned to Jimenez. "Lieutenant?" He looked at me expectantly, barely able to contain his excitement. It was a sign of youth, but, damn, he'd just turned twenty, so it wasn't unexpected. "I'm gonna need a problem solver with a keen scientific mind manning my tactical station. Only the best. Know anyone who could do the job?" His countenance fell for moment before he realized I wasn't serious. I extended my hand and a pip promoting him from second lieutenant to first.

I thought that smile might split his face in two as he responded. "Thank you, Captain!"

Now it was Lamiraux's turn. She met my gaze without expression, her countenance serious and hard. She'd just lost her former commanding officer and friend, so I expected any promotion would be met with a measured response. "Gunny, I know you've lost a lot. But I need you. I need you now more than ever. You're the best damn Marine I've ever met. If I had to choose one person to bring on a mission to cover my ass, it'd be you. No question. That's how we all feel." I motioned to the others in the room. "But we have a little bit of a problem." I turned to Simms and Zhao. The vice admiral arched an eyebrow and shrugged. I took his noncommittal response as the liberty I needed and ran with it.

"Gunnery Sergeant Jeanne Lamiraux? For valor and exceptional execution of duty under extreme duress, and in recognition of your professionalism and competence, by the authority granted me as captain of this vessel, I hereby grant you a field commission to Lieutenant Second Class." I grabbed a pip from the box and tossed it at her. "Put it on, Lieutenant." She did as I ordered without even a hint of emotion. Then, I saluted her and held her at attention until she met the gesture with her own. "I may only be a spacer," I said, "but, to paraphrase a great man and friend, I don't give two wet shits about that. How many stars you see on this collar?" I asked, pointing to my captain's pin.

"Five," said Lamiraux. To my surprise, tears welled up in her eyes, and a single drop skittered down her cheek, splashing onto the deck at her feet.

Then I pointed to her collar. "And how many do you see there?"

"Two, sir."

"B Company is yours, Lieutenant. You'll do Major Chan proud, I'm sure," I said, as another teardrop hit the deck.

Tanaka stood still as stone at the end of the line. He turned his head slightly to meet my gaze. "Private? There's an opening in B Company for the position of Gunnery Sergeant." I tossed a chevron pip to Lieutenant Lamiraux. "See the commanding officer of B Company if you wish to apply."

Lamiraux, smirked and strode over to Tanaka, removing his former rank and pinning him with the promotion. "As long as you never miss, Sergeant," she said.

Then, I did something I don't think anyone expected, but afterward, everyone agreed was the right thing to do. I placed the pips, chevrons, and stars representing everyone's former ranks on the deck in two piles and grabbed a cutting torch from the emergency kit on the starboard wall. I lit it up and melted the pins into two irregular clumps of metal. "There wasn't just *one* hero of White Star Beta," I said, removing a handkerchief from my pocket and scooping up my little creations into the velvet box. "Forged in the heat of battle, our friendships shall endure. And so that their actions are never forgotten, to their memory, I posthumously award Captain-Commander Patricia Simms and Major Anthony Chan the Hades Star of Valor." I presented the first one to Admiral Simms, and the second to Vice Admiral Zhao. And for the first time—and likely the last—the two highest-ranking officers in Galaxia Corps saluted me *first*.

I was feeling a strange mixture of intense emotions at that moment. Zhao had earned and kept my respect. He'd given me chance after chance and rewarded me beyond my merits. Simms, on the other hand, was a duplicitous, ravenous businessman masquerading as a military leader. I didn't trust him as far as I could throw him. But when we locked eyes, for a moment, I saw into the soul of a man who knew genuine pain and loss. A man, who, it would seem, was more human than I'd thought.

"Captain," Admiral Simms said. "Do you remember the first order I gave you when we met on the bridge of the *Icarus* so many months ago?"

How could I forget? He'd just relieved Captain Zhao and sent me to do a private's duty— painting the Galaxia Corp insignia on the hull of the ship. "Yes, Admiral. I remember."

"Good," he said. "I'm renewing that order." He pointed to a pile of canisters and a laser paint gun against the opposite bulkhead. "There's a blank spot on the hull that needs painting."

The room erupted in smiles, and even I couldn't keep a serious face. Zhao cocked his head to one side and shot me a musing look. "What will you name her?"

Captains didn't normally get to name their ships. I recognized the special dispensation being granted me here and made sure to get it right. I pictured my grandpa on his horse in that ancient-looking straw cowboy hat. I caressed the handle of his Beretta on my thigh and nodded firmly. "Montana, Sir. She'll be known as the *GSS Montana*."

And that was the moment that I looked around me, at my colleagues, at the friends I'd made, and realized that I had something incredibly rare. Despite being stranded in a new-and-sometimes-hostile galaxy, despite the ever-present threat the Cerbs and rival corporations represented, I'd found what I was looking for. Some say I have the soul of an explorer. Truth is, I've just never fit in. Except in *this* family. And on *this* Montana. In Hades, I'd finally found a home.

EPILOGUE

The *GSS Montana* still had that new ship smell when Ensign Adebayo eased her out of orbit for the first time. There was a slight vibration in the deck beneath my feet when she pushed the throttle forward. I loved that even though most systems on the *Montana* were controlled via state-of-the-art capacitive consoles and touchscreens, the control to make us move was still a lever with haptic feedback for the pilot to *feel* the ship's acceleration and power. Adebayo was grinning from ear to ear. Apparently, she appreciated that feature as much as I did.

"A little different than shuttling passengers to orbit in a shoebox, eh, Ensign?"

"Yes, Captain," she replied without even attempting to regain her countenance. That was fine with me, though. *Uniform Codes of Conduct* and military regulations had their value, but I wasn't about to stymie emotion on the bridge of *my* ship. Feelings were what made us human, and until we had sentient robots and aliens among the crew, *human* was what we got.

Speaking of robots, I turned to Stohl, who sat in the XO's chair to my left, head down, reviewing pre-launch protocols. "You're certain it's Cerberus?" I asked. Sensors had picked up a single non-friendly entering the outer limits of the Prospera system. It wasn't unheard of for enemy ships to stray into our space, but they usually came in small groups. A solitary Cerb was unusual.

"Yes, Captain," he said. "It appears to be a lone Sentinel."

"Plot an intercept course, Ensign Adebayo," I said. "Let's see what this enhanced Alcubierre drive can do."

The graviton cascade was quick and smooth. We were at speed in less than ten seconds, and the tug of inertia was almost imperceptible. With a flick of his finger, Lieutenant Jimenez sent a tactical display to the main viewer. The Cerb Sentinel was headed to a tightly-packed cluster of asteroids about forty AUs from the sun. But that's where it seemed to be stopping. "Hasn't it seen us?" I asked. "It's not like a Sentinel to just sit back and wait." This was new behavior, and it had gotten our attention.

There were several nods of agreement, and everyone doubled their efforts to find out why. After a few minutes, Jimenez's head shot up from his scan results, eyes wide with amazement. "Sir," he said almost frantically. "I just picked up a communication from the enemy ship."

I turned to Lieutenant Miller, who was

manning the coms station until I could find a suitable officer for the posting. It's not that Miller wasn't suitable himself. He was. But his heart was set on joining B Company, so I hadn't pushed the issue with him. "What channel?" I asked.

"That's just it, sir," Miller said. "All channels are clear. I mean, there's plenty coming from deeper in-system, but nothing out here."

I turned back to Jimenez and raised an eyebrow. "Lieutenant?"

"He's right, Captain. Nothing over laser or wide beam. But I happened to be scanning the lower RF bands and ran across this." He hit a command and the bridge was filled with the sound of a rhythmic tapping.

"Is that what I think it is?" Stohl asked.

"Yes, Commander. It's *Morse code*," Jimenez said.

I was dumbfounded. How in the world could an alien ship from a distant galaxy know an ancient military code from Earth? "Translation?" I barked. We all knew Morse code, but the three days spent on it in officer training at the Academy had been so long ago. All I could remember was it sounded like a shorted-out headset.

Jimenez nodded and began typing on his console, his words appearing on the main display: G-T-S-1-9-0-2. "It's a ship designation. One of ours," he said. "A transport. But the hull configuration and energy signatures are that of a Sentinel, sir. One moment while I cross reference the designation with Galaxia ship records..."

"No need," I said. "I know it."

Without noticing I'd stood from the captain's chair and descended the command dais. "Send a response on all RF bands," I ordered.

"Message, sir?" asked Miller.

I took two steps toward the coms console and typed in my response: *Border Mule?*

Then, the com crackled to life with so much static I could hardly make out the voice of the sender. "We can barely read you. *Who is this*?" I asked.

When the transmission finally cut through the interference, I immediately recognized the Imperial British accent on the other end.

"This is Captain Patricia Simms. Paul? Is that really you?"

Ten sets of eyes darted my direction. "Patricia? We all thought you were dead! How…? But you're in a Sentinel broadcasting a friendly ship designation over RF."

"I'll explain it later, Commander." She had no idea I'd been promoted. "Right now, I need a warm shower and some real food. You won't believe what I've had to eat in order to stay alive on this thing. It might be surprising, but they don't serve cheeseburgers on a Cerb ship."

"Is Chan with you?" I asked, making no attempt to hide my eagerness.

"I'm sorry, Paul," she said, almost too quietly. "He didn't make it."

I turned to Miller and nodded firmly. "Get word to Command…to Admiral Simms that his daughter is alive."

"Belay that order," Patricia said. "Paul, I'm invoking Order Twenty-one-B."

Twenty-one B? The protocol for covertly accepting a request for asylum? Patricia was an officer in Galaxia Corp. She was Admiral Simms's daughter for crying out loud. Why would she ask for asylum?

"Patricia, just so I'm clear, you said Order *Twenty-one-B*? You're asking for asylum?"

Our tactical display flashed an alert as she plotted a waypoint to the asteroid we were orbiting, and the Cerberus ship began to move our direction.

"I have information crucial to the war effort, and the safety of every person in the Hades Galaxy. But we need assurances. *Order Twenty-one-B* assurances."

I didn't know what to say. Jimenez had run a voiceprint analysis and it came up a positive match. So, this *was* indeed Patricia. But who was the *we* in her request?

"I thought you said Chan was dead?" I said.

"Not Chan. I have a prisoner of sorts," she said.

A *Cerb*? Patricia had commandeered a Cerb ship and captured its pilot?

"I hope you can trust the crew on that bridge," she continued, a trace of coldness in her voice. "I know what the Cerberus are, and who our mole is. And I have a feeling you aren't going to like either one."

ABOUT THE AUTHOR

Doug Wallace is an author of sci-fi and fantasy. His award-winning short stories have been published in several anthologies and magazines. This is Doug's third full-length novel. When not writing, he can often be found wandering about the Wasatch Mountains of Utah where he lives with his four children.

Manufactured by Amazon.ca
Bolton, ON